I'D KILL
FOR THAT

also edited by Marcia Talley

Naked Came the Phoenix

by GAYLE LYNDS, RITA MAE BROWN, MARCIA TALLEY,
LISA GARDNER, LINDA FAIRSTEIN, KAY HOOPER,
KATHY REICHS, JULIE SMITH, HEATHER GRAHAM,
JENNIFER CRUSIE, TINA WAINSCOTT, ANNE PERRY,
KATHERINE NEVILLE

EDITED BY MARCIA TALLEY

I'D KILL
FOR THAT

a serial novel

St. Martin's Minotaur ⚔ New York

Chapter 1 copyright © 2004 by Gayle Lynds
Chapter 2 copyright © 2004 by Rita Mae Brown
Chapter 3 copyright © 2004 by Marcia Talley
Chapter 4 copyright © 2004 by Lisa Gardner
Chapter 5 copyright © 2004 by Linda Fairstein
Chapter 6 copyright © 2004 by Kay Hooper
Chapter 7 copyright © 2004 by Kathy Reichs
Chapter 8 copyright © 2004 by Julie Smith
Chapter 9 copyright © 2004 by Heather Graham
Chapter 10 copyright © 2004 by Jennifer Crusie
Chapter 11 copyright © 2004 by Tina Wainscott
Chapter 12 copyright © 2004 by Anne Perry
Chapter 13 copyright © 2004 by Katherine Neville

www.minotaurbooks.com

ISBN 0-312-29057-8
EAN 978-0312-29057-3

First Edition: May 2004

10 9 8 7 6 5 4 3 2 1

To the millions of
breast cancer survivors everywhere,
in hope of an imminent cure

acknowledgments

Like its predecessor, *I'd Kill for That* is in every way a collaboration. First, I must thank the twelve extraordinary women who carved time out of their own incredibly busy schedules to write a chapter for this book: Gayle, Rita Mae, Lisa, Linda, Kay, Kathy, Julie, Heather, Jenny, Tina, Anne, and Katherine. Month after month, as each chapter hit my mailbox dead on time—or even early!—I was grateful to be working with such talented professionals.

To my friend Sherriel Mattingly of Annapolis, Maryland, who stopped by my house one day with a head full of amazing characters all clamoring to audition for parts in the novel—several of whom made the final cut—you have a weird and wacky sense of humor. Don't ever change.

To Lt. Cmdr. Cindy Silberblatt, U.S. Navy, retired, whose generous bid at a charity auction sponsored by the 2002 Malice Domestic Convention bought her the right to be a character in our novel, thank you! We hope you enjoy being dockmaster of Gryphon Gate.

To our skateboarding guru, Neil Sutherland, of Warrenton, Virginia, for introducing us to the tricks of the trade—thanks, dude. It was a hoot to have thirteen successful female authors trolling the Web to learn the meaning of "nollie backside lipslide" or "crouch and ollie while turning backside 180."

To Lawrence Baker, R.I.P., and to Saul Woythaler, senior principal electrical engineer at Raytheon, for explaining how it could be done.

ACKNOWLEDGMENTS

Thanks to our editor at St. Martin's Minotaur, Jennifer Weis, and her talented assistant, Stefanie Lindskog, and as always, to my agent, Jimmy Vines, who listens, smiles, and instead of saying, "No way!" asks, "Why not?"

INTRODUCTION

I'd Kill for That is my second expedition into collaborative serial novel territory, and what an adventure it has been! For the uninitiated, let me explain that the novel, like its predecessor *(Naked Came the Phoenix)*, was written in round-robin style: One author writes the first chapter, then passes it to the second, who picks up the story where the first author left off, then passes it on to the third, and so on.

For me, coming up with the scenario—murder in an exclusive gated community—and creating a smorgasbord of fascinating characters for the others to play with were just the beginning. The fun really started when I turned it all over to my fellow authors, then sat back and waited to see where my dream team would run with it. And they didn't disappoint me.

Under the talented pen of Gayle Lynds, the "greedy real estate developer" suggested in my proposal leapt to life "with a clash of cymbals and a drumroll" as Vanessa Smart-Drysdale, a petite, chestnut-haired beauty in black leather slacks who possesses all the compassion of Cruella de Vil. Little did I know what Lisa Gardner had in store for poor, tormented Roman Gervase, and Julie Smith's take on Sunday services at St. Francis of Assisi Interfaith Chapel had me chuckling for weeks.

As you might guess, my job as editor/contributor resembled a cross between tour guide and traffic cop, as I assembled the team and worked out the intricacies of scheduling—each author had just a month to complete her chapter—and made sure, for example, that each author received packets of background information and copies of the chapters that preceded hers. Timing was critical. We met at conferences, spoke on the telephone, and exchanged e-mails at a furious rate. As we raced to the finish line, Anne, Katherine, and I kept the transatlantic telephone lines hot as we brainstormed and worked out plot details. Anne pointed out that the novel needed a love story, and she was right, so we put one in. Often we found ourselves revisiting an earlier chapter to plant a clue or clear up a discrepancy, and it fell to the amazing Katherine Neville—who volunteered for the job, I should point out—to tie up all the loose ends as our novel sprinted to its stunning conclusion.

The history of the collaborative serial novel goes back, as far as I have been able to determine, to the early 1930s, when Britain's famed Detection Club produced *Behind the Screen*, which first appeared as a serial in the *Listener* in 1930. Written jointly by Hugh Walpole, Agatha Christie, Dorothy L. Sayers, Anthony Berkeley, E. C. Bentley, and Ronald Knox, *Behind the Screen* was followed in quick succession in 1931 by *The Scoop* and that classic of the genre, *The Floating Admiral,* where G. K. Chesterton, Canon Victor L. Whitechurch, Freeman Wills Crofts, Clemence Dane, Anthony Berkeley, and several others joined the usual suspects.

It wasn't until 1969, however, with the publication of the now classic *Naked Came the Stranger,* that the words "Naked Came . . ." became synonymous with a novel written by multiple authors in a serial fashion. Its author was "Penelope Ashe," a fictitious suburban housewife who turned out to be two dozen *Newsday* reporters headed by mastermind Mike McGrady. In 1996 another group of reporters, this time from the *Miami Herald,* revived the form with their slapstick novel, *Naked Came the Manatee,* and soon "Naked Cames . . ." were cropping up all over, including Philip José Farmer's *Naked Came the Farmer,* a benefit for the Peoria Library described by author Barbara D'Amato as a "high-octane blend of humor, talent, and hog farms!" *Farmer* was followed in 1999 by *Naked Came the Plowman,* a similar effort by twenty-five Midwestern writers.

There were not-so-Nakeds, too, as in *Pete And Shirley: The Great Tar Heel Novel,* sponsored in 1995 by the *Raleigh News & Observer,* with such writers as Clyde Edgerton, Lee Smith, Kaye Gibbons, and

Margaret Maron. In 2000, *The Putt at the End of the World* became a worthy addition to the canon where nine authors drawn from a spectrum of genres, including Dave Barry, Tami Hoag, Tim O'Brien, Lee K. Abbott, and Les Standiford, contributed chapters to this farcical thriller about golf. And in 2001 William Bernhardt and ten others devised a legal thriller, *Natural Suspect,* with this twist—the author of each chapter was not identified.

It has been suggested that the Irish cornered the market on the serial novel with such romps as *Finbar's Hotel* and its sequel, *Ladies Night at Finbar's Hotel;* yet these are essentially collections of short stories linked by a central theme—each author is given a room in a fictitious Dublin hotel—rather than a true serial novel like the more traditional *Yeats Is Dead,* described by Claire Dederer reviewing for Amazon.com as "a protracted pub crawl in the company of fifteen hyperarticulate writers" where each writer seems intent on outdoing the last by killing off as many characters as possible.

Most recently, harking back to that 1931 mystery classic, *The Floating Admiral,* and in homage to it, Elizabeth Foxwell has put together an English country house murder mystery for Malice Domestic, Inc., entitled (appropriately) *The Sunken Sailor.* Published in 2004, this collaboration features an introduction by Anne Perry and chapters by Simon Brett, Jan Burke, Deborah Crombie, Walter Sattersthwait, Sarah Smith, and nine others, including Dorothy Cannell, who also wrote a chapter for *Naked Came the Farmer.*

It's common for serial collaborations to benefit a worthy cause and *I'd Kill for That* is no exception. Like *Naked Came the Phoenix* before it, a percentage of our royalties is earmarked to support breast cancer research.

I'D KILL
FOR THAT

1

ALEXANDRIA, VIRGINIA, CITY Of cobbled streets and graceful door lamps, of austere Federalist architecture, and at least one millionaire per block—guaranteed. Quaint, expensive, highly desirable—that was Alexandria. History and the future met in this tony metropolis with a clash of cymbals and a drumroll, or at least that was the way Vanessa Smart-Drysdale imagined it.

Today was lovely, a perfect May afternoon, and Vanessa was determined to not let her worries ruin it for her. With her cell phone in one hand and a cup of fresh espresso in the other, she walked past her desk and out onto her balcony, where she gazed east across Alexandria's gabled roofs, over the silvery expanse of the Potomac River, and onward over the rolling hills of Maryland, where her fortune and revenge lay. It was only a matter of time.

She owned the penthouse condo here, an opulent hideaway high above Alexandria, with hand-knotted Berber rugs, Impressionist paintings, museum-quality antiques, and walls of glass that co-opted the blue sky into a priceless backdrop for her pricey decor. The penthouse was also the perfect getaway from Gryphon Gate, where her ex-husband was mayor. The selfish fool wanted her to sell her house there, but she wouldn't do it. At least not yet. Her county residency helped legitimatize her as a local developer. He just wanted to get rid of her.

She felt herself grow irritable as she tried to savor the panorama.

She sipped her espresso, the rich aroma scenting the spring air. Still, she hardly noticed it. Instead, as she studied Maryland's forested countryside in the distance, she found herself imagining murdering the Chesapeake County planning board. The entire board. All of them, even the ones who supported her rezoning request. They were too damn much trouble. She wanted to slice them, dice them, and asphyxiate them under the mountains of papers her lawyers, engineers, architects, landscapers, and environmentalists had to generate at an appalling—and costly—rate.

Her cell phone rang. With an angry flick of her wrist, she opened it. "Yes?"

"Vanessa, you bitch."

She smiled. "Yes, Peter. I thought it might be you."

"How could you *do* this to me!"

"Darling, I didn't do it. You did. All by yourself, I might add."

"This is extortion!"

"Well, not really all by yourself," she went on as if he'd said nothing. "Sorry. There was Mignon, too. Silly of me to forget her. I'm sure her husband hasn't. Such a beautiful body under that ridiculous Burberry trench coat. I hope she didn't catch cold. Oh my, I'm wandering off the point. Sorry again. We're talking about adultery here, of course. Not just hers, but yours. Tsk, tsk. Screwing around with someone not your spouse. Bad boy, Peter. Stupid, too, to both be caught in flagrante delicto. What will your congregation *think?*"

"Vanessa!" His voice was a cry of outrage. Then there was a sound in his throat, something between a growl and a choke.

She drank espresso.

At last he managed, "What's this going to cost me?"

"Relax. You won't have to murder anyone."

Without another glance at her glorious view, Vanessa Smart-Drysdale turned on her heel and walked back into the condo. Her nerves were on fire. This was dirty work, and part of her hated it. But another part of her felt incredibly alive, excited.

As she realized that, and enjoyed it thoroughly, she caught sight of herself in the decorative mirror at the end of the hall. She looked like her usual self—small, slender, and sophisticated. But now there was more: Her eyes were particularly large and bright, snapping with hot blue light. Two spots of rosy color had appeared on her cheeks.

Her chestnut hair—long and casually loose today because she was working at home—seemed unusually vibrant and glossy. Altogether, she was more than attractive in her black leather trousers and vest. She was appealing, perhaps even magnetic. Not too bad, she told herself modestly, then grinned.

He assured her, "I wouldn't murder anyone. I couldn't. I had one little slip, a tiny moment of weakness. As you said yourself, Mignon Gervase is—well—impossible to ignore." His voice hardened. "And the way you soften me up for whatever you want is to say it's *not murder?* I'm shocked, Vanessa. I thought better of you."

She laughed. "Guilt, Peter? How amusing that you're trying to make *me* feel guilty." She continued around to her Chippendale desk, sat, put her cup on a hand-painted Delft tile, and leaned back.

He retorted, "How many affairs did *you* have while you were still married?"

"There's a big difference. I'm no hypocrite. I never said I was any better than I am. You, however, hold yourself up as a paragon." She was growing angry again. "You could go public about everything. Then we wouldn't be having this conversation." Of course, she thought, if the Reverend Dr. Peter Armbruster let his wife and the world know of his sexual frolic in the woods, he'd lose his place at the helm of the St. Francis of Assisi Interfaith Chapel, the most popular church in Gryphon Gate. And, considering his wife—the pinch-faced Laura Armbruster—he'd probably lose her, too. On the other hand, that might not be such a bad outcome for him.

He announced firmly, "I want your video of us. I'd like to take away your camcorder, too, but I'm determined to be reasonable about this."

"It's worse than that," she said cheerfully. "I've just upgraded my equipment, and I'm all set to put the video and audio on RealPlayer and post it to the Gryphon Gate Web site. What that means, of course, is that not only all the 250 homeowners in our little exclusive enclave can watch you and Mignon in living color and hear all your coos and squeals, but anyone who checks out the Web site can catch the show, too . . ."

"Stop, Vanessa. *Stop!*" He groaned loudly. "What exactly do you want from me?"

Without hesitation, she told him, "Your vote on the county planning commission to rezone Forest Glen for greater density. I've spent a fortune to develop that land. When the houses are built and the project's finished, it'll be a sweeping monument to art and livability, a place that developers from around the world will come to study and copy. I'll make it the best of everything, far better than even Gryphon Gate."

"And bigger, too," he said bitterly. "A gargantuan sprawl. And right next door. You know I've already taken a public stand against it. We need to protect our open space. That's why the homeowners association offered to buy it from you. Forest Glen is bad on every level, from the additional stress on the Chesapeake watershed to increased traffic and pollution. I can't change my vote. I'll look like an idiot."

"Well, darling, you *are* an idiot. Or you've been one. Truth in advertising and all that. Be grateful I caught you before you jammed yourself up with a serious zipper problem. Next thing, it'd be cigars."

"*Vanessa!*" It was a scream.

"Do I have your vote? Or do I send a friendly E-mail to all our friends in Gryphon Gate, letting them know about the sexy addition to the Web site?"

He erupted, "I'll do it, dammit. I'll vote to rezone your land. But I want all your evidence. *Everything.*"

"Of course. And I'll throw in a nice cup of espresso, too." The phone on her fax line rang. "I've got to go, Reverend Armbruster. It's been a delight. See you in church."

"When can I come over and get that video?" he demanded.

"Once Forest Glen breaks ground."

"That could be years!"

"Not if you help me." Vanessa hung up and pulled the fax from her machine.

As she read, her throat tightened, and fear made her heart pound like a kettledrum. There was just one sheet of paper, and in the middle were typed four words: *I know about Carbury.* The meaning was horrifying. She stared, shocked. How could anyone have found out? Then lower down the page: *8:00 P.M., sixth hole, sand trap. Tonight. Come alone.*

She looked for a name, a return phone number, anything to indicate who'd sent the fax. But the paper was otherwise completely blank. Her hands trembled as she read the message one last time. Then she checked her watch. It was nearly six o'clock. A murderous rage shook her. There wasn't much time. She tore the fax into small pieces, grabbed her purse, jumped to her feet, and ran out the door.

Born in controversy, Gryphon Gate, Maryland, was an elite community with sky-scraping house prices, tight security, and sentry-guarded kiosks at its three arched entries. Many in Chesapeake County had fought its construction intensely, complaining it would denude the bucolic countryside, planting houses where Mother Nature's towering timber had thrived for millions of years. It was blasphemy, they claimed. They were right, and they were wrong.

Nestled in rolling woodlands, Gryphon Gate was now a fait accompli, home to briefcase barons and political pundits, philanthropists and society mavens, and young families boasting large investment portfolios because they'd sold their tech shares before the market went south. The township spread along the banks of the tranquil Truxton River, just minutes from the nation's capital. Residents here enjoyed the finest of everything—neighborhood clubhouses, hiking and riding trails, a championship golf course, a yacht-filled marina, an interior forest of some twenty-two pristine acres, even a five-star restaurant. Trees were everywhere. So were *Southern Living* flower gardens, lush shrubbery manicured into topiary shapes, and delightful wildlife, especially deer.

For Antoinette "Toni" Sinclair, the township was pure magic. A paradise. She, her husband Lincoln, and their daughter Miranda had moved in six years ago. While she vaguely knew all about Gryphon Gate's contentious history, her fundamental belief in live and let live erased its significance from her mind.

Even more important, she didn't like to think about the past. It was too painful. Shortly after they'd settled into their wonderful new life here, Lincoln was killed in a terrible accident at his dot.com start-up in Alexandria. He'd been wearing his headphones, which were plugged directly into his office TV so he could get the highest quality sound, while he put in thirty vigorous minutes on his Nordic-trak, working off the double cheeseburger and fries he'd had for lunch. He was still wearing the headset when he went into his private bathroom to wash up. The headset, which he prized not only for its technical virtues but because it was a birthday gift from his employees, had been made of an experimental polymer. Flexible, light . . . who knew it would conduct electricity? Ordinarily, it wouldn't have mattered, except that the stereo amplifier custom built into the bathroom wall had been faultily wired, according to the police. So when Lincoln sat on his stainless-steel toilet seat and plugged himself in, he was electrocuted.

It still brought tears to Toni's eyes, thinking about Lincoln writhing on the cold ceramic tiles, his heart fibrillating wildly. If only someone had been there to administer CPR! If only *she* had been there! She'd been devastated to lose him, especially in such a pointless mishap. But then Lincoln had always been cutting edge, and everything about his work and his business had been the most modern. Why he thought stainless steel toilets were avant garde she had no idea. What an unusual buying choice. But his goofiness was just one more reason why she fell in love with him.

In the long, moist shadows of afternoon, Toni stepped out onto the grass in front of her colonial-style manse and threw out handfuls of birdseed mixed with corn.

"Miranda, sweetie!" she called as she dug into the Egyptian cotton grain bag. "It's feeding time. All of the Bambis will be here soon!"

As she tossed out another handful, Toni Sinclair gazed up at the clear afternoon sky, the sun's warmth on her face. Dressed in her Mephisto loafers, Donna Karan jeans, and open-necked Escada shirt, she felt so completely at home that she could never imagine living anywhere else. She was thirty-two years old, a willowy woman with auburn hair. Her only makeup was lipstick. Natural and unassuming, she reveled in all of the stately homes, the verdant grounds, and the lovely gardens of Gryphon Gate.

As white-tailed deer approached from neighboring properties up and down the winding street, she sang happily to herself. "Whistle while you work. Ohhhh, whistle while you work."

Soon Miranda was at her side. "Look, Mommie! Thirty-four deer. More every day. Hurray!"

Toni's daughter peered at the grazing animals, her plump little face shining with excitement. A streak of dirt creased her forehead, and twigs stuck to the back of her Sundance Festival T-shirt. She was eight years old, an earnest, freckle-faced, redheaded child who loved nature, M&M's, and sneakers that lit up when she walked.

"Yes, sweetie. We're popular," her mother assured her proudly.

The deer—all females, many with fawns—circled the thick lawn, their velvet muzzles delicately vacuuming up the food. Toni Sinclair had begun feeding them just three days before, because, unfortunately, not everyone in Gryphon Gate had her tolerant attitude about life. Some time ago a noisy group of residents had formed to complain about the deer: They were a traffic hazard; they crapped on the golf greens; they ate the flowers and the very costly shrubbery.

Then last week, the group decided they should "harvest" the animals. That's when Toni went into shock. They were planning to hire sharpshooters to kill the defenseless deer, which completely and irrevocably broke her live-and-let-live code.

She'd put her mind to the problem, finally deciding that all of the troubles arose because the deer were hungry. Which meant the solution was simple: She'd feed them, and they'd stay off the streets and quit rummaging for meals on other people's estates.

Miranda chirped, "May I have some, Mommie? Please?"

"You bet."

Toni opened the bag and Miranda dove in with both hands, her short, freckled arms disappearing. With a triumphant smile, she threw the seed and grain in a long arc.

As the deer moved to sweep it up, Toni heard a car on the quiet street. She stared. It was one of the official white-and-periwinkle blue BMWs that the Gryphon Gate police drove. On each side was painted a proud gryphon—half eagle and half lion. Beneath was written GRYPHON GATE POLICE DEPARTMENT.

Little Miranda gave a shiver. "We like the police, don't we?" She slipped her hand inside Toni's.

"You bet," Toni Sinclair said again. But this time her voice was less assured.

The car stopped at the curb in front of her elegant colonial, and two grim-faced policemen in full riot gear jumped out and ran toward Toni and Miranda, their guns flopping against their pant legs until they clamped the grips to their belts.

Miranda stepped back, and so did Toni, feeling a moment of intimidation.

"Stop!" ordered the first policeman. He had a square jaw and a face shaved so smooth that the pink skin glowed. He turned his head, his reflecting sunglasses surveying the lawn and the deer as if they constituted a crime scene. On the collar of his flak vest was embroidered a name: Leland Ford.

"We've stopped moving, Officer Ford," Toni told him. "See?"

"We're not moving at all, are we, Mommie?" Miranda asked. She clutched Toni's hand tighter.

Toni gave the small hand a reassuring squeeze. "What can we do for you officers?"

The second policeman also wore reflecting sunglasses. He was shorter, about Toni's height, with thick shoulders and splayed feet. The name on his vest was John D. Carnegie.

Both men's heads rotated like lighthouse beacons.

"I count thirty-four," said Officer Carnegie. "Hell, she's got a friggin' zoo here."

"We may have to arrest you, ma'am," Officer Ford informed her. "You're harboring deer. You'll have to come down to the station house with us."

"Shouldn't we read her rights to her first?" asked Carnegie. He was the older of the two.

"We have to wait until we officially arrest her," Ford informed him.

At that moment it seemed to Toni that her heart stopped beating. She gave a little gasp. "*Arrest* me? For harboring *deer?*" She gulped. "But how can I 'harbor' them? They're wild animals. I can't control them. No one can control them. That's the problem!"

"Your yard's full of 'em, ma'am," Ford said loudly. "You're *feeding* them," he accused.

The deer had been watching the new human arrivals suspiciously. When Ford raised his voice, they began to move away.

"That's just seed and corn!" Toni said indignantly. "I could tell the deer not to eat the birdseed, but you just can't convince them. Besides, they're hungry. Look at them. Would you deny a starving animal? The Nazis did that. Surely you're not that heartless."

"Mommie?" Miranda had been studying the policemen's forbidding expressions. When she looked up at her mother, her petite face had gone white, and her freckles stood out like black polka dots. "If they take you to jail, will I ever see you again?"

"Shame on you," she scolded the men. "Scaring a little girl. And you're scaring the deer, too. Look, they're leaving. They're your only witnesses, and if they won't talk to me, they certainly won't talk to you."

"Ma'am!" Carnegie exploded, exasperated. "Did you deliberately feed those deer?" He looked around quickly. All had vanished.

Toni lifted her chin stubbornly and put the grain bag behind her back. "I take the Fifth. You really should learn to be more flexible, you know."

The officers exchanged a long look. Then they gazed up the brick driveway to where Bertha and Bill, Toni's household help, had come out to watch. Up and down the leafy street other residents and their servants were beginning to appear, too.

All of this unsettled both policemen. Gryphon Gate was supposed to be an easy gig. Usually, the only arrest each month was of that wacko Roman Gervase, who was convinced he was a werewolf. When the moon was full, he'd rip off his tuxedo and howl, and all of the phone lines at the station would light up like a Christmas tree. Of course, there were drunken parties here and there celebrating deals and retirements and divorces. But a polite police visit was usually enough to send everyone indoors, where heavily insulated walls contained the disturbing good cheer. There were smaller problems, too, that required simple warnings—broken golf clubs that sailed through the air when a particularly easy putt was missed, the infrequent disagreement about reservation times at the bridge tournaments, that sort of thing.

However, arresting a mother on her front yard, with her minor daughter for a witness, on a charge of feeding "starving" animals that had already dispersed could explode into something far larger. Neither policeman wanted to be caught in the cross fire. Not in Gryphon Gate, where the residents had all the wealth, education, and savvy in the world to back up any crazy notion.

"You know, ma'am," Carnegie told her, mustering as much authority as he could considering the situation, "the new antifeeding ordinance is serious. Next time, we'll definitely have to arrest you." His expression was glum.

"We can't let you off a second time," Ford agreed. He shook his head, unhappy. "You look like a nice lady. Can't you find some other hobby?"

Toni Sinclair was insulted. "Life isn't a hobby! Come to the town meeting tomorrow night, and you'll see how serious this is!" She looked down at her daughter. "Let's go, Miranda. We'll phone the other mommies."

"What for?" Miranda wondered as she skipped along at her mother's side. They were headed up the drive toward the house.

"A candlelight vigil," Toni explained, thinking rapidly. "We'll hold a candlelight vigil for the deer at the meeting. We'll buy tall white candles and notify all the newspaper, radio, and TV newscasters. Would you like to be on TV, sweetie?"

"Ohhhh, Mommie!" Miranda said, excited. "We'll be stars!"

Ahead of them Bertha waved a sheet of paper at Toni. She was a heavyset woman with a kind, soft face, who wore her usual black housedress with white apron and white lace collar. "Mrs. Sinclair," she called. "You have a fax."

Toni took the paper and sent Miranda into the house with Bertha and Bill, chuckling about the poor policemen, although she felt a wee bit sorry for them. They'd looked so dejected when they'd driven off.

As she strolled toward the side door she read the fax—and stopped cold in the driveway, horrified. It was impossible! No one knew. No one! Sweat broke out on her forehead, and her chest tightened with terror. She stared at the words in the middle of the page: *I know about Salinger.* Then she forced herself to read the rest of the message. *8:00 P.M., sixth hole, sand trap. Tonight. Come alone.*

She gazed at the message longer, still not quite believing. Her breath emerged in panicked little pants. She looked at her Rolex wristwatch. It was after six o'clock. Thank God she didn't have long to wait. She forced herself to walk calmly into the house, rending the fax into smaller and smaller pieces.

Jerrold "Jerry" Lynch lived in the rarified world of the DOW and the NASDAQ, of short calls and stock puts, of electronic trading that could break the heart or make a fortune in the flash of a keyboard stroke. For years he'd thrived. An investment banker during the go-go 1990s, he'd retired to Gryphon Gate to use his fat portfolio as a launching pad for even greater wealth. At first, all of his plans had succeeded.

His French Renaissance chalet was enormous, one of the largest properties in the township, with eight bedrooms and twelve baths, plus maids' and nannies' quarters, a media room, a two-lane bowling alley, and a swimming pool with a retractable roof. He and his wife, Renée, were the proud parents of their first baby, a green-eyed little charmer named Samantha. He was crazy about those unusual green eyes. He had all the accoutrements and toys of the genteel suburban fast lane: On one side of him lived a curvy German duchess (very blond; he wondered whether she was blonde all over), on the other side was the estate of the renowned U.S. ambassador to Great Britain, and across the street stood the mansion of one of the world's most prominent rock stars—rich, drugged out, with gorgeous babes always in tow. No one missed the neighborhood barbecues, especially Jerry.

At one time he'd had it all. But now he was two months behind on his mortgage. Just a moment ago, he'd lost the final hundred thousand in his bank account. He'd borrowed on everything, and there was nowhere else to go. He was only fifty virile years old, but he was finished. It was enough to make a grown man shed a tear, and—as he sat there behind his top-of-the-line IBM computer staring at his flat screen that showed the commodity transaction that had finally wiped his portfolio clean—he considered it.

He remembered an old Wall Street joke: "Now I'm in real trouble. First the laundry called to say they'd lost my shirt, then my broker called to tell me the same thing." With electronic trading made easy, he had managed financial ruin entirely on his own.

He swore loudly and picked up the telephone. There was that mysterious little click again. It was so quiet that he usually didn't hear it, but right now, in his sensitive state, the sound rang loudly in his ear. He'd have Renée get the phone repair people in. He cursed again and punched the extension to the maid's room.

"Hullo?" she answered.

His voice was husky and full of need. "Come down here, Anka."

They made love on his massive desk. Right on the leather-trimmed, merlot red blotter. In the initial throes of her gratitude, Anka knocked the phone off its hook, but Jerry was busy and ignored it. He breathed heavily, devouring the sight of her beneath him. He liked her silky unblemished skin, her rounded thighs, her long, exposed throat, her lavish breasts, but most of all, he prized her sharp little cries of ecstasy. With a shudder he exploded, arching his head back.

He opened his eyes and looked down. Instantly she smiled.

"That's better," he decided.

He stood up, sweaty, his pants around his ankles. He pulled them up. Suddenly, he had a renewed fondness for life. He liked his dark walnut moldings, the Venetian crystal lamps, his handmade walnut desk, and his black leather sofa and two matching side chairs that formed a conversation grouping across the room. Right now his office seemed particularly masculine. He even liked the plantation shutters that lined the big bay window that overlooked his back acreage. He decided he must be feeling a sort of paternal acceptance of this wayward world.

"Would you like a cigarette?" Anka asked as she sat up and rearranged her clothes. She was a leggy brunette, with thick black eyelashes and pouty lips that he had to admit were a big turn-on.

"Smoking again, Anka?" Jerry tucked in his shirt and zipped up his pants. He might be fifty, but he could still perform as good as the next guy. Better, if Anka's response was accurate evidence, and he was sure it was. "You've gotta quit hurting your lungs like that," he advised. "Respect your body and your mind. That's what I always say. Your individuality. Your importance as a person. You hear me, Anka? I'm just telling you this for your own good."

"Yah," she agreed. "Would you like a cigarette, too, Jerry?"

Just then his fax machine rang. He glanced at it. "Might as well. Leave me one. Scoot on out of here. You can smoke yours up in your room. Just keep the door closed. Otherwise, Renée'll be pissed." He gestured at the fax machine, where a sheet of paper was feeding into the tray. "Might be a big business opportunity." He prized optimism. Next to money, optimism was the largest source of wealth.

"Right, Jerry. Thanks a lot. You're the best." She gave him a quick kiss on the cheek.

"You're welcome. Where's my cigarette?"

She produced it from a pocket in her skirt, slid out of the room, and the door closed quietly behind her.

He was alone again. He sighed with satisfaction. Smoothing back his hair, he hurried to the fax machine. The transmission had ended. But there was only one piece of paper, which was disturbing. Good faxes—the ones that meant potential deals—came with cover sheets. If this were just a cover sheet, what the hell use was that?

He snapped it up. As he read, his face turned tomato red, and he could feel his blood pressure shoot through his skull. For a moment he was paralyzed by terror. He read through a second time: *I know about Roach.* Then: *8:00 P.M., sixth hole, sand trap. Tonight. Come alone.*

"Who in hell's been digging into my past?" he complained aloud.

He was outraged and horrified and frightened all at the same time. He stared at the polished brass captain's clock on his desk, which had cost five hundred dollars and kept perfect time. It was nearly six-thirty. He dropped the fax into his electric shredder and watched until its destruction was complete. That's when he noticed that his phone was off the hook. He replaced it and ran for the door, lighting the cigarette. He was going to get to that damn meeting early and case it all out.

At exactly 7:55 P.M. Toni Sinclair drove her champagne-colored Mercedes SUV toward Gryphon Gate's championship golf course. As was her habit, she would be exactly on time. She was still dressed in her jeans and shirt, but she'd replaced her loafers with her Nike running shoes. They were just a precaution, she told herself soberly. She'd left little Miranda at home with Bertha, who was feeding her a nice meal of hot wings, arugula salad, and homemade, multigrain bread. Miranda was fond of hot wings, which she explained were among Britney Spears's favorite foods.

As she drove into the golf club's parking lot, Toni worried again about what awaited her at the sand pit near the sixth hole. Her throat tightened.

Pine trees and decorative granite boulders lined the parking area. Dusk was spreading, casting a gentle lavender light across the tree-dotted golf course, which rolled out in three directions. The hour was sufficiently late that even the most addicted duffers were leaving for stiff drinks and fine dinners at homes or in clubs. She passed several in their cars and on their bicycles, speeding out of the lot.

One was Vanessa Smart-Drysdale, who was in her usual red Corvette. Toni waved. Vanessa didn't spend all that much time at

Gryphon Gate these days, but then that wasn't unexpected. Between her divorce from Henry Drysdale and that ambitious development she wanted to build next door, Vanessa didn't have many friends left in the community.

When Vanessa finally noticed her and waved back, Toni gave her a genuine smile. She liked Vanessa. She was spunky, Toni thought, although right now she looked distracted and worried. No doubt due to all the problems with rezoning Forest Glen.

And there was that strange Mr. Lynch—Jerry Lynch, a handsome fellow who used to be some kind of hotshot international financier. He was racing away, too, in a predatory-looking Humvee. Toni wondered whether he had agoraphobia, because she seldom saw him. He seemed to stay holed up in that elegant French chateau of his, although she'd heard that he regularly attended the local social gatherings that all the neighborhoods in Gryphon Gate held. She'd spot his wife, Renée, much more frequently, mostly at the pediatrician. They had a darling baby girl with the same color of jade green eyes as the Upshaw twins and the Anderson boys. When she'd told Bertha what she'd noticed about the eyes of all those children, Bertha had laughed and said it must be the Gryphon Gate water.

Thinking about the pleasures of ordinary, worry-free conversation brought Toni's troubles back in a rush. Her mouth dry, her brow furrowed, she parked, grabbed her shoulder bag, and headed around the clubhouse and out onto the putting greens. She didn't play much golf, but Lincoln had. Sometimes she'd gone with him, so she had a good idea where the sixth tee was.

The place was deserted. She checked her watch. Two minutes until eight. She pressed her hand against her chest and felt her heart hammer. She tried not to think about what she was facing.

There was a foursome in the distance, over near the eighteenth tee. She broke into a lope across the greens, heading in the opposite direction. The pungent scent of pine was heavy in the air, and a twilight breeze was rising. Tree shadows were long and black and chilly. She felt uneasy. Who would be waiting for her? What would they want?

Maybe she should've phoned Sigmond Vormeister. He might know. He was a Ph.D. sociologist and was secretly studying the residents of Gryphon Gate for some kind of exposé book he wanted to write. She knew that only because he'd gotten tipsy at one of their neighborhood parties and confided it as sort of a lame apology after he'd tried to grab her butt and she'd stomped his wingtips hard.

She had her checkbook with her. The only thing that made sense was that the person who sent her the fax intended to blackmail her. One of the sweetest things about Lincoln had been that he'd planned wisely and left her filthy rich. Still, an insightful part of her knew it was unlikely she could ever pay enough. Once anyone allowed themselves to be blackmailed, there'd be no end to it. After all, decent people didn't go digging into things that were none of their business. Decent people didn't threaten to reveal other people's secrets. Decent people didn't blackmail. Whoever was waiting for her was an awful, despicable person, more to be pitied than feared.

Nevertheless, she was scared. She clamped her teeth together to keep them from chattering. As she caught sight of the sixth hole, she slowed, watching as a family of deer stepped quietly from a stand of willows. A creek ran through the willows, and they'd been drinking from it. Their black noses glistened in the waning light. They were sleek and velvety and looked friendly. She wanted to stop. Maybe they'd let her pet them.

But there was no time. Regretfully, she loped past, searching the shadows ahead for whoever was waiting. When no one was standing at the tee, she stopped on the springy grass, peered all around, scrutinizing. No one.

She headed for the sand trap about twenty feet away. It lay in a shallow hollow, and if anyone was standing next to it, she'd easily spot him. There were no trees or bushes around there either, which meant there were no shadows for her to fear. Heart thudding, she closed in—and stopped abruptly. Someone was lying in the sand. There was still enough light to tell it was a man lying on his stomach, and he was wearing a rumpled suit. There was something vaguely familiar about him.

"Are you all right?" she called.

There was no answer.

She raised her voice. "Hey! Are you okay?"

There was neither answer nor movement. In fact, now that she studied him, his face seemed to be straight down in the sand. No way could he breathe. She dashed to his side, fell to her knees, and rolled him over. And stared. It was Sigmond Vormeister, the sociologist, his broad face twisted in fright. There was a gash on his forehead. Blood with a generous dusting of sand coated his face.

"Oh, poor Dr. Vormeister!"

She put her ear against his chest, hoping his heart was still beating. But there was only silence. "Oh, my God!" She pulled her cell phone from her purse and hit the buttons for 911. Shuddering, she looked around. She had a horrible, sinking feeling. Why were hers the only footprints in the sand?

2

TONI NO SOONER PRESSED THE
"send" button than she pushed her thumb down hard on the "end"
button. Yes, why were hers the only footprints in the sand?

Lincoln, who had loved her impulsiveness most of the time, recognized that it catapulted her into trouble at other times. "Look before
you leap," he'd counsel.

She was looking now.

Kneeling down, she was assailed by the odor of fresh blood as she
squinted at Sigmond Vormeister's wound. Deep though it was, the
gash on his forehead couldn't have killed him. She was tempted to roll
him back over, but she knew better.

Surprised that this proximity to a corpse didn't unnerve her, she
slung her purse over her back and dropped the tiny phone in her
pocket. She reached for the sand rake, hesitated, dropped her purse
back in front of her, plucked out an embroidered handkerchief,
wrapped the handkerchief around the sand rake, and carefully obliterated her footsteps from the sand.

Every noise or rustle of wind grated on her senses. She prayed as
she raked that no one saw her. She gently laid the rake beside the
sand pit and slowly walked toward the curving line of azaleas nestled
under handsome pines.

It was bridge night at the club. Her hope was to slip into the ladies' room at the end of the hall and then emerge just as the group took their break. She'd smile, chat, and go to the bar for a drink.

As she breathed deeply, calming herself, a slow tendril of anger crawled upward inside her.

Salinger. She'd jumped at the bait. *I know about Salinger,* that loathsome fax said. The only other person to know about Salinger was Salinger, a relationship she chalked up to her impulsive nature and her youth. Who else could know?

Sucker. She had been suckered.

Fool me once, shame on you. Fool me twice, shame on me. She wouldn't rise to the bait so quickly the next time. Toni, though impulsive, was capable of cold logic. She knew there'd be a next time.

It occurred to her that whoever sent her the fax had also killed Sigmond Vormeister. She opened the side door to the club. The coast was clear to the ladies' room. As she scooted down the hall, she thought about it again. Maybe whoever sent that fax *didn't* kill Vormeister, he was such an odd one.

She splashed water on her face then held her wrists under the cold running water. "Assume nothing," she whispered. "Assume nothing."

All she knew was that Sigmond Vormeister was glassy-eyed dead and she didn't kill him. She cut off the tap, shook her head for the tousled look, and stepped into the long hall toward the main interior corridor.

"Toni," Renée Lynch called out as she crossed the hall.

"You look wonderful in coral," Toni complimented her. "How are you doing tonight?"

"Pretty good." Renée winked. "So good that I need this break to pinch myself."

The tinkling of a small bell alerted both women. "I don't believe Laura Armbruster does that. She puts on more airs than any white woman I've ever met."

Up until the seventies, wealthy Maryland families employed African-Americans in their households. A cherished ritual was for a smartly dressed man, sometimes in livery, to carry bells on a crossbar. These emitted a melodious sound as he made his stately progression through the lower floors of the house. It was the call to dinner.

"Maybe because she's not white. She's going to remind us how it's properly done." Toni smiled.

"Actually, I think she'll do anything to divert herself from Peter. Any of us could have told her marrying a preacher is a one-way ticket to engulfing boredom. Marrying a white preacher is boredom under-lined three times."

"Renée, God will get you for that."

She laughed, the sound not unlike the tinkling of Laura's insistent bell, calling the players back to the bridge tables. "No doubt, but I'll have a whale of a time before Judgment Day. Well, I'd better get back in there before she has a conniption."

"Wouldn't want that." Toni winked right back at her then sighed, sighed again with deep relief as she made her way to the bar.

The bar curved around the gracious room, paneled, filled with gilt framed photographs of members in moments of triumph on the golf course, tennis courts, hunt field, or sailing. One wall, encased in glass, held the silver trophies, colored banners, and other paraphernalia of sporting prowess.

Vanessa perched at a small table under the trophies.

The bar was otherwise empty, as bridge night traditionally was a light night at the watering hole.

"Toni."

Toni walked over. "Didn't I just pass you?"

"You did. Then I pulled a U-ey. Couldn't face the kitchen." Vanessa clicked her fingers and Tiffany, a young waitress, appeared.

"Martini." Tiffany smiled at Vanessa.

"You are so smart, Tiffany. That explains why you're going back to Maryland this fall. Stinger for Toni."

Tiffany looked at Toni to make certain she wanted a Stinger.

"Vanessa, you remember the smallest details." Toni glanced up at Tiffany. "Stinger."

As Tiffany walked back to the bar, Vanessa leaned toward Toni. "Let's have something sinful to eat. My treat."

"Well, only if you'll let me take you sailing first really good day." Toni had a spectacular forty-foot boat built in the 1920s and com-pletely restored by Lincoln as an anniversary present.

"Deal."

The drinks appeared, and the two women said they needed time to study the menu.

"Are you girding your loins for the battle tomorrow night?" asked

Toni, referring to the Gryphon Gate council meeting concerning their action on Vanessa's proposal to the county for Forest Glen.

"I'd rather gird my loins for something far more pleasurable. But yes, I am ready for battle, and more, I intend to win. God forbid a woman succeed."

"I suppose there is that," Toni paused, "but you can't so easily dismiss the environmental concerns."

"I wouldn't do that. I love the Chesapeake Bay and all her tributaries." Vanessa sipped her martini, deliciously cold. "I grew up in these parts." Vanessa rattled off the details of the environmental impact study she'd commissioned, her wetlands preservation plan.

She'd foolishly been lured back from Alexandria, but as she drove, her mind had revved as fast as her engine. Who knew about her condominium? Senator Carbury of the great state of Maryland. He wouldn't be dumb enough to discuss their deal or their affair even to Parker Upshaw, his best friend. She sipped her drink thoughtfully. Parker Upshaw was becoming the best friend to many people in Congress, thanks to his management consulting firm.

Vanessa didn't believe anyone else knew about her arrangements with Carbury. But then politics and treachery were bosom companions. *Someone* knew.

She had paid off Ned Carbury in crisp new bills as well as with her perfectly maintained body. If the Rev. Dr. Peter Armbruster hadn't been such a ninny, she would have paid him off, too. Bills only. Laura could keep his body. However, it was proving amusing to torture the devout member of the God Squad. She stifled a laugh, which made her drink go down the wrong way.

"Are you okay?"

Eyes watering, "Windpipe," Vanessa gasped.

"Hate that." Toni handed her a glass of water.

"Made myself laugh. I was thinking that I'll drop the Drysdale and return to my maiden name, Smart. But then if I'd been smart, I'd have never married Henry in the first place."

"And you wouldn't be sitting in Gryphon Gate with a pile of money. You were plenty smart," Toni replied evenly.

Vanessa, recovered, coolly assessed Toni. "I underestimate you."

"Everyone does." Toni smiled brightly.

Barbara "Babs" Blackburn, late twenties, swept into the bar. Her close-cropped blonde hair gave her the air of an adorable waif. Henry Drysdale certainly thought so when he ran his fingers through those artfully sculpted locks.

Vanessa's eyes narrowed for an instant, "Ah, the lady of the moment, or perhaps the lady of the evening."

Babs, lovely, had not yet mastered the art of emotional repression. She had mastered few arts, except for her computer and golf. Her handicap of two attested to her skill. But she had little direction in life, which tended to erode whatever gifts she may have been granted.

"I can't believe you'd show your face in here, the way you're trying to ruin Gryphon Gate," Babs sneered with the indignation of the righteous.

"Better my face than my ass, and I'd advise you to cover yours," Vanessa slyly replied.

"You'll get yours." Babs stomped off.

"I truly hope so." Vanessa tightened the back of her pierced earring.

"She's so young," Toni remarked.

"And that's all she has in her favor."

"With men it seems to be enough," Toni ruefully said.

"I resent that." Jerry Lynch had walked up behind the two well-groomed women. "But you're dead-on."

"And what are you doing here?" Vanessa queried him.

"I promised Renée I'd watch the second half of her little contest and that I'd bring her a very large, very frosty daiquiri."

"Sit down while Tiffany gets your daiquiri." Vanessa pointed to a chair.

"And a single malt on the rocks for me, Tiff," he called to the young woman.

"Okay." She flashed a genuine smile.

Jerry stared at Toni Sinclair, realized what he was doing, and smoothly covered. "You're so attractive, Toni. You need to get out more."

She blushed. "It takes time."

He smiled and thought what a cool customer she was.

Jerry had driven to the golf course, feared what might await him, and then cruised away, which was when he passed Toni. But the fax and the implied threat drove him crazy. He parked his Humvee in Bob

Satterfield's driveway. Bob and his wife Sue were in France for a month. Going through their backyard, he could easily get on the front nine. He crept up on the back side of the sixth green, hunkering down in the willows. No one came out of the gathering darkness.

Crouching, Jerry loped to the sand trap in five strides and nearly fell over when he saw the body. Breathing raggedly, he stared, trying to make out who it was. A man, for sure, who looked a lot like Sigmond Vormeister, but impossible to confirm without getting closer. No thank you! Jerry backed away, keeping low, and then caught sight of Toni walking across the fairway. He couldn't see her features, but the way she walked, the purse over her shoulder, it had to be Toni Sinclair. He dropped into the creek, used the high banks as a cover. He saw Toni walk into the sand trap, walk out, and drop the rake.

When he reached his vehicle, he drove home to change his clothes, then returned to the club. He *had* promised Renée he'd cheer her on. For all his philandering, he tried to please his wife. He loved her. But he also loved risk, both sexually and financially. He had just encountered a little more risk than he imagined.

What was Toni Sinclair doing out at the sixth hole?

She didn't kill whoever was in the sand, that was clear, but she didn't report it either. She was becoming very interesting to Jerry.

"I'm surprised you haven't asked me about Forest Glen?"

"Sorry?" Jerry blinked at Vanessa.

"For or against?"

"Uh, against; but I won't stand in your way. Business is business, and it doesn't devalue my investment."

"That's big of you," Vanessa purred.

"I'm a big guy." At six foot four inches, Jerry could say that. He turned his attention back to Toni. "Still being Mother Teresa to the deer?"

"Oh, they are so beautiful. I can't bear the thought that they might be shot."

"Not the killer type, are you?" His voice deepened.

Startled, then back to herself, Toni replied, "I suppose I could kill to save myself or my daughter, but no, I'm not the type. Are you?"

"Me? Violence comes more naturally to men."

"Balls." Vanessa laughed.

"Exactly." He laughed, too, as Tiffany appeared at his elbow. "Ah, the magic potion. Thank you, Tiffany." He stood up, inclined his head to the ladies, picked up the two drinks. "Renée's dying to get the better of Laura tonight. Ladies, I enjoyed seeing you both."

As he walked away, Vanessa smiled. "Cocksure."

Later that evening Vanessa opened the door to her Gryphon Gate home and breathed in. The wonderful orangey odor of her house pleased her as well as its grandeur.

She kicked off her shoes, and before she could click on the news, she heard the grinding of the fax machine in her downstairs office.

A furrow creased her brow, which had been expertly unwrinkled with BOTOX. She padded down the thick carpet to the office and plucked the fax out of the machine.

I don't like being stood up. You'll hear from me.

"Asshole." She crumpled the fax and threw it into the wastebasket.

Renée, curled up at home in their overstuffed sofa, was replaying her brilliant night. "Jerry, are you listening?"

"I am. You said, 'Laura smiled through clenched teeth when you beat her ass.'"

Renée clapped her hands. "She really is a hypocrite."

"I suppose we all are to some extent."

"Jerry!"

"All right. You're not." He hoisted himself out of the enveloping sofa. "The kitchen calls. Can I get you anything?"

"No, dear, just yourself."

Jerry passed his home office on the way to the kitchen. A lone white sheet stood at attention in the fax machine.

He hesitated just an instant, then strode in and yanked the goddamned thing right out of the machine.

I don't like being stood up. You'll hear from me.

"What is your game?" he muttered under his breath as he fed the message to his shredder.

He returned from the kitchen, Coca-Cola in hand, and sat next to his wife, absentmindedly listening. He hadn't enlightened her concerning his financial crisis. He was confident he could pull that chestnut out of the fire. Balls! He really did have them, as well as nerves. He wasn't going under. But whoever knew about Roach could command a hefty sum of money. What else does anyone want but money? At least that's what he wanted, what he worked for all his life. But Sigmond Vormeister was probably dead, and whoever was sending the faxes probably killed the socially inept academic. A flash of fear zigzagged through Jerry's brain. What was the game?

Bertha evidenced no interest in Toni's business, but if Toni had a fax, a FedEx, or mail, Bertha always alerted her employer. Much as Toni wanted Bertha and Bill to live with her in the servants' quarters, they owned a tidy trailer five miles down the road on two acres of land. No amount of cajoling could pry them off *Quittin' Time,* as they styled their little place. Even bonuses and promised raises didn't sway them.

But as Bertha left, she said there was a fax. And so there was. Toni found it in her office after she'd kissed Miranda, already sound asleep in her bed.

Her hands shook when she read it. "Why now?" she said aloud.

The image of Sigmond Vormeister sprawled in the sand trap made her hands shake even more.

She scanned the top of the fax. There wasn't a sending number. A bitter smile crossed her lips, because, even if there were, what could she do about it? Whoever knew about Salinger probably wasn't stupid enough to be tripped up by a fax machine.

She tore up the paper and walked into her bedroom. She turned on all the lights, which made her feel safer. On the other hand, if someone were outside, she'd make a better target. She shut the plantation shutters and sat down on her bed.

"I was just a kid when . . . ," she drew in a deep breath, "when all that happened. Just a kid. Who in the hell *is* this?" She put her face in her hands, took them away, and shook her head again. "I am not going to cry."

The next morning Silas Macgruder, eighty-eight years old, stroked balls on the putting green. Although he was slightly bent over, his eyesight was excellent. He came to the course early in the morning to practice. Eighteen holes taxed him these days, but he could knock the ball around for nine and he wasn't slow about it, either.

This morning Mignon Gervase was to go out with him. Just the two of them. That pleased him enormously. Mignon Gervase oozed sex appeal. The nearness of her, the fragrance of her perfume, rejuvenated him.

As Silas watched Mignon pull into the parking lot, he heard a bloodcurdling scream from the area of the sixth hole. He chuckled. The good Reverend Doctor Armbruster must have sliced the ball to kingdom come.

Then he noticed a greens keeper driving like mad for the club-house, the go-cart swaying dangerously on the swells and rolls of the course.

The young driver, Ray Flynt, cut the motor and vaulted out of the white cart. He ran into the pro shop.

The next minute, Bill Oberlin, the golf pro, shot out the door, heading for the cart, but was overtaken and passed by Ray. As Ray was the star quarterback for Chesapeake Community College, Bill couldn't keep up with hir   .ooks on their faces alerted Silas to the fact that this might be more serious than yet another tantrum on the course by Peter, a man convinced the devil invented golf. Yet Peter couldn't give up the game.

Turning his back with some reluctance on the delectable Mignon, Silas dropped his putter and hustled, joining Ray and Bill at the lip of the sand trap. The three men peered down at Dr. Sigmond Vormeister, now in rigor mortis. Doctor Vormeister didn't look good in death, Silas thought, but then the poor fellow hadn't looked very good in life, either.

Capt. Diane Robards regarded Officers John Carnegie and Leland Ford as wannabes. Security in gated communities overflowed with creaking ex-cops on the way down or young kids hoping to make the grade. She'd made the grade fifteen years ago. Being a woman had set her apart from the other trainees in her class. They'd let her know it, too. She'd kept her mouth shut, her head down, and she'd worked like a dog. She'd graduated at the top of her class. Now she'd made captain, and those young men who had once made her life miserable answered to her.

If Diane had been a vengeful person, she would have taken pleasure in that. She wasn't. She lived for her job. The apprehension of criminals, the solving of crimes, the meting out of justice on those few occasions when she could, commanded her attention.

She loved her job.

"Very good of you officers not to allow anyone near the body," Diane complimented Ford and Carnegie. Praise a fool that you might make him useful.

"Been dead awhile." Leland Ford pushed his right fingers into the palm of his left hand.

The medical unit awaited orders from Diane. Her team was finishing up a careful, complete inspection of the body and the site.

John Carnegie nervously laughed. "We should be thankful he wasn't here too long." He pinched his nose.

"What time did you two go off duty last night?"

"Twelve," Leland Ford answered.

"Do you have a routine before you leave, a checklist?" She folded her arms across her chest.

"Well, we, uh, drive down the main street and usually the side streets. Then we park at the station," John Carnegie replied, irritated and nervous.

"You pass the clubhouse on your way to the station?"

"Yes."

"And you did so last night?"

"Yes," Leland Ford again answered.

"Nothing out of the ordinary?" Diane smiled, trying to lessen their tension. She knew she'd gain more if she didn't act superior to them.

"No," John Carnegie said.

She lowered her voice. "What did you think of the victim?"

Being asked an opinion brightened John Carnegie. "A whiner. He'd call two and three times a week. Someone was playing their music too loud. A car drove past his house and he didn't recognize it. One of those."

"I see." She smiled again. "But he sounds like an observant person."

"You got that right." Leland tipped his hat back on his head. "One nosy SOB."

"So, he offended people?" she continued.

"That's one way to put it; but you know he'd try to suck up to them, too." Leland was pretty observant himself.

"Captain Robards." The medical officer called her.

"Excuse me a moment. I'll try not to keep you much longer, but I'm going to need your help."

"No problem." Leland beamed.

Diane walked over to the edge of the sand pit, marveling at how the groomed grass felt like a spongy carpet. "Jordan."

"We're done."

"Okay, take him away. Guess you'll need an extra big bag. Always difficult when they're in rigor."

"Hey, we come prepared." Jordan climbed out of the pit, slipping a bit. "Did you notice there were no footprints in the sand? When we arrived, I mean?"

"I did. Had Greg fingerprint the rake. Nothing."

"Odd one, isn't it?"

"Yeah, it is." She breathed in the fragrance of early morning laced with a top note of the Truxton River not a quarter of a mile away as the crow flies. "Most of what we see is pretty straightforward. A shoots B or stabs B or bludgeons B. The truth is, most murders are spur-of-the-moment, loss-of-control kind of events. This doesn't have that look. In fact, we won't know what killed Dr. Vormeister until the lab work comes back. It wasn't the gash on the forehead."

"No."

"And, Jordan, was he killed here, or was he dumped here?"

"That won't take too long to figure out. The autopsy ought to tell us that. Why, you got a feeling?"

"I do."

Jordan put his hands on his hips. "Well?"

"I got a feeling we'll be doing a lot of work and we'll be besieged. The kind of people who live at Gryphon Gate aren't used to their world being rocked."

"Uh-huh. Here comes one now."

Striding across the manicured grass, filled with the importance of his mission, came Henry Drysdale. He introduced himself as the mayor. Wanted information. He could have been more offensive, Diane supposed, but as it was he was offensive enough.

"This is terrible. Terrible," the mayor sputtered. "We've never had anything like this happen at Gryphon Gate. Must have been some intruder."

Leland Ford, overhearing, took this as a slur. "Mayor Drysdale, John and I were on duty last night and everything was in order. I took the precaution of checking with the gatehouse. No one not sponsored by a member came through that gate, and after seven in the evening only residents drove in or out."

"Good work, Officer," Diane praised him. She judged Leland to be in his middle twenties, well-built, and methodical. He could make it on the regular forces if he wanted to. She wondered why he hadn't. Money? Trouble getting the time to go to school, then the police academy? Or maybe he was burdened with some family problem. The other one, Carnegie, well, he was filler mostly.

Henry Drysdale's mouth twitched. "Prescient of you." He glanced toward the parking lot where Bill Oberlin and Ray Flynt were preventing people from coming into the club. Nothing they could do about Silas Macgruder, now sitting patiently on the bench at the putting green. He'd been told to stay put.

Henry returned his attention to Diane. "I'll have to issue a press release. Would you like to be there?"

"Mayor Drysdale, you aren't going to issue a press release until we clear the crime scene. And no, I don't want to be there. The media will be camped in front of headquarters. You've got to watch those people. Sharks."

"I can handle them," Henry bragged. "In my twenties I was station manager at Channel Six in Baltimore. Worked my way up. Bought the station. Bought some more. Finally sold them all to Metromedia."

"I'm sure you can handle anything." Diane thought quite the opposite. "What is your relationship to the victim?"

"Sigmond? An involved citizen. Never missed a council meeting. Served on the board. Very academic man, as you would suppose, given that he has, had, his Ph.D. in sociology."

"Did you like him?"

John Carnegie and Leland Ford, perhaps twenty yards away, held their breath, hoping not to make a sound. They wanted to hear this.

"Well, he was a very dedicated resident."

"Did you like him?"

"Uh, I got along with him."

"Did you like him?"

"Am I a suspect?"

"Mayor Drysdale, a resident of your community has been murdered. Your thoughts, your impressions are important to the case. Did you like him?"

"No."

"Can you think of why anyone would like to kill him?"

"Not really. He didn't irritate anyone that much. It would make a lot more sense if *I* had been the victim." He laughed. "Lightning rod. All you have to do is be in a position of authority and you're a lightning rod."

"Thank you for your time." She adroitly dismissed him, although he had been the one to barge in to put her in her place.

"Uh, any suspects?"

"I'll be in touch."

Henry reluctantly retreated toward the clubhouse.

"Officer Carnegie, would you make sure the ambulance can get out? It appears that your golf pro and the other fellow, Ray,"—she was good with names—"can keep them out of the parking lot, but they can't keep them from clogging up the road leading to it."

"Sure thing." John, with a lift to his walk, now that he was in charge of something, moved toward the parking lot. He heard the medical crew grunt as they hoisted Vormeister in the body bag into the ambulance. The bag was stretched out, due to the deceased's arms and legs being at right angles.

"Let's you and I talk to this elderly gentleman at the putting green. What do you know about Silas Macgruder?"

John smiled. "Neat old guy. Sharp as a tack. Plays golf almost every day. They say he made his money at IBM. I don't know. And," his smile broadened, "he loves the women."

"I like him already." She smiled back at John, noticing that his eyes were the color of dark honey.

"Captain Robards, thank you for giving me the chance to observe proper procedures."

"It's a lot of legwork. Kind of like putting together a puzzle. I know that sounds trite, but really, that's what solving a murder is. People become enamored of pathology, high-tech stuff you see on TV, but it's still a lot of legwork and a little luck."

As they approached Silas, he looked Captain Robards up and down. He liked what he saw.

So did Leland Ford.

When Vanessa Smart-Drysdale heard the news about Sigmond Vormeister, she hung up the wall phone in her sunny kitchen and wondered if, by sending her to the sixth hole, the sender of the fax had intended to frame her for murder. A lump rose in her throat. She swallowed hard. Yes, she suffered a knot of fear, but she wasn't a wimp. She'd survive to spite whoever had sent her that fax, and if she could, she'd do him in first.

Whoever it was knew her movements and knew about the condominium in Alexandria. Damn.

When Jerry Lynch heard the news, he feigned shock. Anka ran into the breakfast room. She'd just heard it from the au pair the Upshaws employed.

"Why would anyone kill that silly man?" Renée was incredulous.

"Maybe he was in the wrong place at the wrong time," Jerry shrugged.

"Jerry, how can you be so cold?" Renée chastised him.

"He was a pain in the ass. I wouldn't wish him dead, my dear, but I can't pretend I liked him."

"May I go down to the club?" Anka's voice rose.

"Ghoul." Renée laughed at her.

"All right by me, unless you have something pressing, honey." Jerry patted his wife's hand.

"Oh, go ahead, Anka, but don't be too long, and don't be a pest. People will be quite upset. They aren't all like my husband."

"One of a kind." She tossed that line over her shoulder and disappeared out the door.

Renée's eyes narrowed. "She's getting big for her britches."

"She's young. This is exciting."

"You're too soft where she's concerned."

Of course, the opposite was the truth.

Toni, driving back from dropping Miranda at school, saw the flashing lights at the clubhouse. She shuddered and prayed she had wiped down the sand pit rake thoroughly.

Why was Sigmond out at the sixth hole? Although she wanted to stick to the facts, she considered that Sigmond Vormeister might also have received a fax. If so, what was *his* secret? Did he attack whoever lured him there? Or, was he an innocent bystander? Her instincts told her he wasn't. Sigmond had been right where *she* was supposed to be. No, Sigmond had a purpose at the sixth hole. And he died for it.

Toni wasn't ready to die. She had a beautiful daughter, lived in paradise—at least up until now—and she had a net worth of many, many zeros. Death wasn't an option. She never thought of herself as a brave person, but it crossed her mind that she would kill to keep all this, kill to keep her secret.

3

"DAMN IT TO HELL!" PARKER
Upshaw snatched a copy of the *Washington Post* off his desk and sent it
sailing across the room, where it settled into an untidy heap on the Yag-
cibedir carpet. His great-grandfather had haggled for that carpet in
Constantinople, rolled it up, lashed it to the outside of his satchel, and
after a week-long trans-Atlantic voyage, it had graced the office floor of
every CEO of Upshaw, Tracey, and Associates since Roosevelt was
president. The first one. If the Upshaw men had been given to pacing—
which they were not—the carpet would have been threadbare.

This is not a crisis. Parker repeated the phrase like a mantra, chair
tilted back at a comfortable angle, his fingers drumming a soft tattoo
on its padded leather arms. *Black Monday was a crisis. So was the tech
meltdown of 2000. And Enron?* It made his head throb to think about
the chunk of his portfolio that had gone south with that gang of
white-collar bandits. No, this was just an annoyance, like a biting fly.
And he'd deal with it. Then back to business as usual.

Upshaw, Tracey, and Associates rescued companies. Turned them
around. When you file for Chapter 11, the first call you make is to your
lawyers. The second, to U.T. and A.

His own damn fault, really. He'd actually *volunteered* for this
headache, volunteered to run for president of the Gryphon Gate
Homeowners Association, never dreaming he'd be elected. Parker
sighed and massaged the bridge of his nose. Only six more weeks until

the end of his term, then those fanatics at the American Wildlife Confederation would be Jerry Lynch's problem.

Parker leaned across the blotter and pressed a button on the intercom. "Kris?"

"Yes, sir."

"Get Manny on the line, will you?"

"Sure. Right away."

"And Kris?"

"Yes?"

"Hold all my calls. If I have to dance the two-step around one more tree hugger, I think I'll blow my brains out."

As if to add insult to injury, the sun suddenly emerged from a cloud, shot across the Potomac River and through his window, fixing the offending front-page article in its beam like a spotlight—ACTIVIST GROUP SPEAKS OUT ON MUTE SWAN PROPOSAL. "Tell them I'm on safari." Parker suppressed an insane urge to giggle.

"Not to worry, sir," Kris said. "I'll say you're busy. Up in the Arctic clubbing baby seals."

Parker laughed nervously. "Bad girl! You will die and go to hell."

"Thank you, sir."

"Let me know when you locate Manny," Parker continued. "The least the SOB can do is hear our side of it. Frankly, I'm surprised. The *Post* is usually a bit more balanced in its reporting. We're not going to *kill* the swans, for Christ's sake, just neutralize their eggs."

"Who's his source, then?"

"Damned if I know. It could be anybody in the Gryphon Gate community." Parker stood, his free hand toying with the loose change in his pocket. "Legally, there's nothing these folks can do to stop us, but they can definitely make our lives miserable."

"I'm sure. And sir?"

"Yes?"

"Can I get you anything? Coffee? A martini?"

"No thanks, Kris," Parker chuckled. "You'll just spoil a perfectly good sulk."

A few minutes later the telephone warbled like a strangled turkey. Nothing in the way Parker stood, hands jammed in his pockets, gazing out his Georgetown window over the Whitehurst Freeway toward Roslyn, Virginia, gave any indication he'd heard it. He was staring at the *USA Today* building, wondering when they'd pluck the story off the AP wire and spread it to every airport and hotel room in the nation. Eventually the phone fell silent. *Thank God for Kris.*

When the intercom buzzed a few seconds later, Parker sighed and picked up the receiver, not surprised to discover it was still warm.

"You got Manny?"

"No, sir. But I think you better take it. It's your wife, and she sounds upset."

Parker punched the blinking green button. "Lydia, I was just thinking about you," he lied.

"Oh, Parker! It's just so awful!" his wife began.

"I know. It's all over the front page of the *Post.*"

On the other end of the line Lydia snuffled then drew in a quick breath. "The *Post?* What are you talking about, Parker? They just found him this morning."

Parker stopped fiddling with his paperweight, suddenly alert. "Found him? Found who?"

"Sigmond!" she wailed. "He was lying on the sixth hole. Oh, Parker, Sigmond's dead!"

In the background Parker heard one of the twins begin to tune up. In another minute the other would join in, and Parker's chances of getting a straight story out of his wife would shrink to nil. While he waited for Lydia to pacify the children, he tried to process the information she had just given him. Sigmond Vormeister. Golf. It didn't compute. Sigmond hung, if he was said to hang out anywhere, at the marina. Sitting on a bench facing the Truxton River, with his ever-present leather-bound notebook. What the hell was Sigmond Vormeister doing at the golf course?

"I don't know why I'm so upset," Lydia sniffed. "I hardly *know* the man. It's just . . . oh, poor Rachel!" Lydia's voice died out.

"I know. I know," Parker soothed. What he knew was that as a founding member of the Gryphon Gate Garden Club, his wife had worked closely with Rachel Vormeister. They often played tennis together, at least until the twins had arrived to happily complicate her life.

Parker waited while Lydia blew her nose. "Nobody seems to know what he was doing on the golf course," Lydia continued, control returning to her voice at last. "But the worst of it is this: Laura got it from Peter, who got it from Bill Oberlin—the police think Sigmond's been murdered."

"Shit!" Across the Potomac Parker visualized platoons of reporters pouring out of the *USA Today* building, cameras at the ready, piling into company cars and heading north up I-395 into Maryland. "Shit, shit, shit!"

"Exactly."

"Any suspects?"

"If they have any, they aren't saying. Laura says the police captain, Diane Robards, has taken over the club—the Wild Goose Room—and is using it to conduct interviews. Laura's been keeping Diane and her two acolytes Ford and Carnegie supplied with croissants and coffee."

"You mean Mutt and Jeff?"

Parker was pleased to hear Lydia laugh. "Seems Mutt is quite fond of Krispy Kremes. Laura's not happy about it."

Parker considered for a moment. "I wonder if we should call off tonight's town council meeting?"

"Parker, you can't! I've spent almost a year putting it together. I've already squandered enough of my maternity leave working on this case. Next month I'll be back at work, and anything I take on pro bono will have to have the blessing of Messieurs Matthews, Jacobs, and Reed.

"If we don't line up enough public support to demand a new environmental impact statement," Lydia chugged on, "nothing short of Hurricane Floyd will stop Vanessa from developing that parcel any way she damn well pleases. You've seen the plan!"

Parker had. Vanessa Drysdale proposed to strip the parcel clean of offending trees, backfill the wetlands, and contract a New Jersey firm to construct wall-to-wall condos that looked like they'd been designed by a student at Chesapeake Community College as a class project. It was obscene. "Okay. Okay. Do me a favor then, would you? Call Laura at the club and tell her to put out the word that the meeting will go on as scheduled." He paused. "Who's doing the Web page?"

"Temple Flynt's son, Ray."

"Right. Ask him to post it there, too. And Lydia?"

"Yes?"

"See if you can't persuade the colonel to put off the report from the deer committee until next month. Tell him I'll explain later."

"Any dragons you want slain while I'm at it?"

Parker grinned and promised himself that after this was all over he'd buy Lydia that diamond tennis bracelet she'd admired at Alan Marcus. "I'll love you forever," he whispered.

"Hah!" Lydia snorted. "That's what all my boyfriends say."

Lydia hung up the phone. It was well past lunchtime, and the twins, sitting side by side in their bouncy seats, were quietly fussing. She'd already wasted one nutritional opportunity by feeding them short-bread cookies full of empty fat and sugar calories. With a damp paper towel, Lydia wiped the evidence off their chins. Where were the whole-grain, fruit juice–sweetened muffins when you needed them? Lydia loved her children, was crazy about them actually, but sometimes she felt that if *Working Mother* gave an award for Uninspired Parenting, she'd definitely be on the shortlist. Lydia couldn't imagine what she had been thinking when, today of all days, she had given Nicole, their au pair, the afternoon off.

Lydia plugged a pacifier into Todd's mouth and distracted Amy with a *Baby Mozart* video while she made the phone calls she had promised. Laura answered at once, but neither Ray Flynt nor Colonel McClintock was home, so she left detailed messages on their answering machines, secretly praying that neither man would call her back.

After the twins were fed and down for their nap, Lydia plopped a fresh Lady Grey tea bag into a mug of water and set it on the turntable of the microwave. While waiting for the *ding,* she rummaged in the pantry until she found a box of Girl Scout cookies she had optimistically hidden from herself. Tea and Thin Mints in hand, she sat down at the kitchen table and considered the orderly piles of documents that were stacked there among a jumble of half-empty baby food jars and a scattering of Goldfish crackers: environmental impact statements, minutes of zoning board meetings, piles of EPA and Maryland state regulations, and a copy of HB278 dotted with strained squash. Nibbling a dainty circle around the edges of a cookie, Lydia reviewed her strategy. She planned to claim that Vanessa's building permit had been approved on the basis of misinformation supplied by the developer that vastly underestimated the effect of the proposed development on the infrastructure of the area. Thus, they would need to reevaluate requirements for power, water, and sewage; revisit issues of traffic and public transportation, not to mention looking closely at the schools.

Lydia sometimes worried that she had pressed her sources too hard. She would willingly confess to being a NIMBY—Not In My Back Yard—but hoped not to be thought of as a BANANA—Build Absolutely Nothing Anywhere Near Anyone.

Yet last night her persistence had borne fruit. Cheryl Madsen, her mole at the Maryland Department of Natural Resources, had discovered that the Forest Glen marshland was home to *helonias bullata,* an endangered flower popularly known as the swamp pink, and to *hyla sanguinea,* a red-toed tree frog as cute as any character out of a Walt Disney cartoon. Now Vanessa and her developers would be up against the Federal Endangered Species Act. Lydia smiled. Bulldozers had been halted by smaller creatures than a tree frog.

As she sat there leafing through the papers and taking notes on a yellow legal pad, she had the nagging feeling she'd forgotten something. Rachel! If Lydia had been any kind of friend, she would have been over there by now, homemade casserole in hand, and with the offer of a comforting shoulder to cry on.

Lydia hauled a turkey tetrazini casserole out of the deep freeze in the garage and set it on the hood of her Volvo station wagon.

Ignoring the fax machine that was noisily churning another page into the tray with several others Lydia had also ignored, she changed, freshened her makeup—such as it was—and roused the twins from their nap. With Todd squirming on one hip and Amy calmly straddling the other, Lydia stood in the garage and considered her options. The Peg Perego double stroller, imported from Italy and a gift from her in-laws, was sporty as all get out with its double yellow canopies, but, considering the inches she'd put on her thighs since the children were born, she settled for the twinner baby jogger instead. Maybe someday neighborhood heads would turn for *her* the way they did for the jogging Yummy Mummies.

Lydia belted the children into the jogger, set the casserole in the mesh basket underneath, punched the automatic garage door opener with her thumb, and when the door yawned wide shot out the door and down the tree-lined drive, her raven hair flying and the children shrieking in delight.

The Vormeisters lived ten two-acre lots away in a three-story, nouvelle Tudor set well back on an aggressively landscaped lot. So many trees dotted the lawn in so many varieties that Lydia couldn't help but think of it as the Vormeister tree zoo.

There were no cars in the driveway, so Lydia was surprised when her knock—on an ornate lion's head the size of a dinner plate—was answered not by Rachel but by a pale woman of Germanic sturdiness, her graying blonde hair caught up at the crown by a pink plastic Day-Glo butterfly clip. Lydia recognized the generous nose and cupid's bow lips and knew who this must be. Rachel's mother.

"Mrs. Kaplan?" With her toe Lydia set the brake on the baby jogger and extended her hand. "I'm so sorry to hear about Sigmond, Mrs. Kaplan. I'm Rachel's friend, Lydia Upshaw. How's she doing?"

"She's in shock, poor child."

Lydia lowered her head. "We all are. It's terrible."

Suddenly remembering her mission, Lydia bent and wrestled the casserole out of the basket. "I've brought this. It's not much, but I wanted to do something. Please tell Rachel that if there's anything she needs, or if I can help in any way . . ." In her own ears, the words rang hollow. Would a stupid noodle casserole make her feel any better if something awful were to happen to Parker?

"Why don't you tell her yourself?" Holding the casserole dish in both hands, Rachel's mother gestured toward the entrance hall. "Rachel's in the kitchen. I was about to make some tea. I hope you'll join us?"

Lydia thought that if she swallowed one more ounce of tea her bright blue eyes would turn muddy brown. Besides, she had the children with her. She had just opened her mouth to refuse when Mrs. Kaplan shrieked, "Aaron!"

Lydia shook her head to clear the ringing from her ears as a whey-faced youth with cheeks sprouting a fine crop of pimples materialized, seemingly from nowhere, a skateboard tucked under his arm.

"Hey, Mom! You seen my lid and pads around anywhere?"

Mrs. Kaplan frowned. "You won't need your helmet just now, Aaron. Take the children around the jogging trail a couple of times, will you, while I give Mrs. Upshaw some tea."

A smile split Aaron's face, and Lydia caught a glimpse of the handsome man he would be in another four or five years. Like his sister,

39

Rachel, the teenager's cap of hair was blond all the way down to the roots. "Sure thing," he said.

Lydia watched while Aaron laid his skateboard, as tenderly as if it were an infant, in the basket where her casserole had so recently rested. She watched without a single pang of concern as her children disappeared into the woods in the custody of someone she had never met. Shouldn't she worry? Even a little? But what could one expect from someone whose own mother would have plopped her down in a playpen and gone off to smoke another Lucky?

The two women found Rachel seated at an enormous white oak table, idly spinning a teaspoon around on the polished tabletop.

"Rachel," Lydia began. "I'm so, so sorry."

Rachel regarded her with red and swollen eyes. "Oh, Lydia, I don't know what I'm going to do!" Her lower lip quivered and her shoulders began to shake.

Lydia pulled up a chair and sat down next to her friend. Taking Rachel's hand in hers, she soothed. "It'll be all right. I'm here. Your mom's here. . . ."

"Bill Oberlin came and got me," Rachel sobbed. "They needed me to identify . . ." She took a deep, ragged breath. ". . . to identify poor Sigmond before they took him away to, to . . ."

The morgue. The word hung unspoken in the air. Lydia rubbed Rachel's hand gently.

"Oh, Lydia, he looked so peaceful lying there, as if he were asleep. I can't believe . . ."

Mrs. Kaplan set cups of hot tea on the table in front of them. When Rachel made no move to pick hers up, her mother added a heaping teaspoon of sugar to the cup, stirred briskly, and pushed it toward her daughter. "You have to drink *something,* darling, or you'll get all dehydrated."

Rachel wrapped her hands around the cup but didn't drink from it. "Things were finally turning around for Sigmond," she said. "He was wrapping up his research and he had made some sort of revolutionary breakthrough."

"Finally!" Mrs. Kaplan huffed. "Although, what anybody can make of all those Martian runes, I'll never know."

Rachel leaned toward Lydia, a slight smile creasing her face. "Sigmond wrote in shorthand. He's got *hundreds* of notebooks, Lydia.

One day he's going to publish them." Suddenly her voice cracked. "Oh, Mother, I won't even know where to begin!"

"Why don't you worry about that later, Rachel?" her mother suggested.

"We were so happy!"

"I know."

"Everyone told us it wouldn't work out." She squeezed Lydia's hand. "Sigmond was older than me, you know."

Lydia nodded.

"And Sigmond so wanted children. We tried and we tried and we tried. Sigmond was so patient with me." She managed a slight smile. "When he decided we needed help, we went to the best fertility doctor in the state. Doctor Jefferson said—"

"Dr. *Charles* Jefferson?" Lydia interrupted.

"Yes. Why? Do you know him?"

"Of course I know him! He helped us conceive Todd and Amy."

Across the table, her eyes bright behind a pale, untidy fringe of bangs, Rachel's mother grinned. "Tell her, Rachel."

Rachel pressed her hands together, as if trying to contain her excitement. Crimson patches appeared on cheeks that were otherwise pale from crying. "Sigmond wanted to keep it secret until we were sure. But I'm pregnant, Lydia. The baby's due in December."

Then her face crumpled. "Sigmond hoped it'd be a girl," she sobbed. "Next month we were going to do the ultrasound. And now he'll never know!" Rachel leapt to her feet and rushed from the room. Flashing a nervous smile of apology, Mrs. Kaplan bustled after her.

Lydia sat. For want of something better to do she sipped her tea— a sprightly ginger concoction—and stared at the wallpaper. Tendrils of ivy snaked under the windows, over the doorways, twined around the copper pot rack, crept across the stone floor, wound themselves up the table leg, curled over her hand and around her neck. Lydia shook herself. She was having a Stephen King moment.

Lydia had decided to head out to the jogging trail in search of Aaron and her children when Rachel returned carrying a large manila envelope. She leaned against the stove, the envelope clasped to her chest. "Can I share something with you, Lydia? That policewoman," she continued without waiting for a reply, "Diane somebody. She really annoyed me."

Mrs. Kaplan stood in the doorway, nodding vigorously. "Not a compassionate bone in her body."

Lydia smiled reassuringly. "We've never had a murder at Gryphon Gate before. Captain Robards is probably just being careful. You wouldn't want her to make a mistake, would you, and have Sigmond's murderer go free on some technicality?"

"Of course not! But, she's in over her head, if you ask me."

Rachel's mother nodded. "Not a job for a woman."

Although sorely tempted, Lydia kept her mouth shut.

"That's probably why I didn't tell her about the baby," Rachel mused.

Lydia forced a smile. "No reason you needed to, Rachel."

Rachel shrugged then crossed to the table. She lifted the flap on the envelope and dumped its contents onto the tabletop. "These are Sigmond's things. Except for his most recent notebook. The police are still looking for that."

Lydia stared as Rachel lovingly touched each item. A Seiko watch with a silver, basket-weave band. A black leather wallet. A monogrammed handkerchief. A ballpoint pen, a handful of loose coins, and a fistful of keys. "I didn't tell Diane Robards about the baby," she repeated almost dreamily. "And I didn't tell her something else either."

"What was that?" Lydia asked.

"Sigmond's Palm Pilot. He took it with him everywhere. It's missing."

Lt. Col. Lance J. McClintock, USMC, retired, a cigar clamped between stubby fingers, fanned out his cards with elaborate care. "One diamond." His bushy eyebrows, shot with gray, settled over his horn-rims like awnings.

Across the table, Camille frowned, whether at her husband or at the cards she held it was impossible to tell. Without looking up she said, "Christ, Lance. I wish you'd throw that damn thing away."

"What?" Lance screwed the wet end of the cigar into his mouth and lounged back in his chair. "It's not like I've lit it or anything, *sweetheart*."

"No fighting, no biting!" Roman Gervase chided cheerfully. "Pass."

"Don't pay any attention to them, Gervase," Mignon said. "It's a clever ruse. Meant to throw us off our game."

"Ha!" Camille squinted at her cards through her half-glasses. "One spade."

"Pass." Mignon twiddled an earring, but if it was a secret signal to her husband he must have missed it. His eyes were glued on Barbara Blackburn, who had sashayed into the bar wearing an off-the-shoulder peasant blouse, electric blue capri pants, and high-heeled sandals.

Lance noticed Barbara, too. "Nice buns."

"Your bid, Lance *darling*," Camille drawled. "If you aren't too, how shall I say, *busy?*"

Lance grunted and returned to his hand. "One no trump."

Roman winked in the direction of Babs's remarkable backside. "Nice scenery," he muttered, "but I miss playing in the Wild Goose Room." He glanced at his watch. "It's six o'clock, for heaven's sake! When do you think they'll be finished in there?"

"Haven't the faintest, Ro baby," Lance commented. "What's your bid?"

"Sorry. Got distracted for a minute. Pass."

Camille straightened in her chair, smiling broadly. "Three no trump."

"Pass," said Mignon.

"Pass," said Lance.

"Pass," said Gervase.

"Well bid, sweetheart," Lance began to arrange his hand faceup on the table. "Do you need me, or may I wander over to the bar for a bit?"

Camille scowled at her husband. "If I didn't know better, Lance, I'd say you actually *planned* to be dummy."

Lance, who took his card playing as seriously as he had the command of his regiment in Kuwait, tapped the ace, queen, eight, and seven of diamonds into a neat cascade. "Cards is cards is cards, my dear. Can I get you anything?"

Camille shook her head.

"Single malt," said Mignon as she led with the jack of hearts. "On the rocks."

Lance observed the play in silence until Camille finessed Roman's king of diamonds and he knew they'd make their contract, with a trick or two to spare. "Carry on," he said.

"It doesn't seem right for us to be going on like this, as if nothing had happened," Mignon remarked, leading a ten of hearts.

Lance laid a hand on Mignon's shoulder and squeezed it gently. "Nothing we can do about it anyway, Mignon. We've told Captain Robards all we know. Life goes on."

Gervase considered his next play, nibbling on a well-chewed thumbnail. "It's Rachel I feel sorry for," he said, sluffing a three of spades. "Those two were like Ron and Nancy Reagan. Inseparable."

"I saw Rachel this afternoon," a new voice said. Lance turned to see Lydia approaching from the direction of Michener Auditorium, looking radiant in a bright yellow pantsuit, her thick dark hair intricately and attractively braided. "She's taking it very hard. But her mother's with her now. And her brother."

Camille gathered up the last winning trick, jotted down the score, and stood. "Why don't we call it quits for tonight? I can use a drink. Lydia? Will you join us?"

"Thanks, but I need to talk to Lance."

Lance smiled. "What about?"

"Didn't you get my message?"

He shrugged. "Don't think so. I haven't been home today." He gestured toward the Wild Goose Room, where, presumably, Diane Robards was still holding forth with Ford and Carnegie. "Ned Carbury and I were last on the links last night, so Robards kept me in there for quite a while. She's still talking to Ned." Lance waved an arm toward a vacant table. "Let's sit."

Lance eased himself into an upholstered chair and flagged down a passing server. "Another gin," he said. "And the lady will have?"

"White wine. Something crisp and cold." Lydia leaned forward, her elbows resting on the table. "I have a favor to ask. Parker wants to know if you can delay your report on the managed deer hunt until next month."

Lance felt as if he'd taken a blow to the solar plexus. "No, ma'am. No can do."

If Lydia was upset by this news, she didn't show it. "Why not?"

"I've got people coming in to testify, that's why. George Carroll from Sea Pines, Georgia, for one. And a guy from the Maryland

Department of Natural Resources. Carroll's going to recommend that we make it a bow-and-arrow hunt," he continued, warming to his topic, "and open it up to young folks. A father-and-son thing."

Lydia winced. "Don't push your luck, Lance." She eased a notebook out of a pouch in her handbag and turned to a fresh page. "I'm setting up the agenda for Parker." She uncapped her pen. "Do you want your guys on before or after we talk about Vanessa's Forest Glen development?"

"After, I think." Their drinks had arrived, and he took a generous sip, savoring the coolness of the alcohol as it lingered on his tongue, enjoying the tart twist of lime that had decorated the glass.

Lydia scribbled something in her notebook. "Good. So we'll put Vanessa on first. Then I'll bring on my experts." She reached for a bowl of mixed nuts that sat on the table between them, picked out a handful of roasted almonds, and tossed a few absentmindedly into her mouth. "I think I've found a way to stop Vanessa cold."

Lance smiled around his glass. "May I ask?"

"Oh, I think you'll want to be surprised, along with everybody else."

"Does it involve weapons?" Lance hooted. "The only thing that will stop Vanessa *cold* is an elephant gun."

"Ain't *that* the truth." Babs Blackburn shouted from a nearby bar stool.

"Babs, baby!" Lance waved his drink high in the air. "Come over and join us!"

"Sure thing, honey. Anybody trashing that trashy Vanessa is *definitely* a friend of mine." Holding her drink, a tall pink concoction, in one hand and a column of paper-umbrella-skewered fruit in the other, Babs wriggled off her stool, weaved across the carpet, and plopped herself down in the chair across from Lydia. In the dimly lit bar something flashed across the ceiling.

"Gorgeous ring, Babs," Lydia said.

Babs extended her hand and waggled her fingers over the table. "It is gorgeous, isn't it? Henry gave it to me." Plump, crimson lips closed around her straw, and Lance watched in fascination as the liquid rose, like a thermometer, into her mouth. "Vanessa is going to be *so* pissed when she sees it!"

"I wouldn't mention it if I were you," Lance suggested. Married or divorced, if he ever gave a three-carat diamond to another woman, Camille would have reduced him to smithereens.

Babs shrugged. "She'll find out soon enough anyway, Lance. We met with Peter Armbruster at the chapel yesterday." Even in the subdued lighting her face was radiant. "The wedding's set for June."

"Congratulations!" Laura Armbruster elbowed her way through the crowd that had been gathering around the bar and bent to kiss Babs on the cheek. "Peter told me about the wedding yesterday. I've been *dying* to tell someone, but . . . well, you know: seal of the confessional!"

Babs beamed up at the club manager. "We'll want to have the reception here, of course."

"Of course." Laura patted the bride-to-be's shoulder. "You and Henry come in next week, say Wednesday or Thursday, and we'll start talking details."

"Oh, Henry's leaving all that to me," Babs said.

Laura's eyebrows disappeared under her bangs. "I see. Well, give me a call. Soonest. We've no time to lose!"

"I'll want you to get that ice sculpture guy . . ." Babs began. She tipped her glass and sucked on her straw until the liquid remaining in the bottom of the glass gurgled. ". . . and whoever you got to do the music for the Steinberg bar mitzvah."

"No problem," Laura called over her shoulder as she turned and headed toward the auditorium. "I've got to check to make sure Ray's set up the projector for tonight. See you later."

"Speaking of tonight," Lydia said, checking her watch. "I wonder where Parker is? He said he was planning to take off a bit early."

"Traffic," said Lance. He gestured toward the large-screen television that hung from wrought-iron brackets over the bar. On the screen Wolf Blitzer was silently mouthing the latest news from Iraq as closed captioning crawled across his tie. "If Laura kept that damn set tuned to anything other than CNN, maybe we'd get the local traffic report." Lance stood and waved over the cluster of heads that separated him from the bar. "Tiffany!"

The young bartender looked up from the blender, where, judging from the pink liquid sloshing around inside, a refill for Babs was being prepared. She pushed a strand of hair out of her eyes with the back of her hand. "Yes, Colonel?"

"Switch to Channel Two, will you?"

"Okay," Tiffany shouted. "But if Mrs. Armbruster asks, I'll tell her you forced me to do it."

"Fair enough," Lance shouted back. "And Tiffany? Another for me, when you get the chance!"

"Make that a *light* one," suggested Camille, neatly extricating herself from a conversation with two women wearing designer jogging suits in which, Lance was sure, they'd never broken a sweat. Camille carried an Irish coffee topped with a generous dollop of whipped cream. She kissed the air next to her husband's cheek. "Careful, Colonel. You have to speak tonight."

"Yeah, yeah." He offered the chair he had just vacated to his wife, then stood at attention behind it, arms folded, his eyes on the television.

"Ummmm," cooed Camille, squirming more deeply into the cushions. "Nicely warmed. Thank you, darling."

Somewhere a cell phone chirped.

Lance reached for the instrument attached to his belt.

Camille rummaged in her fanny pack.

Babs patted her pocket.

Lydia bent over to retrieve her purse. "Mine, I think. I set Parker's number to *The William Tell Overture.*"

"When my mother calls, Camille's phone plays 'The Dead March' from *Saul,*" Lance muttered cheerfully.

"Get out!" Babs giggled.

"Guilty!" Camille laughed. *"Dum dum de dum, dum de dum de dum de dum.* It's a hoot."

Across the hall from the bar the green baize door that led to the Wild Goose Room burst open. As they watched open-mouthed, Leland Ford spilled out, his hand resting on his weapon as he sprinted down the hall toward the lobby. Next came John Carnegie, moving slowly but deliberately in the same direction. Behind John, Diane Robards paused to speak into the two-way radio that crackled from a clip attached to her left shoulder. "Tell them not to let anybody in until I get there." And then she, too, was gone, leaving Sen. Ned Carbury sitting in a leather armchair, framed in the open doorway like a prisoner on death row. Carbury unfolded his long legs, shook them as if to get the circulation going, and wandered out of the Wild Goose Room and into the bar.

"What the hell?" Lance asked the senator.

"Damned if I know," Carbury replied. "She got this call, then they took off." Carbury whomped Lance on the back. "'Scuse me while I get a drink, old friend. Talking to that lot," he hooked a thumb in the direction of the front door, "one works up a thirst."

Meanwhile, Lydia had located her cell phone and flipped it open. "Hey, ho." She listened for a while, her face morphing from cheerful anticipation, to puzzlement, to astonishment, and finally to disbelief. "Switch to Channel Four," she shouted to Tiffany behind the bar. "And turn up the sound. Parker says there are TV cameras and mobs of demonstrators at the gate. He can't even get his car through."

Lance watched as, one by one, heads turned in the direction of the TV and fifty-some pairs of eyes focused on a reporter wearing a bright red blazer and sporting a hairdo reminiscent of the seventies. Babs pointed with her glass. "Call Channel Four and tell them that Barbie wants her hair back," she jeered.

Camille poked Babs with an index finger. "Shhhhh! I want to hear what she's saying!"

"... also the scene earlier today of the mysterious death of Dr. Sigmond Vormeister, a prominent sociologist and scholar."

As they watched, the reporter turned and, with a broad sweep of her arm, indicated the crowd behind her. The camera followed, panning the line of demonstrators, three deep in places, that blocked the drive leading to Gryphon Gate. Some carried signs: *Speak Up for the Swans!* and *Stop the Slaughter!* and *S.O.S.—Save Our Swans!*

Camille gaped at her husband. "Thank God they don't know about the deer, Lance."

The reporter paused to interview an untidy woman holding an S.O.S. sign, who had it on good authority that the Gryphon Gate Town Council was planning a mass slaughter of the mute swans living and breeding within its community boundaries. As the reporter moved on to the next demonstrator, those watching in the bar could see John Carnegie and Leland Ford holding back the crowd to allow Parker's dark green BMW to ease through the gates, followed by a limousine and a car bearing the distinctive logo of the Maryland Department of Natural Resources.

"That'll be my guy," said the colonel.

"And mine," said Lydia.

"How about the fellow from Georgia?" asked Camille.

"Henry's at BWI picking him up in the helicopter," said Babs. "He called about an hour ago. They're on their way."

"And now," the reporter with Barbie's hair was saying, "we switch to John Mann, on the scene inside the exclusive Gryphon Gate community. John, I understand you've talked to some of the residents. What do they have to say?"

"Thank you, Jean. I'm standing outside the Gryphon Gate Community Recreation Center, and I have with me here Toni Sinclair and her daughter, eight-year-old Miranda." The reporter, fresh-scrubbed and gently moussed, thrust his microphone toward the little girl. "Miranda, please tell the people why you're holding a lighted candle."

"What the hell!" Lance erupted. While Miranda patiently explained to the 350,000 viewers tuned into Channel Four's seven o'clock news about the bad men who were going to murder Bambi's mother, the camera followed a train of Gryphon Gate residents, all holding candles and singing something to the tune of "Oh Christmas Tree."

"How did that reporter get in?" Babs sputtered. "Henry will be absolutely furious!"

"Oh forest deer, oh woodland deer, how lovely are your antlers," Miranda sang in a high, clear voice.

Lance was already on his feet. "I'll take care of this," he said. "Either someone invited the bastard in," he waved a finger at the television screen, where Toni, holding her candle high, was beaming at her daughter, "or, he climbed over the wall. Either way, he's toast!"

Freed at last from the clutches of the mob, Parker Upshaw escorted the little caravan of cars up the tree-lined drive that led to the country club, circled around the parking lot, pulled under the antebellum-style portico that protected the lobby from the capriciousness of the Maryland weather, and cut off his engine. He was just wondering when the nightmare was going to end when Lance McClintock, with Camille on his heels, spun through the revolving glass doors and erupted onto the driveway.

As he passed, Lance rapped on the hood of Parker's car. "C'mon," he shouted. "There's a reporter loose outside the rec center!"

Parker was weighing whether to follow Lance or see to his guests, when Sen. Ned Carbury burst through the door followed by half a dozen stalwarts of the Gryphon Gate community, some with drinks still in their hands. "Go get 'em, tiger," Parker called as Jerry Lynch flew past, comb-over flopping and ice cubes rattling. Parker didn't know what reporter they were talking about, but he felt sorry for the guy if that drunken mob ever caught up with him.

By then his companions had stepped from their vehicles and were watching, wide-eyed, as what must have seemed like half the population of Gryphon Gate streamed past, making a hullabaloo like sixth graders on the last day of school. "They're racing to the rec center," Parker explained, thinking fast. "Probably playing Catch the Pig and somebody lost."

"Catch the Pig?"

"A bar game. Uses dice."

Cheryl Madsen gazed at the pack receding in the distance and laughed, "Where do I sign up?"

Ray Flynt, wearing tan pants and a red jacket, came loping up the drive from the direction of the parking lot. "What the hell? Not another murder I hope?"

Parker handed Ray his car keys and indicated that the other drivers should do the same. "Just a few high-spirited citizens, is all." He turned to Cheryl and to Glenn Gibbs, Lydia's expert from the U.S. Fish and Wildlife Service. "We've been under a bit of pressure, lately. One of our residents has been killed."

Glenn paled. "How terrible!"

"Yes. It'll be all over the *Post* in the morning, I'm afraid."

Parker deposited his experts in the bar and went to find his wife. After a hasty consultation with Henry Drysdale, who had just arrived via go-cart from the helipad with George Carroll in tow, they decided that the meeting would go on. And if Lance hadn't returned with his posse by the time they were scheduled to begin, tough.

When Parker thought about it later, he chided himself for not seeing it coming, for not doing something, anything to prevent the tragedy. In hindsight it seemed so predictable, like a B-movie script with characters straight from central casting.

At the meeting, Vanessa pulled out her biggest gun—the head honcho of the Chesapeake County Zoning and Planning Board—but was poleaxed by Lydia, the U.S. Fish and Wildlife Service, the Maryland

Department of Natural Resources, a little pink flower, and a frog the size of a ping-pong ball. She left the meeting early, in a huff, and headed for the bar to quench her rage with a martini, straight up.

Poor Lance never knew what hit him. Before he could even introduce George Carroll, he was drowned out by Toni and her organized band of saboteurs. Time and again he'd straighten to his full six feet four, crew cut bristling, and wait, steel gray eyes drilling into the crowd as if they were a platoon of raw recruits. Gradually the heckling from the back row would die down, and he'd open his mouth, only to have his words drowned in a new wave of protests. Finally, he'd had enough. "I'll be back!" he muttered like a latter-day Arnold Schwartzenegger as he hopped from the stage, strode down the center aisle, and retreated to a dark corner of the bar, as far from Vanessa as possible.

Much later Parker and Henry found him there sprawled in a chair, balancing a long neck Corona on his six-pack abs. In the chair next to her husband, Camille was babbling amiably to Babs about the tickets she'd snagged for *The Producers*. At the St. James Theatre! In New York!

"Sorry, Lance," Parker began.

Lance raised his bottle in a mock toast. "To bitches everywhere."

Across the room Vanessa grimaced as if he meant her personally, and waved down Tiffany for her tab.

Camille shot her husband an anxious glance. "Lance is taking this deer business very personally."

"Well, the deer aren't going to go away," offered Henry philosophically. "A few more collisions, a few more tomato plants nibbled down to the roots, an outbreak of Lyme disease . . ."

Camille patted her husband's knee. "See? I told you that Henry's on our side."

Lance set his empty bottle on the table and stood up. "That's just what we need," he said. "Fuckin' Lyme disease." With two long strides, he stepped around his wife's chair and headed for the door. "As far as I'm concerned, you can give it all back to the red Indians! I'm going for a walk," he said, easing a cigar out of his pocket.

Camille's eyes followed her husband's broad back until it disappeared around the corner. She shrugged and drained her wineglass in a single, long swallow. "Just wait until next time." She centered her glass carefully on a square of napkin. "Ladies' room, I think. Lydia? You coming?"

Lydia shook her head.

"Another round?" asked Henry. Camille waved affirmatively and disappeared down the hall.

Ten minutes later, just as Tiffany was signaling that their drinks were ready, a terrible scream paralyzed her arm in midwave. Everyone in the bar looked up, stupefied.

"It's from out back!" someone shouted. "By the pool!"

Parker scrambled to his feet and raced down the hall—past the newsstand, past the pro shop, past the billiard room, and into the snack bar—with Henry wheezing right behind. Parker shoved aside the sliding glass doors and stepped onto the concrete apron that surrounded the pool. He squinted helplessly into the dark, scanning the shadows as the screams turned to moans and then to sporadic whimpers. "Somebody get the lights!" he shouted.

One by one the lights came on, gradually illuminating the area around the pool: the tiki bar, the towel hut, the outdoor spa gently gurgling. Suddenly, near the shrubbery by the cabanas, a dark shape stirred.

Parker rushed forward to find Camille kneeling beside the body of a man, his muscular arms limp at his sides, his long legs akimbo.

"Oh, Lance, Lance," Camille crooned, cradling her husband's bloody head in her arms. "You just *had* to go and smoke that damn cigar, didn't you?"

4

CAPT. DIANE ROBARDS, CALLED
out to Gryphon Gate for a second suspicious death in only twelve
hours, wasn't happy. For one thing, she still hadn't finished pro-
cessing all the paperwork on the last body, Sigmond Vormeister. For
another thing, this new body came with way too many lights, cameras, action. She'd already had to call the station and request secured
airspace to clear out all the media choppers. Then she'd wasted valuable manpower securing a twenty-foot perimeter while Henry Drysdale wrung his hands and whined that reporters weren't even allowed
inside the gated community. The third time a camera flash unexpectedly exploded in a nearby bush, he'd cried, "Damn those vultures!"
and gone running off into the trees to personally chase away every
irresponsible vagabond from the fourth estate.

That was about it for entertainment this evening.

Robards headed back to the small cluster of shrubs next to an outdoor teak cabana that was larger than her entire apartment, and resumed her inspection of Lt. Col. Lance McClintock's prone body. U.S.
Marine Corps, retired, she'd been told. Used to lead troops in Kuwait.
Was equally proficient with a handgun, an assault rifle, and a machine
gun. Could disarm a missile with a paper clip; probably pilot a Har-
rier, too; but then something had to remain classified.

Now the lieutenant colonel was sprawled faceup on the edge of
the clubhouse's concrete patio. His blue eyes were open. His forehead

was bloody. His right hand lay outstretched, as if still reaching for the faintly glowing cigar lying just three inches away.

The wife had gotten to the body first. Then three or four of the lieutenant colonel's richy-rich neighbors. In other words, the scene was shot to shit before the call had even gone out to the station. Second scene in one day, too.

Robards was getting a really bad feeling about this overpriced place. She straightened slowly while noticing that there was no blood on the white concrete patio. She inspected the nearby bushes. No dark splotches on those waxy green leaves, either. So, plenty of blood on McClintock but none on the ground. Yeah, she really didn't like this place.

"Make sure you bag the hands," she ordered.

Jordan from the M.E.'s office raised a brow at Robards's needless request. She responded with a stern look of her own—*I'm tired, I'm cranky. Don't make me kill you.* Jordan bagged the lieutenant colonel's hands.

Some women had this kind of perfectly assimilated relationship with their loving husband of fifteen years. Robards had it with her fellow death investigator. That didn't say anything about the quality of her life. If her mom happened to call tonight, Robards was hanging up before the word "hello."

"You think he put up a fight?" Carnegie asked nervously. Robards ignored the rent-a-cop's question and continued her inventory of the scene.

The second half of Gryphon Gate's dynamic duo, Leland Ford, was prowling around the thatched tiki hut next to the clubhouse. Like Carnegie, he was careful not to trespass beyond the yellow crime scene tape, but was also shamelessly trying to sneak a peek at McClintock's body. Supposedly, Carnegie and Leland had been working the front gates of the neighborhood when this latest mishap had occurred. Notified by radio, they'd rushed back to the pool area in time to hustle all the gawking patrons back inside the clubhouse and solemnly request for everyone to remain calm.

Now the majority of Gryphon Gate's illustrious homeowners were gathered around the club's U-shaped bar, where they furiously gulped very expensive booze and tried to pretend they didn't know what was going on forty feet away on the other side of the wall of windows. Every now and then someone would break away from the herd and peer out through cupped hands as if waiting for something, anything, to happen next. Crime scene investigation was very tedious work, however, so eventually each Peeping Tom abandoned his vigil and returned to the welcoming noise of the bar.

Only McClintock's wife, Camille, remained outside. She sat on the edge of a lounge chair, hands clasped limply in front of her, eyes focused on nothing in particular. There was a dark stain on her cheek, more on her hands. Her husband's blood from when she discovered his body. She didn't seem to notice.

"He was a fighter," Camille murmured now. Robards turned towards her.

"He stay in shape?"

"Absolutely. Did a full P.T. regimen every morning—ran six miles, did one hundred push-ups and two hundred sit-ups. Lance took a great deal of pride in aging well. Except for his cigars of course. Those damn cigars . . ."

"Mrs. McClintock, you said your husband had been drinking."

Camille snorted. "He had a few beers, Captain Robards. Lance was a marine. He could down a fifth of whiskey and still hold the walls of Guantanamo Bay."

"Did your husband have any enemies?"

"Absolutely not!"

Leland Ford, however, expressed a different opinion. "S.O.S." he said.

Robards flicked a glance in his direction. Leland was wearing all black tonight. Tight black T-shirt, black dress slacks, high-gloss black dress shoes. The upscale muscle look. It worked for him.

"S.O.S.?"

"Save Our Swans. They were the ones picketing the front gates earlier in the evening. They don't like Gryphon Gate's policy of reducing the local population of mute swans."

Henry Drysdale returned to the pool area, breathing heavily. He had caught the tail end of Ford's statement and was already shaking his head. "We don't have a policy! We love swans. We love deer. We have no policy! At least not yet."

Camille shot the mayor an impatient look. "For God's sake, Henry. We were investigating options for reducing the swan and deer populations, and everyone knew it—or at least knew enough to rope in a bunch of nature freaks." Her attention went back to Robards. "Lance was in charge of the managed deer hunt. It's a very civilized event with bows and arrows. The whole intent is to make the deers' life better by reducing an overpopulated herd. Lance went out to reason with the protesters tonight, but they wouldn't even let him speak." Camille snapped her fingers as if a thought had just occurred to her. "Toni Sinclair. She's the one who organized the rally, and she definitely didn't approve of the deer hunt. You should talk to her."

"She a resident?" Robards wrote down the name. It sounded familiar, though she wasn't sure why.

"She feeds the deer," Carnegie volunteered eagerly. He had moved closer to the crime scene tape, and was now looking inside the perimeter almost longingly. "We caught her yesterday evening. She and her daughter had spread deer feed all over their yard. And they were *not* very cooperative with us when we asked them to stop, if you know what I mean."

"She knew Vormeister," Leland commented. "A few weeks ago, I saw them talking intently at one of the neighbors' parties. Of course, this community isn't that big."

"And Lieutenant Colonel McClintock?" Robards directed her question at Camille. "Did he know Vormeister?"

"Only in passing. Lance was a man's man. Sigmond . . . well, not to speak ill of the dead, but Sigmond probably didn't know his asshole from his elbow, as the saying goes."

Robards made another a note. Two suspicious deaths in the same neighborhood on the same day were probably a bit much for coincidence, but linking the crimes this early would only start panic. Then again . . .

"Oh my God," Carnegie said and started pointing excitedly at McClintock's fallen body. "His head, his head. He has a bloody head. And so did Vormeister! It's like a, like a . . . what do they call it? A signature. A serial killer's signature!"

Robards skewered Carnegie with her best shut-the-bleep-up stare. "You watch a lot of TV, don't you, Carnegie?" she said pointedly. He didn't take the hint.

"Books!" he said enthusiastically. "And in novels it's always a serial killer who did it!"

"Oh brother," Leland murmured.

"A serial killer?" Camille's head came up; she appeared even paler and more shell-shocked than before. "Oh poor Lance. He never stood a chance."

"Let's not jump to any conclusions," Robards tried to caution, only to be ignored for the second time.

"No! No, no, no!" Henry Drysdale moaned. "We are *not* that kind of neighborhood. We do not have those kinds of incidents. Lance tripped and fell. I'm telling you, he had a few too many beers, he went out for his nightly cigar, and *boom*. Purely accidental."

"In the bushes?" Camille cried. "My husband was not that big an oaf, Henry. Though I don't speak for others on this patio."

"There's no blood," Leland spoke up. "McClintock has blood on his forehead, but there's none on the patio. If he tripped and fell, how did he manage to die so neatly?"

"Listen!" Robards tried to interject.

"This is obscene!" Henry said.

"Oh my God," Camille was rocking back and forth now. "Lance, poor Lance."

Henry laid a comforting hand on Camille's shoulder, his dark eyes skewering Robards. "It's a serial killer, I tell you. A serial killer who preys on middle-aged white men. Maybe it's one of those black widow–type killers. Or a homosexual maniac who lusts for passive partners."

"*Hey!*" Robards shouted.

Henry's mouth slammed shut.

Leland and Carnegie stood, arms folded.

Camille simply stared.

Finally, she had their attention. Robards took a deep breath, reminded herself to use her happy voice when dealing with well-connected civilians, and said, "These are interesting possibilities, but as a general rule we like to wait for the evidence before building a theory of the case. Now then, I'm going to need to talk to everyone in the clubhouse."

"Of course," Henry said.

"We'll help!" Carnegie offered brightly.

"*No!* I mean, I'm sure that won't be necessary. Given the high-profile nature of this case, I'm sure the department is willing to expend whatever resources are necessary to resolve this matter expediently and quietly. Very quietly. Got it?"

"Absolutely!" Henry said vigorously, and looked relieved for the first time all night.

Carnegie, on the other hand, appeared forlorn. Robards gave him another hard stare, until he finally, reluctantly, nodded. Camille and Leland followed suit. Robards allowed herself to breathe again. Order restored, she was just about to approach the clubhouse when Jordan ruined the moment.

"Captain," Jordan said, in a tone that was much too quiet. "You're going to want to see this."

Robards turned slowly. She took in Jordan's grave expression. She took in McClintock lying with his bloody face on the much-too-clean concrete. *This damn neighborhood,* she thought for the second time this evening, and headed mutely for McClintock's body.

She had just taken her second step when an unearthly howl pierced the night sky. Followed by another and then another. Robards froze, one foot still in the air and goose bumps suddenly racing down her spine. "What the hell?" she demanded.

"Lord have mercy," Camille gasped.

"Damn!" Henry Drysdale said. He sighed, then hung his head. "Just what we needed—a full moon."

Running. Heart beating, blood pulsing, veins bursting.

Racing. Trees slapping at face, vines tugging at ankles. Jacket, gone. Shirt, gone. Shoes—so painful. Feeling flesh swell, split, burst.

Panting. Hard. Hot. Tongue lolling out of mouth. Could taste the night. Cool and icy, like a slice of moon. He inhaled, felt himself take the shadows deep inside, and his senses expanded, grew sharper and keener. Like a wolf's.

Roman Gervase, fourth generation European royalty and product of three fine boarding schools, finally dropped into a crouch behind some bushes. He was breathing hard, his skinny white chest expanding and contracting rapidly. He had a stitch in his side, but ignored it, as werewolves did not get side aches from running three suburban blocks. Werewolves could run forever. Werewolves ruled the night!

"Oooooow, ow, ow, ooooooooow."

Roman focused. He swore he could hear the garden snake slithering across Silas Macgruder's yard four houses down and the young buck chewing the tops off of Laura Armbruster's azalea bushes six blocks the other way. He jerked left and watched an owl, perched a dozen trees up ahead, suddenly spy a mouse. He jerked right and saw the mouse tremble with fear beneath the quivering fronds of a woodland fern.

Roman threw back his head once again. "Ooooooow, ow, ow, ooooooooow." *Children of the night, hear my roar.* He howled again. *Children of the night, fear me!* And then he trembled all the way down to his toes—er—claws. Which reminded him, real werewolves didn't wear Kenneth Cole loafers.

Time out. Roman Gervase ditched his shoes. Okay again. He resumed the crouched position and sniffed.

Dirt. Ferns. Deer droppings. Ooooh, cat!

He debated giving chase, then decided not yet. Tonight was a special night, after all. Tonight there was plenty of prey. He sniffed again, flaring fine aristocratic nostrils, and finally caught the odor he'd been seeking. Beer. Chlorine. Death.

Ooooh, death. He licked at his hand, tasted blood, and in a frenzy of savage emotion burst from behind the bushes.

Running. Into the joy of the night. Into the dark of the shadows. Into the glory of the moment. Trees slapping, dirt pounding, bushes trembling.

"Ooooooooow, ow, ow, OOOOOOOW."

Whoa, car!

Jerry Lynch, investing time in something far more interesting than his stock portfolio, slammed on his brakes, just as a shape careened off his hood. "What in God's name?"

For a moment, a man's face was frozen in Jerry's headlights, then the beast was off and running again.

Anka's head popped up. "What was that?"

Jerry slowly expelled his pent-up breath. "Roman Gervase," he muttered. "Fruitcake."

"Did he see anything?" Anka wiped her lips with the back of her hand.

Jerry put the car into drive. His wife was home with Samantha, so he'd volunteered to run out for milk.

"No one would believe him anyway."

"Hey, Jerry, what's with all those flashing lights?"

"He just fell and hit his head."

"Are you kidding? A former marine dying outside a country club because he 'tripped and fell.' It's murder, no doubt about it. Probably killed by the same person who did in Vormeister."

Nervous laughter around the bar. Parker Upshaw made a quick motion with his hand, and Tiffany promptly started pouring a fresh round of drinks. The police were still outside. So was Camille. So was Lance, or rather, Lance's body. They were all trying not to notice the morbid scene, but as the hour grew later, their efforts were becoming more and more futile.

"How long are they going to keep us here?" Laura Armbruster demanded. Her face was pinched, her normally uptight features even more constricted this evening. "My God, first Lance is murdered, and then we're all held at the scene like . . . like common criminals!"

"It ain't a bad prison," Silas Macgruder commented, and nodded at Tiffany for a fresh brew.

"Of course it's not a bad prison!" Laura snapped. Humor always had been lost on her. "But I want to go home! Besides, it's not like *I* did anything."

"It's awful, just awful," Babs murmured. Trauma had driven her from her normal fruity fizz to Cosmos straight up. Now she knocked back her fourth martini, then slammed down the empty glass and pushed it forward for more. The bar's overhead lights caught the sparkling facets of her three-carat diamond. She stopped, stared at the oversized stone, and then giggled at something only she understood. Babs was more than a little tipsy. Then again, after an hour and a half of serious drinking most of them were.

"We need to keep calm," Parker stated flatly. He was the unspoken host of this impromptu shindig and considered it his job to maintain order.

"Calm?" Ned said beside him. The senator's voice was shrill, his forehead covered in a sheen of sweat. When he held out his glass for another dose of Johnny Walker Gold, his hand trembled like an addict who'd gone too long without a fix. "Two men found dead. *In only twelve hours.* It's like that morbid Agatha Christie story, *And Then There Were None.* Which one of us will be next? My God, I didn't even think Vormeister and McClintock were that close."

"Who said they were close?" someone asked from the other side of the U-shaped bar.

"Who said the deaths were related?" Parker asked more relevantly. He frowned at his friend. What was up with Ned tonight? Carbury was a senator, for God's sake. You would think he'd show a little more courage under fire.

"We shouldn't jump to any conclusions," Lydia murmured. Parker gratefully patted his wife's hand for her support. Lydia's lips were bloodless, her features pale, but she was holding it together. It was more than he could say for most of their neighbors. *Overbred snobs,* he thought, not for the first time since moving into this place.

"Maybe it was them tree huggers," Silas Macgruder said. "Never can tell with those nature types. A lot of them wouldn't hesitate to ax off a man's foot if it would keep him from stomping an ant."

"Swan goons?" Mignon Gervase offered up, then twittered nervously.

"Well, it can't be one of us," Parker said firmly.

"Why not?" Babs asked.

"We were all here. We have an alibi."

"We weren't all here," Ned said immediately. "Where's the reverend?"

"He has a very important meeting," Laura said.

"That's what he thinks," Mignon muttered.

"What?"

"Nothing."

Laura narrowed her eyes. "And where's your husband, Mignon? I didn't see him at our meeting tonight. Doesn't he care about our community?"

"Full moon," Mignon said carelessly. "Roman's probably enjoying our community just fine right now—running around peeing on everyone's foundations."

"And Toni Sinclair never made it," Ned continued. "Guess she was too busy playing with Bambi. Other people?"

"Vanessa," Lydia said quietly. "Vanessa went home early."

Vanessa. Conversation ground to an immediate halt. The newest candidate for homicidal maniac was considered, then in the spirit of the drunken moment, accepted wholeheartedly.

"Vanessa," people started murmuring. Yes, bloodthirsty, hard-as-nails, grate-on-your-nerves Vanessa. Everyone's mood picked up for the first time since Lance's tragic passing. Vanessa was evil; order in the universe was restored.

Tiffany shook her head at the whole lot of them, wondered if all rich people were this stupid, and poured a fresh round of drinks.

In another dark corner of Gryphon Gate. No lights here. No cops. No bar. Just a half-dressed woman, a half-crazed man, and a loaded handgun.

"What the hell are you doing?" Vanessa hissed as she opened her front door to find Rev. Peter Armbruster standing on her shadowed steps. "You're going to ruin everything."

"*I'm* going to ruin everything? You bloodthirsty bitch."

"Peter, get lost. I don't know why you're soiling my property, but I've already had an atrociously bad day, and I refuse to top it off by dealing with you. You heard me. Shoo, shoo. Go *away!*"

"I want the videotape."

Something in Peter's voice finally brought Vanessa up short. She frowned, standing in the foyer of her Gryphon Gate home in nothing but a peach peignoir, and wondered if she'd made a miscalculation regarding the loving reverend. She'd always considered him a spineless bastard, henpecked by his shrewish wife and desperate for a little action on the side. At the moment, however, Peter didn't look ready to back down. In fact, with his harsh-planed face lit only by the icy glow of the full moon, he appeared almost menacing.

"What's in your pocket, Peter?"

"I'll show you mine if you'll show me yours."

"Peter!" That was it. She went to slam the door in his face. Peter, however, kicked his foot forward, blocked the door, then shoved his way forcefully into her home. He was shockingly strong for a reverend. Shockingly tall, powerful, determined. Vanessa fell back, panting heavily.

"What are you doing, Peter?" Her voice had gone up a notch. She could feel her control of the situation slipping away, and she still wasn't sure where she'd gone wrong.

"I want that tape!" Peter repeated shrilly. He dug into his pocket, then waved a small, silvery pistol in front of her eyes. A .22 maybe. Or, knowing Peter, a stainless steel cigarette lighter that only looked like a firearm. Still, did she want to take that chance?

Peter was advancing. Vanessa automatically fell back, already wracking her brain for a plan of attack. Yelling for help would get her nowhere. Her nearest neighbor was three acres away, and she didn't keep her Gryphon Gate home staffed anymore, as she spent the majority of her time in her Alexandria penthouse. Just her bad luck she'd chosen to spend the night here. After tonight's community meeting, however, she'd been too tired to head back into the city. After her sip at the clubhouse bar she'd retired to her Gryphon Gate abode, wanting nothing more than to curl up in her silk-draped bedroom and nurse her wounds. Frogs, for God's sake. Some rare flower named swamp pink, for crying out loud. Vanessa Smart-Drysdale did *not* get thwarted by tiny amphibians or poorly named weeds.

A nervous reverend with a peashooter, on the other hand . . .

She came up against the back wall of her foyer. Hardwood trim from the rich mahogany panels dug into her spine. No place else to go, and Peter was still waving his gun like a maniac.

"When I break ground on Forest Glen, you get the tape," Vanessa tried gamely. "That's our deal, Peter. We've already been through all this. Now get out!"

"What deal? You already reneged on the deal!"

"I've done no such thing. Now put down that gun, Peter. Or better yet, if you really feel like inflicting violence, I know of some tree frogs that would make perfect targets!"

"You'd like that, wouldn't you? Have me fix all your problems." His voice had gained a dangerous edge. Now that Vanessa was paying more attention, she could discern the glassy sheen in his eyes. Dear God, Peter had been drinking. Oh, this was just not her day!

"Peter," Vanessa said crisply, "once Forest Glen goes in, the sweep of high-end homes will boost the property values of the entire area, including this community. Your house will be worth twice as much. The situation is win-win for everyone."

"Mignon left me."

Vanessa faltered, digested this latest news, and once again tried to find the proper strategy.

"Mignon is a fool," she said.

"She called me the world's most unimaginative lover. According to her, I'm even sanctimonious when I sin."

"Ouch," Vanessa murmured.

"What did you say?"

"I said posh. Pish-posh. Mignon married Roman Gervase. What could she possibly know about good men?"

That seemed to be a better tactic. Peter stepped back, appearing slightly mollified. He exchanged his menacing tone for a drunken whine. "The bible's right, you know. Women are evil."

"Hey, we came from your rib. Garbage in, garbage out, I always say."

Armbruster frowned at her. He was definitely too drunk to follow that thought, so he waved his gun instead. "Now you're trying to screw me, too."

"Peter, I have a tape you need. You have a vote I need. I'm not screwing you, I'm conducting business. You hold up your end, I'll hold up mine."

Whatever she had just said, it was not the right thing. Peter's face went dark. He swung his right hand forward, and Vanessa found herself staring down the barrel of what definitely looked to be a real .22 semiautomatic. She sucked in her breath and watched Peter's finger tremble on the trigger.

"Lying bitch!"

"Peter—"

"Why the hell did you send me that fax?"

"What fax?"

" '*I know about Mignon. Ten P.M. Pool house. Tonight. Come alone, bring your wallet.'* What are you trying to do, suck me dry?"

"Peter, I swear—"

"You lying bitch! I'm not paying you any money! I'm through, I'm through, I'm through!"

Peter's hand tightened on the trigger. And Vanessa cried out quickly, "Peter, I got a fax, too!"

"What?" His finger froze.

"Fax. Got a fax. Just like yours. Last night. Honest, Peter, I'm telling the truth." Vanessa was breathing hard. And she was thinking faster than she'd ever thought in her life.

Very slowly, Peter lowered the gun. "You got a fax?"

"Yes, it said . . ." Vanessa paused, then lied effortlessly, "it said, 'I know about Armbruster.' Don't you see, Peter. Someone not only knows about you and Mignon, but that same person knows that I know."

"Huh?" a drunken Peter Armbruster said.

Vanessa sighed. Well, you had to work with what you had to work with. "Someone is trying to blackmail me, too, Peter. The same person who is blackmailing you. But now that we both know what is happening, we can stop it. We'll work together, identify the blackmailer, and make sure he never screws around with us again."

"But you're a bitch," Peter said stupidly.

Vanessa sighed again. "Trust me darling," she said, and led Peter into her living room, "the feeling is mutual."

It seemed to Toni that she had no sooner fallen asleep than she was awakened by pounding on her front door. For a moment she lay in her bed disoriented. Isn't Bertha going to get that? Then she realized that it was one in the morning and Bertha was sleeping peacefully in her trailer next to Bill. Toni glanced over at the vast emptiness of her king-size bed, feeling a familiar pang. Then she was egged into action by further knocking down below.

Toni rose blearily to her feet, yawned, and grabbed a rose-colored silk bathrobe and her favorite pink bunny slippers—a gift from Miranda—from the chaise lounge next to her bed. She had been so invigorated after the rally in front of Gryphon Gate she'd had to take Nyquil in order to finally fall asleep. Now she felt muddleheaded and sluggish.

What kind of people went around banging on doors at one in the morning anyway? Thank God Miranda was a heavy sleeper.

Toni navigated her darkened house with the natural deftness of a mother—and a widow—who'd spent her fair share of sleepless nights. She passed down the yawning hallway to the gracefully sweeping staircase that was the focal point of her home's foyer. Only when her bunny slippers touched down on the oak parquet floors of the first floor did she snap on the overhead chandelier. Then she looked out the peephole and saw the flashing red and blue police lights.

Déjà vu hit her hard and fast. She staggered back, one hand reflexively clutched against her chest while she struggled to get her bearings. No, it couldn't be. That was a long time ago. She was thirty-two now, safe in Lincoln's house, safe with Lincoln's money. Safe, safe, safe.

I know about Salinger.

The knocking sounded again. Toni frantically worked the locks, more intent than ever now on not disturbing her daughter.

A woman stood on the front porch, clad in khakis, a light blue shirt, and a brown suede jacket that had definitely been bought off the rack. She appeared close to Toni's own age, with beautiful thick dark hair. Her eyes were harder though, her face held more lines. She had not married into money, it was clear, and she was already giving Toni the disdainful look career women reserved for kept wives. The woman flashed a police badge. CAPTAIN DIANE ROBARDS, it said. HOMICIDE.

"Toni Sinclair?"

"Yes?" Toni fought to keep her face composed and her voice steady. She was suddenly, acutely aware of her silly little robe and pink bunny slippers.

"I have some questions, Mrs. Sinclair."

"Has someone been hurt?"

"If I could come inside for a moment." The woman gave her a cajoling look. Don't make a scene, the look said. Just do as I say and everything will be all right.

Toni stiffened her spine. "What is this regarding, Captain Robards?"

"It really would be best if I came inside. You know, before your neighbors start noticing."

"My daughter is asleep."

"Well, you can always come down to the station."

That did the trick. Toni opened her door and let Captain Robards into her home. *It's okay,* Toni reminded herself. *You've done nothing wrong. This time.*

Toni led the policewoman into the den. It was the most secluded room in the house, with heavy cherry doors she could close to dampen the sound. The den boasted a gigantic bird's-eye maple desk Lincoln had had custom made the year before his death. Across from it were two deep-cushioned chocolate suede chairs and roughly one hundred thousand dollars in rare antiques. Toni crossed to the built-in bar, discreetly tucked into the room's cherry wood paneling. She took out a bottle of Evian water and offered the captain the same. Diane Robards shook her head.

"Where were you this evening?" the police captain asked.

"I was at a rally at the front gates of the community. I joined people from Save Our Swans to protest the slaughter of innocent animals within my neighborhood. Why do you ask?"

Captain Robards produced a small spiral notebook. She ignored Toni's question and made a note. "What time was this?"

"We started at five. The protest lasted until eight."

"What did you do after eight?"

"What happened, Captain? Do I need a lawyer?"

Captain Robards looked at her impatiently. "Where were you after eight P.M., Mrs. Sinclair?"

"I was home with my daughter! We ate a late dinner, I read her a few stories, I put her to bed. Then I went to bed. I'm a single mother, Captain Robards. It's hardly a glamorous life."

"Do you have anyone who can corroborate your activities?"

"You mean an *alibi?*"

Captain Robards simply stared at her. Toni grew flustered again. Her hands self-consciously gripped the edges of her robe. She forced herself to take a deep breath, then had a sip of water. She had done nothing wrong. She was safe in Lincoln's home, safe with Lincoln's money.

I know about Salinger.

Stop it, stop it, stop it! Toni took another, longer, drink of water.

"The protesters," she said shortly. "They can vouch for my whereabouts. And then, after that, my daughter."

"How old is your daughter?"

"Eight. Miranda is eight. Listen, I have no idea what happened, Captain Robards, but my daughter and I had nothing to do with it. We attended a peaceful protest, which is our right under the U.S. Constitution, then we ate dinner. Simple as that."

"Did you feed the deer dinner, too?"

Toni paused, tried to follow that question to some sort of logical conclusion, then gave up. She said more warily, "I don't see how what I do on my private property is anyone's business but my own."

"Your neighbors don't care for the deer."

"My neighbors need to spend less time in their Mercedes and more time in the great outdoors."

"Sounds like some of them were going to take you up on that advice. Who is it? Someone is going to lead an organized deer hunt?"

"Lieutenant Colonel McClintock," Toni said immediately. "As if that man didn't get enough violence as a marine."

"You were opposed to the hunt?"

"That's why they call it a protest," Toni said wryly.

"He didn't care for that. Sounds like he went down and tried to reason with your S.O.S. friends, but they weren't interested."

"He wanted to defend shooting helpless animals. You can't defend that. The deer were here first. We're the ones intruding on their habitat. We should adapt, not them." Toni smiled sweetly. "We have another rally scheduled in three days, if you'd like to join."

"One protest wasn't enough?"

"Hardly. Lance McClintock didn't become a lieutenant colonel by going down without a fight. We have a long uphill battle in front of us."

"Interesting you should say that: go down without a fight."

"He's stubborn," Toni said seriously. "Ask his wife."

Captain Robards regarded her more intently. "Do you take disappointment well?"

"I don't know what you mean."

"What about being stood up? Do you like being stood up?"

Toni paused for the second time. She still couldn't follow the line of questioning, but once again she could sense a trap. Do you like being stood up? Something about that phrase bothered her. And then she got it. The second fax that had arrived first thing this morning. *I don't like being stood up. You'll hear from me.*

Toni stared at Captain Robards and was suddenly very sorry she had let this woman into her home.

"I don't know what you're talking about," Toni said, but she knew she must look stricken now, and her tone didn't even convince herself.

"Were you sleeping with him? Is that what this was all about?"

"Who?" Toni cried. "What? I swear I don't know what you're talking about!"

"Lance McClintock. Were you sleeping with him?"

"*Lieutenant Colonel McClintock?* He's sixty if he's a day. Besides, Camille would kill me."

"Lance is dead," Captain Robards said matter-of-factly. "Someone caved in his skull earlier this evening."

Toni felt all the oxygen escape from her lungs. One moment she was a perfectly fine single mother, the next she couldn't even draw a breath of air. Lance. Killed. *I don't like being stood up.* The room was spinning away from her. She had to grip the arms of her chair. "But Lance," she murmured weakly. "Lance was a former marine, strong as an ox. Who could attack, who would attack . . ."

Captain Robards leaned forward. "We found the fax folded up in his inside jacket pocket. *'I don't like being stood up. You'll hear from me.'* You know that phrase, don't you, Mrs. Sinclair?"

"No, no, why would—"

"You sent that fax, didn't you, Mrs. Sinclair?"

"*No!* I liked Lance. He was a good man, even if he wanted to shoot deer!"

"But you know about the fax," Captain Robards pounced. "You know that phrase!"

Toni couldn't talk anymore. She stared at Captain Robards mutely while the policewoman slowly smiled in triumph.

"Where were you after eight P.M. this evening, Mrs. Sinclair? And what did you do to Lt. Col. Lance McClintock?"

5

TONI SINCLAIR WATCHED FROM
inside her foyer as Captain Robards tried to stare down the ten-point
buck that stood on the walkway between her house and the Gryphon
Gate patrol car. Toni had been smart to remember what the lawyer
had told her after Lincoln's fatal accident. She simply took all the in-
sults that Robards spit out at her, but didn't answer any more of those
ridiculous questions.

The buck won. Hoping for a nocturnal feeding opportunity, he
stood his ground and forced Robards onto the lawn. He would be re-
warded for his tenacity.

"Shit."

You said it, Officer. Toni smiled for the first time in an hour as she
peeked from behind the French lace runners bordering the front door
and saw Diane Robards sink into piles of deer droppings that had
been deposited all over the yard these past few days. Step after
sloppy step, the officer made her way to the pavement. It was slippery
stuff, and would take hours to dig out of the pleated rubber soles of
those shiny patent leather lace-ups that set off her uniform so smartly.

Toni waited until the taillights of Robards's car disappeared from
the quiet cul-de-sac. She needed to calm down before she placed the
call.

She made her way to the mudroom, exchanging her bunny slippers for gardening clogs. She unlocked the garage door and headed

for the corner where half a dozen bags of grain and four of Purina Deer Chow were lined up. She scooped a few helpings of deer chow into a pail and went out onto the lawn, where the buck still waited, trailed by a small army of followers.

Toni held out her hand, and the deer approached, nudging each other to get at the food. She patted the side of a small doe. "So I lied to the captain. Lance wasn't a nice man at all. I didn't kill him, but I'd rather see a mean old fool like him dead than any of you with an arrow between your eyes."

It calmed her to be among the gentle brown animals. She tossed the chow across the lawn and went back inside, stopping to replace the clogs and snuggle back into her bunny slippers.

Toni stood at the bottom of the staircase and listened for movement from above, but Miranda seemed to have slept through Diane Robards's visit. She returned to the den and shut the heavy cherry doors behind her again. Ignoring the lukewarm Evian, she reached into the wine cooler and searched the labels for a bottle she wanted.

This wouldn't be an easy phone call to make. Something rich, something smooth. She had to sound relaxed and in control. The wine would help to soothe her. Corton Charlemagne, Grand Cru. She uncorked the fine burgundy and braced herself with a glassful.

Funny, Toni thought, *that there are some telephone numbers you just never seem to forget, no matter how long it's been since the last call.*

The phone rang three times as she continued to sip the cold wine. A mechanical voice grated against her ear. "The number you have reached is no longer in service. If you think you have reached this recording in error, please . . ."

Toni pressed the receiver and dialed information. Now she was guzzling the wine. After ten or twelve rings, an operator got on the line. Probably one of only three live bodies working for any of the phone companies in the entire country.

"Salinger," she asked the operator. "Jason Salinger."

"Checking for you."

Toni swiveled on the bar stool at the sound of something brushing against the window behind her. Out of the corner of her eye she glimpsed a shadow, the shape of a man, gliding out of sight into the bushes.

"Probably just Roman Gervase, baying at the moon," she mumbled to herself as she took another swig.

She turned back to the bar to pick up a pen as the operator spoke to her. "I'm sorry, ma'am, but that residence is an unlisted number."

"This is an emergency. There's been a death. A—a—murder—I need to get in touch. . . ."

"I'll connect you to 911 immediately, ma'am."

Toni dropped the receiver back in the cradle. "That's the last thing I want right now, you nitwit."

A tapping noise again, and Toni turned to the window. Maybe it was just the branches scratching against the glass, the light from the moon dancing off the leaves.

She dialed information a second time. "A business listing, in Chesapeake County. Salinger. Jason Salinger."

"Nothing for Jason. I have a Salinger Solutions. Could that be it?"

"I thought it was a solution at the time," Toni mumbled.

"Excuse me? Do you want me to connect you to that number?"

"Please."

Toni listened as the automated menu at Salinger Solutions gave the list of options, then she pressed the number eight. Jason's deep, velvet-toned voice suggested that she leave a message.

She started to record but realized that she had better be cautious. The little upstart had his own business now, and if the menu was any indication, he had at least seven employees. Maybe he had a secretary who screened the calls and passed the information on to him. Or a wife who worked in the office with him.

"Mr. Salinger? This is Antoinette." *He was the only one who called me that,* Toni thought to herself. It was their own private joke. Marie Antoinette is what he dubbed her, in fact. Except, this queen was unhappily married to the Dot.Com King, as Jason was among the first to observe, and when devoted employees were kept out of the lucrative deal that took the company public, it was Toni who whispered to Jason, "Let them eat cake."

"You did some work for me a few years back, Mr. Salinger. I'm sure you remember." It was work that had profited both of them handsomely. "I've got a new project for you. I'd like to install a new system. It's Friday morning, about two A.M. Sorry to call at this hour, but I'm having trouble sleeping. I expect you'll get this message when you get into the office later today. I'm hoping you can put this on the front burner. Get out to me immediately. I think you know where I live."

Toni was about to hang up, but then she had a better idea. "Not to the house actually. I'd like you to do some work on my boat." She thought quickly, timing the appointment for after Miranda left for school and before the S.O.S. planning session at the club at noon. "Can you meet me at the marina at ten? Can't miss her. It's a forty-foot sloop. Only one that big."

She hung up the phone and emptied her wineglass in one long swallow. This time when she heard the tapping at the window, she spun around quickly. Dozens of pairs of eyes crowded around the bay window. Deer everywhere. They seemed jumpy and skittish. She had that creepy feeling that someone had been watching her the entire time. Was it Roman? Or was there someone else secreted in the bushes? This was not just about their hunger. Something—or someone—must have spooked the animals.

Toni poured another glass of wine. After several minutes she walked to the window, but the deer had gone back to quietly grazing. She drew the curtains closed and reclined on the sofa, stretching out and leaning her head back against the pillow. Jason Salinger. She hadn't thought the sound of his voice would arouse her again after almost five years, but it was working its old magic. She kicked off the bunny slippers and ran the toes of her right foot up and down the inside of her left knee, remembering the spot where Jason used to kiss her so tenderly.

Toni wondered if he had outgrown that grad student look that had so endeared him to Lincoln in the early days, when the business was just taking off. He had seemed so earnest when he showed up at the house that first time, at his boss's insistence, to personalize Toni's system.

Jason was a few years younger than she. He had a shock of long, straight, dark brown hair that she used to brush off his forehead whenever he leaned over her to pull her close. He had a total geek affect, from the wire-rimmed glasses to the plaid flannel shirt to the ripped jeans. He looked so meek and harmless that even she was shocked when he suggested a solution—both for her unhappiness and his ambition.

Lincoln had been unfaithful to Toni before she became pregnant with Miranda, but he had sworn off teenaged girls after the first Lamaze class. When she caught him surfing the Britney Spears Web site and answering E-mails from fifteen-year-olds while pretending to be a cheerleading coach, she knew he was incorrigible.

Perhaps Jason was being blackmailed now, too. Why else would his name have been mentioned? There must be a Salinger solution to this mess.

Leave it to Lincoln to find the smartest guy in the field. And leave it to Jason to find the foolproof way to hot-wire that stereo system, to convince the other employees that the mean bastard deserved a birthday present from all of them, and to sell Lincoln on the fact that the stainless steel toilet seat was state-of-the-art. They don't come any more brilliant than Salinger.

The Reverend Dr. Peter Armbruster pulled into his garage shortly after 2 A.M. He had been so surprised when he passed Diane Robards parked on the side of the road, barefoot and scraping something off the soles of her shoes, that he didn't even notice that the light was on in his own kitchen.

Peter felt absurdly grateful that Vanessa had made a pot of coffee to sober him up before sending him on his way. No point making good on his threat to kill her as long as she still had a copy of the videotape.

Peter eased himself out of the driver's seat and braced himself unsteadily against his John Deere riding mower. He was fumbling for his house key when Laura's voice cut through the quiet night air like a carving knife. "Get in here fast," was all he heard, after she screamed out something to him about Mignon.

Not another confrontation tonight! He moaned at the thought. His head ached as he stalled, trying to think of answers to the questions she had so obviously waited up to have answered. How could she possibly know about Mignon? Had Vanessa called Laura after Peter left her?

His hand tightened on the grip of the pistol for the second time. He repeated each of the Ten Commandments to himself over and over again—lingering on the most relevant ones—as he let himself into the mudroom and made his way to the kitchen, about to come face-to-face with the tight features on his wife's screwed-up little face. He was sweating now, formulating his own question to try to deflect his wife's palpable anger.

"What a surprise to see you up so late, my dear," Peter said. "Is everything all right?"

Laura looked up from a yellow legal pad she'd been scribbling on. "Lance died tonight, at the club."

"He *what?*"

"Dropped dead. They're not sure how."

Peter was dumbfounded. It was hard to think of the mortality of his poor friends as Laura Armbruster rose to her feet and pointed a long metal barbecue fork at him. He flinched and covered his face with his hands. "Another death in our little village. Now I'll have two memorial services to write. They've asked for me, haven't they?"

"They were certainly asking for you last night. Everyone wanted to know where you were. I told them you had an important meeting, but I don't know myself what you were doing, and it's time I did."

"How in the Lord's name can I show my respect for the dead while you're waving that tool of the devil at me? It looks like a pitchfork, for goodness sake."

It was clear she had found out about his affair and was ready to skewer him.

He tried to pull the gun out of his pocket, but it snagged and ripped the lining. "I can explain it all," he pleaded. "You don't need to scream. All the neighbors will hear you."

"Stop whining, Peter. I was just trying to get you in here so I could shove this in the microwave and get to bed." She turned to the counter and stuck the fork in a prime piece of beef. "Filet mignon. They had some leftover at the club tonight so I brought a few steaks home. I was afraid you missed dinner and I didn't want you to go hungry."

Peter collapsed onto a kitchen chair and removed his hand from his pocket, resting his elbows on the table and wiping his brow with a checkered blue napkin. Laura didn't know a thing. "Bless you, my dear."

There was a place setting ready for Peter, and Laura cleared her papers from the rest of the tabletop.

"What are you working on at this late hour?" Peter asked, his breathing growing steadier.

"An article for the *Gryphon Gazette*. The deadline's tomorrow. I promised to get a piece together about Sigmond. About his—um . . ."

"His passing. About his passing, my angel. Still no word on what it was?"

"Not that we've been told. And now there's poor Lance, too. That's why everybody wondered where you were."

"God's work, my dear, God's work. Better that you don't put yourself in the middle. If my parishioners wish me to tell the police anything more than that I was doing God's work, I'm sure I'll be able to get their permission."

Laura leaned to put the plate down in front of him, then handed him a printout of her story. THE GRYPHON GRIEVES, the banner headline began.

Peter sliced his filet and started to read aloud. "'Tears streaked down the eagle's beak and the lion's roar softened to a whimper as the Gryphon, guardian of all treasures within its gates, mourned the loss of two longtime residents, Sigmond Vormeister and Lance McClintock.' Lovely, my dear, lovely image."

"Well, someone has to protect us," Laura sniffed. "The *Washington Post* will be on doorsteps all over town in a few hours, talking about murder in our little community. We've got to keep this in perspective. So far as I know, nothing's to say Sigmond didn't have a heart attack and Lance didn't trip and fall."

"To everything there is a season, my beloved. You're absolutely right. The bible tells us so." Peter pushed the meat around on his plate, barely able to think about eating.

"We've got so many big events coming up this month. Here I am, the club manager, with our first national golf tournament scheduled for the end of May," Laura's lips pulled down in a tight frown and her nose pinched in even further. "What if Tiger Woods cancels on me, just because someone uses the word 'murder' around here?"

"Frightful." The Reverend Doctor Armbruster put Laura's story down on the table. He pushed away the filet and let his thoughts return to Mignon. Laura could babble on all she wanted. How foolish he had been just fifteen minutes earlier to think she was worried about his affair. Now he had something more serious to consume him. How could he go about regaining his lover's affection?

"Don't you think we need more diversity here, Peter?" Laura

planted herself in the chair next to him and tried to get his undivided attention. "Everyone else gets to tell you things in confidence. I might as well do the same."

"What's that, my sweet?" It would be too perfect if Laura were about to confess an affair of her own, he mused. Maybe she had fallen for the mad Roman Gervase. The reverend could simply perform a series of divorces and remarriages at St. Francis of Assisi Interfaith Chapel. Later today. Screw civil law. His fantasies carried him off in Mignon's arms and planted Laura squarely against Roman's hairy chest.

"That American Medical Union Awards Dinner at the clubhouse next week?"

"Yes."

"Did I tell you who's getting the award?"

"Afraid I don't recall if you did."

"Jefferson, Dr. Charles Jefferson. You know, the famous obstetrician and fertility expert? He's done so much amazing work with artificial insemination. He's actually helped all these families in Gryphon Gate—the Upshaws, the Lynches . . ."

"Then he deserves the award," Peter interrupted, "and you'll be there to cheer him on, I'm sure of it." Peter was delighted. It would provide another evening's opportunity for him to slip away and try to patch things up with Mignon Gervase. "What night did you say that would be?"

"Next Wednesday. But here's what I have to tell you. I confided in Sigmond, but now that he's gone . . ."

"What ever possessed you to tell Sigmond anything? The man was constantly making notes and writing things down. You might as well have told the town crier. Some people around here think he was going to expose all the dirty little secrets he knew about."

"Sigmond was a sociologist, Peter. He studied people. That was his business, just as spiritual healing is yours. I wanted his advice about what to do when I met Dr. Jefferson."

"Doesn't *my* advice count?"

"You'd just discourage me again, dear. That's why I wanted a professional opinion."

"Discourage you again, you say? Oh, that. You mean, he's one of *those* Jeffersons?"

Laura Armbruster had been born a Hemings. She was one of the great-great-great-great-grandchildren of Sally Hemings, the smart and beautiful young slave who had given birth to at least one of Thomas Jefferson's children. Although many of Jefferson's white descendants still battled the realities of the roots of the family tree, twenty-first-century DNA technology had confirmed the blood relationships and paternal heritage.

"What exactly did you tell Sigmond?" Peter pressed.

"I told him about my ancestors, all of whom are still denied burial rights in the family plot at Monticello. And I told him I had traced the genealogy of Charles Jefferson, and could prove that we were indeed related to one another. I asked his advice about how to tell Dr. Jefferson the story when I meet him next week."

"Why in damnation do you want to tell him the story?"

"To enlist Dr. Jefferson's help. To lean on him, if you will."

"And was Sigmond more encouraging than I've been?"

"Indeed he was, Peter," Laura Hemings Armbruster answered. "Sigmond actually encouraged me to study some of the new arrivals in Gryphon Gate—the Upshaw twins, little Samantha Lynch, those darling Anderson boys. I've seen them all over at the pool. Sigmond was right."

"About what?"

Laura focused her pale green eyes on her husband. "There are far too many babies who look alike around here for that to be an accident of nature. I'm going to talk to Doctor Jefferson about that while he's here. And about getting his help to see that my relatives finally have their proper burial."

Vanessa Smart-Drysdale telephoned the clubhouse as soon as the switchboard opened at 7 A.M. on Friday morning. She asked the operator to transfer her to the valet parking area.

Ray Flynt picked up the phone. "Good morning, ma'am. How can I help you?"

"I woke up in knots today, Ray. I'll be there in an hour. I'd like a massage, please."

"Kimberly doesn't work on Fridays, ma'am."

"I know that. That's why I'm calling you."

Ray blushed, remembering what had happened one time last year when Vanessa had asked him to rub her shoulders. "I'm not licensed to do no body work, ma'am."

"Let me be the judge of that, Ray. I'll meet you in the spa at eight. Get someone to cover you in the parking lot."

"But—"

"Don't worry, we'll just talk business. I've got some ideas for the Web site." Her voice softened. "A star quarterback like you has probably had more massages than anyone I know. I just want you to knead some tightness out of my calves before I go out on the course this afternoon. Besides, you're gonna *love* what I'm going to have you do on the Web."

"The Web?"

"Sort of a sneak preview of a coming attraction that I want you to post over the weekend."

Ray was excited just thinking about talking to Vanessa. He tried to tell himself that it was her enthusiasm about his Web design that made him so happy, but then he had a flashback to the way her small, slender body had responded to his large, firm hands when he rubbed her down just before the New Year's Eve party.

At five minutes to eight, Ray spotted Vanessa's red Corvette heading for the valet stand under the clubhouse canopy. He bolted to the driver's side and opened the door for her.

"Any problems?"

"No, ma'am. Bill Oberlin's gonna send one of the guys over from the pro shop to take my shift for an hour. You wanna change and get set up, I'll be ready to go in about ten minutes."

Vanessa strolled through the lobby. A black bunting was draped around the board that listed the club members' names, and standing on the bar was a posterboard with Lance McClintock's photograph above the words *Semper Fi.*

She continued into the ladies' locker room and had just removed her heart-shaped diamond necklace and unscrewed the back of her pierced earrings when Babs Blackburn pushed open the swinging door and walked into the bathroom for one more look at herself in the mirror before heading out to the first tee.

"Well, well, well," Vanessa drawled. "I hear congratulations are in order, Babs. Anything I can do to talk a little sense into you before you take the big step?"

"Henry says I shouldn't even listen to you for a minute—that you have nothing nice to say to anyone about anything."

"Maybe we should bury the hatchet on our own. You can scratch my back and . . ."

"Henry says you'll just try to twist me around, to use me against him in the development plans for Forest Glen."

"No such thing, Babs. Careful."

Vanessa pointed at Babs's pink leather golf glove that had dropped to the floor. A large black spider was crawling into the open end.

Babs squealed. "I hate those things."

Vanessa lifted the glove by a finger and shook out the bug, smashing it with the heel of the shoe she had removed minutes earlier.

"Don't be so squeamish, kid. Better get used to it. Those red-toed tree frogs thrive on big, juicy spiders. They're everywhere in Gryphon Gate. Can't see the deer tick, but these guys get into everything and really sting when they take a bite. The mayor didn't warn you?"

"Henry says—"

"I'm so damn sick of what Henry says. Have been for years. You got the best part of this bargain. That rock you're flashing on your finger. You sure it isn't a CZ? Get out while the getting's good. Take the rock and run."

Babs opened her mouth to speak but nothing came out.

Vanessa kept going. "Let's have a drink together one day. Our little secret, okay? Don't tell Henry. I'll answer all the questions you ever had about him."

Babs belonged in Gryphon Gate, Vanessa thought. She looked just like a doe caught in the headlights.

"Next time he decides to spend an hour up in his helicopter, you call me and drop by my place. Spiders are just the tip of the iceberg."

Vanessa clicked the combination lock into place, wrapped the bath towel around her body, and padded down the hallway toward the massage therapy room, leaving Babs's mouth flapping soundlessly.

Vanessa dropped the towel in a heap on the floor, lowered the dimmer on the light switch, lit an aromatherapy candle, flipped on a New Age tape of gushing waterfalls and rain forest bird sounds, and climbed onto the table. She lay on her stomach, her face in the hole in the headrest.

Dammit, she thought, *the only thing Henry Drysdale ever bought me was a one-way ticket to my mother's house when I told him it was over. I had to wait to meet Ned to get any real jewels. God knows who he put the squeeze on to get the stuff.*

She heard the door open. "Don't be shy, Ray. C'mon in. We've got a lot to talk about."

Ray's shoes squeaked as he walked to the table and stood beside her. She heard him pick up a bottle, unscrew the cap, and begin applying lotion to her back. Ahhh! His hands glided across her shoulder blades and down the bumps on her spine, yet somehow they seemed smaller than Ray's, and more gnarled.

She lifted her head. "Silas Macgruder! You sick old goat. Pushing ninety and you're still looking for cheap thrills. Get your hands off of me. How the hell—where's Ray? What happened to Ray?"

"Just shows you the value of a good tip, Vanessa," Silas chuckled. "I've been generous to that boy since he started caddying for me almost ten years ago. You can't take it with you. Start spending some of that dough you've got."

"Where's Ray?" She was sitting up now, gathering the sheet from underneath her and wrapping it around herself.

"Sent him on an errand. Gave him twice the price of a massage. Something we need for the memorial service for Sigmond and Lance. Duty before pleasure."

Vanessa's eyes narrowed. "What do you want, Silas?"

"Want? I'm here to do you a favor." Silas winked at Vanessa. "Always try to help the pretty ones. Never know when they'll be willing to help me in return. Watch your putter, young lady. That's what I came to tell you."

"Watch your own," Vanessa snarled, glancing down at the fly on Silas' pants.

He laughed. "Now, that's my driver. You ought to know that."

Vanessa squirmed on the table. "I'll count to ten and then I'm going to scream for Laura Armbruster."

"Don't you understand what I'm telling you? It's about the senator." Vanessa froze.

Silas had her attention now. "Lance McClintock was clubbed in the head. A putter's my guess."

"How do you know?"

"I've been around a long time, seen a lot of things. I'd say, if you're as smart as I think you are, you'll take your golf clubs and drive off into the sunset. And if you've got a way to get in touch with Senator Carbury . . ."

"Me?"

"I may be old, but I'm not blind, dammit."

Vanessa shivered. She and Ned Carbury had been so discreet. "You know Ned every bit as well as I do," she sputtered. "Tell him yourself."

"I wouldn't say I've been quite as intimate with him as you have. Tried to find him myself this morning. Thought he'd be sleeping off that expensive hangover he must have picked up last night."

"Try his office, Silas."

"Did that. Won't be there until this afternoon. Has a tryst. Well, his secretary called it a business meeting, come to think of it, on his way into D.C. Somewhere in Alexandria, if I had to guess." Silas headed for the door.

"Wait a minute."

Silas stopped in his tracks, turning to look at Vanessa. He laid his hand on the light switch and the room was flooded with light. "If I can't touch, do you mind if I look a bit?"

Vanessa's grip on the towel loosened. The least she could do in exchange for some information was show the old man a bit of cleavage. "So, if I should happen to bump into Ned, what should I tell him?"

"The senator might want to secure his Big Bertha and all his other clubs, too."

"But—but—surely everyone knows how fond Ned was of Lance McClintock?"

"Used to think so myself, Vanessa. But that was some racket they were kicking up on the seventeenth green last night. I almost expected fisticuffs."

"How'd you—?"

"Wasn't just me. Mignon and I were teeing off right behind them. She heard it, too."

"What else did she hear? And you?" Vanessa was peeved. She had ways of dealing with Silas, but there was no guarantee about who Mignon Gervase might spill her guts to.

"My hearing's not so good. I couldn't make out what it was about. Deer hunting? Swan shooting?"

Vanessa reached her left arm above her head to throw her rich chestnut brown hair over her shoulder. The towel slipped off her breast. "You said Alexandria, Silas. Whatever made you mention Alexandria?"

"Live as long as I have, and someday, young lady, you'll be treated to the joys of a sigmoidoscope. It's a medical device that lets the doctor see right up—"

"Spare me."

Silas took a step closer, fixing his gaze on Vanessa's porcelain skin and the firm, taut lines of her breast. "Well, I used to tease Vormeister all the time. I called that little handheld computer his Sigmondoscope. Boy, was he into everyone else's business. Monkey business. And all there on that little black device. You could get a rear end view of everyone in Gryphon Gate. Bottoms up."

"He let you look at his Palm Pilot?" Vanessa found that hard to believe.

"Just played with it for a minute or two." Silas stretched out his arm and tweaked Vanessa on the nipple. "Told him I couldn't see well enough to read anything. Just wanted a quick feel of the little gadget, know what I mean?"

Toni Sinclair pulled her desert silver Mercedes SUV into her designated parking space at the marina. In a community where size truly mattered, her boat was indeed the biggest.

She looked to the end of the dock, where the white hull of the sloop glistened in the morning sunlight. *Sans Sin*. She had renamed the graceful vessel after her husband's death. Not only was she without sin, but without guilt as well.

Well, well, well. There was Capt. Diane Robards herself climbing out of the cabin of Bob Satterfield's sleek little cat boat. Toni remembered that the Satterfields were out of the country on vacation for the entire month of May. Their house, sitting near the front nine of the golf course, was empty, and there was no reason for anyone to be snooping around their boat.

Toni shut off the motor and watched as Captain Robards scanned the dock before stepping onto it. Topsiders had replaced her soiled patent leather uniform shoes.

Maybe I'll turn the tables on her, Toni thought to herself. *Ask her what she's doing on Bob's sexy little wood-hulled twenty-two-footer.*

She opened the door but stopped with her foot halfway to the ground. Someone else was coming out of the cabin. Beneath the black-rimmed baseball cap and dark lenses of the wraparound sunglasses, Toni recognized the strong square jaw of that other young cop. What was his name? She had seen it on the plate attached to his flak vest the night he had come to her house to stop the deer feeding. Leland Ford, that's who it was.

The young security guard took a step up onto the deck of the boat. The tight black T-shirt showed off Leland's impressive abs, and the ebony jogging shorts revealed the same solid musculature all the way down to his heels. Leland may have been off-duty, but he was definitely on the job.

Leland came up behind Robards, who was about to jump from the boat onto the dock. Toni blinked. Was it her imagination, or had Diane's young protégé just given her a friendly pat on the butt?

Toni Sinclair had seen all she needed. She grabbed her canvas sail bag from the backseat, nestled the chilled bottles of wine between the folds of her cashmere sweatshirt, and set off on the narrow walkway to the dock. She was an hour early for her assignation, and praying now that Jason would be late. Planning ahead was one of her signature traits.

"Good morning, Captain." Toni was certainly in a better position at the moment than during the awkward situation a few hours earlier in the den of her own home. She greeted Robards cheerfully.

The grin that Diane Robards had flashed back at Leland Ford vanished altogether when she came face-to-face with Toni Sinclair.

Toni smiled sweetly. "Why, Captain Robards, didn't you get any sleep after you left my home last night? Those frown lines look like they're embedded in your jawbone. Some of the women at the club have a wonderful new cosmetic surgeon who does BOTOX." Toni turned her smile on Leland. "Oh my—aren't you the officer who stopped by at the house the other day? About the deer? It's Mr. Ford, isn't it?"

Toni took a step closer to the Satterfield boat but didn't stop chattering for a minute. "Is one of my marina neighbors pouring goldfish food into the water? Are you against feeding fish, too, Captain?"

Ford smoothed his shirt into place and adjusted the waistband on his shorts. His pink face had deepened to scarlet.

Before Robards could answer, Toni Sinclair held her forefinger against her lips. "How foolish of me to forget. The Satterfields can't be to blame. They're in the south of France right now. Has someone committed a crime on their darling little boat?"

Robards seemed to be struggling for an answer. The loud whirring noise of an engine, almost directly overhead, nearly drowned out her reply. "Got a call that there might have been a break-in on the boat," she shouted. "Just came by to secure it."

"What?" Toni asked, cupping her hand to her ear. "What did you say? You came by to screw in it?"

The backwash of the hovering helicopter lifted Robards's thick, dark hair and blew it back in her face. With her thumb and index finger she picked strands out of her mouth so she could respond to Toni. "False alarm, Mrs. Sinclair. Everything's fine on board."

"Sue will be *so* relieved! I must give her a call tonight," Toni shouted over the roar of the rotors. "I've got to tell her about Lance, anyway. And poor Sigmond. They might want to cut their trip short and come home for the memorial service. What shall I tell the Satterfields about this ship-to-shore emergency, Captain?"

The helicopter veered off toward the country club.

Robards directed Leland off the dock. "No need to mention it at all. No need to upset her, Mrs. Sinclair."

"So glad to know you're willing to take such good care of us on your time off, Officers," Toni called after the pair as they climbed into separate cars and drove out of the marina parking lot.

Still smiling, Toni scurried down to the end of the dock and walked the short gangplank onto her beloved sailboat. She went below deck into the cabin and unpacked her bag.

Plenty of time! She opened one of the bottles of wine and placed it in the sterling silver cooler that Lincoln had won in the club's first regatta, the year they moved into Gryphon Gate. She stored the second bottle in the fridge. She slipped out of her jogging outfit and into a leopard print bodysuit that showed off her still-willowy figure to perfection.

In the bottom of the bag was a microcassette tape recorder small enough to be concealed between the cushion of the bunk bed and the wall beneath the starboard porthole.

Toni slid a Jimmy Buffett CD into the stereo, surveyed her image in the mirror behind the bathroom door, and declared herself ready for her reunion with Jason Salinger.

But the helicopter had come back with a vengeance. The metallic whirring of its rotors drowned out Buffett, and it completely over-whelmed the gentle lapping of the waves against the side of the boat.

Toni climbed onto the deck. Shading her eyes from the morning sun, she squinted at the chopper hovering directly overhead. She could clearly make out Henry Drysdale in control of the joystick.

Damn it, she thought, *what the hell is he looking for?*

The helicopter lurched to the right, the motor sputtering. Toni tried to make out who was sitting in the passenger seat next to Henry. Before she could get a fix on the facial features, the giant gray ma-chine heaved back on its other side, away from her and her prized possession.

Toni wondered if Henry was having trouble with the controls. He can't *want* to be thrashing around like that. If he didn't watch out, he'd crash-land the damn thing in the shallow water of the marina basin.

Toni checked her watch. Although she had forty-five minutes be-fore Jason was due to arrive, she ducked back inside to freshen her makeup.

Fifteen minutes later there was a knock upstairs on the cabin door.

One more check in the bathroom mirror. Toni looked at herself proudly. So many of the young mothers her age had lost their body tone; the youthful luster was gone from their hair. "Either this boy has finally learned something about being punctual," she said, admiring what she saw, "or he's still excited about the prospect of being with me."

She stopped to turn on the tape recorder, then bounced up the companionway to greet Jason Salinger. The helicopter still bobbed in the sky above the boat. She worried that it would interfere with the tape she was hoping to make of their conversation. All of their conversation. She was beginning to hope that the blasted thing would break away from its wildly rotating blades and drop into the water. What would be the difference if one or two more Gryphon Gaters bit the dust?

Toni Sinclair twisted the handle of the door and stepped back in surprise. "Why, Senator Carbury, whatever brings you out here to *my* little boat?"

6

"TIME OFF, HELL," LELAND FORD grumbled, but not as though it was really a complaint. "See anything?"

Diane Robards kept the binoculars trained on the *Sans Sin* for a moment longer, then swore under her breath. From their position one street back from the marina, and sheltered by a small stand of trees where they'd been able to park their cars without being noticed, the angle wasn't the best. But given a choice between having the surveillance noted and not having the best possible view, Diane chose the latter. There were just too damned many watching eyes in this place—and way too much attention being paid to the activities of cops. "No, not since the senator went on board," she replied at last.

Ford was silent for a moment, then said, "You know what she thought."

"It was fairly obvious," Diane responded dryly, unwilling to betray her own feelings about . . . possibilities. Knowing there was a spark was one thing, doing something about it in the middle of a murder investigation was something else entirely. "Tell me something. Do the residents of Gryphon Gate think about anything but sex?"

"Not so you'd notice." Ford sent her a faint grin when she turned her head to look at him. "Activity-wise, I mean. Oh, there's golf and there's bridge—but sex does seem to be the, er, driving interest."

Ignoring the bad pun, Diane turned her attention away from the rent-a-cop who was earning her growing respect and gazed upward to watch the helicopter still buzzing around above the marina.

"Henry Drysdale," Ford commented.

"Yeah. But who's that with him?"

"Got me."

Diane trained the binoculars upward, trying to catch a glimpse of Drysdale's passenger, even as she thought about the man beside her. Ford had reacted beautifully when Toni Sinclair had intercepted them coming off the Satterfields' boat, fidgeting with just the right amount of embarrassment like a man caught with his hand in the cookie jar. He accepted the part she offered and ran with it.

Pity he was only a glorified security guard. He'd make a damned good homicide detective, unless she missed her guess.

Briefly, Diane wondered if Ford would see it that way. If she was any judge at all, he had the instincts of a real cop—which was why she'd involved him in her little extracurricular activities today—but he had expressed no interest in actually becoming one. Not, at least, to her. He was alert and engaged in what they were doing, but she had to wonder if he was helping her out because of his interest in the investigation or in her.

Not that Diane was at all vain, it was just that it had happened to her before. She had great instincts about crime and about who she could trust, but lousy ones when it came to relationships other than the professional ones. Reasonably attractive, single, career-minded professional women, she'd discovered, were quite a turn-on to a lot of guys, especially those not interested in strings or promises. Plus, she apparently gave off signals that invited ambitious men to at least try to use her to boost themselves higher up the food chain. Especially younger men.

So, was that what was in Leland Ford's mind? Was he at least considering the possibilities of upward mobility, and did she look like his best opportunity to gain a toehold inside the department? It never hurt, after all, to have a rabbi inside, a mentor willing to help an up-and-comer rise through the ranks.

Or was he what he seemed, a smart guy whose rather mundane and predictable job had taken an abrupt and unexpected turn into something very unusual and a lot more important?

"Can I see those a minute?" Ford asked. "Maybe I can recognize whoever that is riding around with Drysdale."

Diane handed over the binoculars. "The way Drysdale's flying, he has to be looking for something. Or someone. And he doesn't give a shit who might figure that out."

"Maybe he got the same tip you did," Ford commented, the binoculars trained on the buzzing helicopter.

Diane looked down into the marina at the *Sans Sin*, still recognizable even at this distance and without binoculars. She frowned. "He does seem to keep hovering around the area near Toni Sinclair's boat, doesn't he? I'm thinking he doesn't know the senator went on board; otherwise he'd clear out fast. Even a small-potatoes politician like the mayor of Gryphon Gate knows enough to keep his nose out of a senator's private business."

"Does a police captain know enough?" Ford asked mildly, lowering the binoculars long enough to send her a quick glance.

Diane waited until he returned his searching gaze to the helicopter, then said calmly, "Risk goes with the territory."

"So you always follow up on anonymous tips?"

"In a case like this? Bet your ass I do. The relationships in a place like this are so tangled an outsider will never make sense of them. But what usually happens is that there's at least one person more pissed off than the others who wants to point fingers. Lots of secrets come tumbling out into the open. Some of it'll be pure spite, of course, but there's always useful stuff as well."

"We didn't find anything on the Satterfields' boat," Ford pointed out.

Diane brooded for a silent moment, then said, "I don't think that's what the tip was all about. I think the Satterfields' boat was just a handy place to direct us so we could be close enough to see Toni Sinclair arrive."

"Meeting the senator on the sly?"

"Well, he is married, so it could hurt him if an affair became public knowledge. That's assuming it's an affair, of course, and not some kind of business meeting. If it *is* an affair, it could also spell trouble for Toni Sinclair. Even though she's a widow, she has a daughter and might not want the kid to know her mom is sleeping with a married man. Besides which, if her name gets blackened, she won't be quite so effective a spokesperson for the other animal rights activists."

"Okay. But that begs the question—who knew Toni Sinclair would be showing up just then? I don't think we're talking about regular meetings on a predictable schedule here, because Mrs. Sinclair is usually doing her animal rights thing during the day while her daughter is at school. Either that or shopping."

"Ever hear any rumors about her and the senator?"

"Not a whisper."

"About her and anybody else?"

"Nope. Devoted wife, by all accounts, and devoted widow since Lincoln Sinclair died in that bizarre accident."

Diane frowned slightly, recalling the details of that definitely bizarre accident, then shook her head to remind herself to concentrate on the here and now. Not every accidental death was a murder—even the bizarre ones.

"So, who knew about today's meeting?" she mused.

"And what does any of that have to do with the murders of Sigmond Vormeister and Colonel McClintock?"

"Hell if I know." Diane grinned. "Yet. Half the fun and most of the frustration of the job is sorting through details trying to figure out which ones mean something."

Ford smiled in return and handed the binoculars back to her. "Well, here's another detail you can sort. The passenger in that chopper with Mayor Drysdale?"

"Yeah?"

"Unless I'm much mistaken, it's Roman Gervase."

"Oh, Christ. The one who thinks he's a werewolf?"

"How'd you hear about that?" Then, remembering, Ford nodded. "Oh, yeah. His howling last night. Drysdale told you it was Gervase, right?"

"Yeah. So I gather they're buddies?"

Deadpan, Ford replied, "Not when there's a full moon."

Diane eyed him. "Please don't try to tell me this guy's anything but a joke." The respect Ford had earned from her so far was in danger of vanishing.

He grinned, then sobered. "Do I believe he turns into a hairy wolf when the moon is full? No. Do I believe he's a seriously disturbed man who *believes* he changes when the moon is full? Yes. We carry a blanket in the patrol car for just those occasions when we have to run him down in the woods, naked and snarling."

"Snarling?"

"Swear to God. As far as I know, he's never hurt anyone or anything. As far as I know, most of Gryphon Gate—those who know at all, I mean—treat Gervase's nighttime wanderings as nothing more than the weirder-than-usual eccentricities of an unusually wealthy and brilliant man. You know what they say about genius and madness being a little too close for comfort? That's Roman Gervase."

"I got that he was some kind of descendant of European royalty."

"Yeah, he's that too. Lived the whole almost-titled-aristocrat lifestyle in Europe for most of his life. Boarding schools, racing cars, jets, yachts, parties where most of the guests were celebrities of one kind or another. Gervase fit right in. But then his life changed. He moved over here, invested his trust fund into a business that took off like you wouldn't believe, married a beautiful and—rumor has it— chronically unfaithful woman, and then wrecked his little red sports car. Head injury. So there's a physical cause, or trigger, according to what I've heard; but he's seeing a shrink, too. Anyway, it was after the accident that he started tearing off his clothes and running through the woods howling three nights a month."

"Three?"

"Night before the full moon, night of, and night after. So, at least he's consistent in his brain-jarred delusions. During the day and every night except those three he seems fairly normal, at least for Gryphon Gate. Plays bridge regularly. I think I've even seen him on the golf course a few times. Goes to the parties, boozes it up just like everybody else. But get the guy started on his business, and you realize about three sentences into the conversation that his I.Q. is off the scale and he might as well be speaking to you in Latin."

Diane considered that for several moments, gazing absently down at the marina. "What kind of genius is he?"

"Well, see, that's the interesting thing about him being up in that chopper with Mayor Drysdale. Roman Gervase is a techno genius, and his very successful company specializes in electronic surveillance."

* * *

Renée Lynch, like most of the other Gryphon Gate residents, believed in keeping in shape. She worked out regularly, but her lifelong interest in horses and frequent rides along the trails Gryphon Gate provided had given her the strongest legs and best ass of any woman in the community. If she did say so herself.

After having Sammie, she had regained her figure in only a few weeks, simply because she was a determined woman and had been determined to do just that. All it took was the willingness to work hard, something she'd always been able to do. So, making the rounds of all the machines in the lavishly appointed exercise room of the indecently huge French Renaissance chalet every morning was a routine Renée had made a sacrosanct part of her life. These daily afternoon rides, with Sammie safe at home with her nanny, were Renée's rewards for how hard she worked at staying in shape. How hard she worked, period.

Methodical and far more coolheaded than most people guessed, Renée was pleased with her deluxe lifestyle and entirely willing to do whatever was necessary in order to maintain it. Even if that meant turning a blind eye to her husband's . . . extracurricular activities.

Her own father had been just the same, banging the maid in the pantry without making much effort to stifle his groans, and expecting her mother to put up with it.

Well, Renée was strong like her mother had been. She could put up with Jerry's philandering. At least for now. Because she knew why he was doing it. Not because Anka was a leggy brunette with big boobs and plenty of enthusiasm—although those were undoubtedly contributing factors in his choice of playmate—but because Jerry's financial risk taking had finally landed him in deep, deep shit.

Riding easily along a familiar trail on that Friday afternoon, Renée handled her thoroughbred with skill and reflected absently that men would get into a lot less trouble if they'd just learn that stupidity couldn't be cured by sex—no matter how good it was. Lots of things could be cured by good sex, of course, but not stupidity.

Still, she had faith in her husband's abilities financially. He would figure out a way to recoup his losses and rebuild his portfolio, and if it took banging the maid to get his creative juices flowing, then so be it.

And if her faith in Jerry happened to be misplaced, well, she had a plan to deal with that eventuality. She always had a plan.

Renée glanced at her watch then tightened her calves slightly to urge the gelding to pick up his pace a bit.

Ten minutes later, she reached a nicely shady, secluded spot on the trail and stopped, dismounting and tying the chestnut's reins to a handy tree. Accustomed, the horse merely relaxed and rested one rear hoof, swishing his tail idly. She patted his flank, then moved away a few yards to lean against the rustic three-rail fence bordering this area of the riding trails.

She didn't have long to wait. Not five minutes later a man rode an elderly bay mare up the trail from the opposite direction. Even with his mount's lazy, smooth gait, it was obvious the man was not a rider by the way he perched uncertainly and stiffly on the saddle. He was a very . . . neutral man. His hair was an indeterminate brown, his features were regular without in any way being remarkable, his build was average. He wore the upscale Gryphon Gate riding attire for men, jodhpurs with riding boots and a polo shirt, obviously borrowed, since the outfit didn't look conspicuously new.

"You're late," Renée said when he reached her. She was determined to get and keep the upper hand at this meeting.

Martin Herbert swung awkwardly down from his patient mount and then led her over to tether her near Renée's horse. Every movement emphasized his unfamiliarity with horses, so much so that it amused her.

"You don't have to worry about Lady. She's the gentlest horse this side of the kiddie rides at the fair."

"I don't ride much," Herbert said unnecessarily.

"No kidding. This probably would have been your last choice for a meeting place. But I ride these trails every day, and I know nobody else comes this way on Friday afternoons."

"I didn't object," he reminded her.

"You couldn't object if I suggested a meeting in the lobby at the country club," Renée mocked.

Gritting his teeth visibly, Herbert said, "Look, Mrs. Lynch, I don't know why you believe your husband is under surveillance, but—"

"I don't believe he's under surveillance, Mr. Herbert, I know he is." Renée reached into the pocket of her well-cut riding jacket and produced a small device which, to the untutored eye, looked like nothing so much as a tangle of fine wires and bits of computer innards. She tossed it to Herbert. "Look familiar?"

A muscle writhed along his jawline. "Mrs. Lynch—"

"I found it in his study at home, beautifully concealed behind a shelf of books Jerry wouldn't touch with someone else's hands. Books for show. I doubt he'd even recognize the titles. Unless it has DOW or NASDAQ across it, or wears a thirty-eight-D cup, Jerry couldn't care less."

"Mrs. Lynch, I'm just a resident of Gryphon Gate like you are. I'm a consultant and work out of my home, so—"

"Bullshit," she said sweetly. "There's a tap on our phone. And I have it from a real expert that the little gizmo I just gave you—plus the others *hidden* in the house, of course—are state-of-the-art and government issue."

Herbert was silent, but obviously both surprised and uneasy.

"FBI? CIA? Or is it the SEC keeping tabs on my husband?"

Carefully, Herbert said, "The SEC is hardly empowered to conduct electronic surveillance, Mrs. Lynch."

Renée smiled. "The CIA isn't supposed to conduct domestic investigations either, but we both know that's just the company line. Still, I'm betting it's the FBI running the show. My only question now is—why? What did my husband do to alert the feds, and why isn't his ass in jail already?"

Capt. Diane Robards hung up the phone then shook her head at Leland Ford's inquiring look. "Autopsy results aren't ready yet. I ordered tox screens and the whole nine yards, and the M.E. was backed up anyway, so it'll take a while."

"Anything preliminary?" He was sitting in her visitor's chair, and, even with the open door behind him, the space felt peculiarly small.

"Nothing helpful. What I want to know is where Mayor Drysdale and Roman Gervase went after they finished buzzing the marina."

"They took off right after that dark guy showed up and headed for the *Sans Sin*," Ford noted.

"Yeah. And if we hadn't had to clear out just then to avoid a few nosy passersby, we could have stuck around and maybe found out if his arrival was . . . expected."

Ford pursed his lips thoughtfully. "Friday afternoon three-way?"

"Toni Sinclair certainly had sex on her mind when she arrived," Diane agreed, remembering the other woman's honeyed drawl and knowing eyes. "On the other hand, I can't see Senator Carbury being quite *that* indiscreet—at least not with a murder investigation taking place on his home turf. He'd have to be incredibly stupid, and despite evidence to the contrary, most politicians are fairly bright."

Ford said, "I wouldn't have said it was in character for him to do anything stupid."

"So there's still a good chance it was some kind of business meeting. Does Toni Sinclair have anything to do with her late husband's business?"

"Lincoln Sinclair didn't have a business. I mean, he'd sold out—something techno, I think—and retired young. One look at that palace of theirs and you know he was filthy rich. Left it all to her."

Slowly, Diane said, "Where there's a lot of money, blackmail is always possible. I dunno. Rich widow, politician scrambling for votes . . ."

"Add in murder and meetings on the sly and I don't know what you've got, but I'm betting it isn't pretty."

Diane grimaced. "Yeah."

Ford looked at his watch. "My shift starts in a couple of hours, and I'm on till midnight. Anything in particular you want me to keep an eye out for when I patrol tonight?"

"Will Carnegie be with you?"

Ford grinned. "Some of the time, yeah, but don't worry—he only sees the obvious."

"Such a fine quality in a security guard."

"In Gryphon Gate," Ford pointed out dryly, "it's considered an asset."

"Yeah, well, it's not an asset in my book." She sighed. "You can move around inside the gates with a lot more freedom than I can, but you still get noticed, so be careful. Watch and listen, but don't change your routine any more than you can help."

"They'll expect some changes," Ford pointed out. "Expect us to step up regular patrols, have a more visible presence. At least, I would."

"You'll probably be stopped a few times. Asked about what's going on, what we know. I doubt many of the fine citizens of Gryphon Gate will expect you to be deeply involved in the investigation, but they'd expect you to know more than they do."

"Any juicy bits I can drop to make myself look more impressive?" Ford asked, more amused than serious.

"Since we don't know which juicy bits might be important," she replied with a grin, "I'm afraid you'll have to at least appear to be as frustrated and confused as they are. But reassuring, of course. Gryphon Gate is an oasis of safety and sanity in a scary, troubled world. You know—the company line."

"Little hard to sell that with two murdered citizens in the morgue."

"Do your best. As for what to be on the lookout for—damned if I know. Anything unusual. Anything that surprises you. Someone in a place they shouldn't be or doing something out of the ordinary."

"I'd expect most of them to behave a bit differently."

Diane nodded, her respect for him inching up another notch. "People get jumpy with an unsolved murder in their circle; two unsolved murders are apt to make them nervous wrecks. Plus, most everybody has a secret or two they'd rather keep to themselves—not necessarily illegal or even sinful, just not for public consumption."

"And murder investigations tend to bring a lot of secrets out into the open."

"They do. They certainly do." She smiled. "So, if you have any secrets you don't want exposed, Lee, you'd better rethink this assignment."

Leland Ford smiled in return. "Secrets? Me? No, no secrets. And too much curiosity not to want to get involved. So I'm in for the duration."

"Good," Diane said. "Good."

Leland Ford would have been happy to have been able to report something interesting—*anything* interesting—to Capt. Diane Robards after his shift, but Friday night was almost eerily uneventful. He and John Carnegie had, as usual, been forced to chase down a naked Roman Gervase and wrestle him into the patrol car around ten and then deliver him home and into the hands of his extremely polite and soft-spoken manservant.

Ford couldn't get over the fact that anyone in this day and age would have a valet, for God's sake; but he had to admit, if only silently, that Roman Gervase needed a keeper of some kind, and his wife was still boozing it up at the club. Plus, the servant seemed to know how to handle his growling employer.

Growling. Jesus.

Anyway, other than Gervase's usual nocturnal wanderings, everything seemed just as it should have been. Nobody got their head bashed in or died in some other fashion. The bridge playing went on as usual, with the usual crowd, and all the usual people got drunker and drunker as the night wore on. Outside the country club those not interested in the Gryphon Gate nightlife stayed peacefully in their very nice houses, with their very well-trained dogs peacefully quiet and their kids all tucked in. Or locked in.

Ford had the weird feeling that he was the only one waiting for the other shoe to drop.

Carnegie talked incessantly about the murders, of course, speculating about the identity of their "serial killer." Ford did what he could to stifle his partner, but it was pretty much a losing battle.

"Middle-aged white men," Carnegie said.

"Place is full of them," Ford agreed.

"No, I mean that's obviously the killer's target. His MO is to go after middle-aged white men." Carnegie considered. "Rich ones."

Ford had elected not to drive on their regular but slightly stepped-up patrols through Gryphon Gate in the hope that it would keep Carnegie occupied, but it obviously wasn't working. "Or," Ford suggested, "they could be grudge killings. Killings for gain or spite. Or, hell, not even murders. Accidents."

"You know damned well they aren't accidents, Lee."

"Okay, so they don't look like accidents. Truth is, we don't know *what* they look like. Not really. You and me, we're amateurs at best; and for all the books we've read and TV we've watched, this is the first time either one of us has been within spitting distance of a murder investigation."

"Yeah," Carnegie agreed reluctantly.

"So we don't know squat," Ford said.

"No." Carnegie was quiet for about half a block, then said, "But we know these people, Lee, you can't deny that. We know 'em better than Captain Diane Robards does. Hell, we probably know 'em better than they know themselves. We've seen 'em drunk and sober, polite and rude, triumphant when they win one of their games and sore as hell when they lose. We've seen them shaking hands with a wink and pinching their neighbor's wife on the ass when nobody seems to be looking. We've watched while they work against each other, sweet as honey one minute and ice-cold the next.

"We've seen them before they've had their coffee in the morning, and tossing their cookies behind the bushes at the country club. We've seen them sneaking out of the wrong house at dawn. We've heard them talk about stuff like we weren't even there." Carnegie drew a breath. "I'm telling you, Lee, *we know them.*"

Ford gazed out the window at the seemingly peaceful houses, most of them still showing a few lighted windows, and he wondered ruefully why it hadn't occurred to him that his slower-witted partner would, once again, see the obvious.

An obvious fact that Ford himself had overlooked.

Quietly, he said, "Yeah, I guess we do know them."

"Bet your ass we do. So, who do you see as a murderer, Lee? Tell me that."

He hadn't thought of it from that angle, hadn't questioned himself about these people and what he knew of them; and having the question posed so bluntly made him consider it for the first time. So he looked out on the peaceful Friday night and seriously asked himself which one of these people could have killed two men.

There had to be only one killer, he was sure of that. Diane was sure, he thought, even though she hadn't committed herself out loud. Logic said it just stretched coincidence too far to think a place like Gryphon Gate would play host to two separate murderers in a bare twenty-four hours. No, it had to be just one—just one person with the will and the motive to kill two men. And one of those victims had been an ex-marine in pretty damned good shape.

McClintock hadn't been drunk, his wife was right about that. The colonel didn't get drunk, period. He might—and often had—drunk enough to put a platoon under the table, but he never got drunk. Which meant he hadn't been staggering around out there helpless and vulnerable. That was an important point. It wasn't likely the killer had snuck up on the colonel, because Ford himself had noticed the man had remarkably acute senses and took notice of what was going on around him, always.

So, odds were he had been taken by surprise only in that he'd known his killer, recognized him—or her—and had not felt threatened in any way.

"Lee?"

"I'm thinking," Ford muttered, doing just that.

An ex-marine could have a lot of enemies, he thought. Big ex-soldier types often rubbed civilians the wrong way. He had certainly made a few enemies by being so vocal in wanting, for all intents and purposes, to shoot Bambi.

Sigmond Vormeister, on the other hand, had seemed too low-key and unthreatening to have made any enemies. Except for his habit of watching everything and either writing constantly in his notebook or else using that little—what were they called? Personal data something-or-other? A Palm Pilot, that's what he'd sometimes carried.

Always watching, always noting down things.

Ford could see how that might threaten a number of the people who lived in Gryphon Gate. And, unlike the colonel, Vormeister would have been an easy target for just about anybody.

"Lee?"

"I'm still thinking." Ford gazed out at the peaceful houses they passed and wondered which one contained a murderer.

Or a murderess.

By Saturday evening Diane Robards was feeling more than a little discouraged. Unless the postmortems turned up something interesting, she didn't have much in the way of viable clues as to who had killed two men. Two very different men.

To the open disgust of a number of fanatical golfers, she had refused to remove the bright yellow crime scene tape from the sixth hole sand trap, and she'd listened all day to complaints about that. At least it had given them something to bitch about while she and her crew took another round of statements in the Wild Goose Room.

Wild Goose Room, for Christ's sake. Either Laura Armbruster had a sly sense of humor, or else she was not so subtly offering her opinion of the investigation. Diane honestly wasn't sure which it was.

Leland Ford had been around most of the day. After endless briefings from her team of detectives and forensics experts, Diane had overheard Ford tell a couple of the club members—when they asked—that he was pulling a double shift for extra cash, an explanation that seemed to surprise no one. He went out on regular patrols, but strolled around the clubhouse as well, smiling reassuringly at the members.

Diane had spent an hour or so in her office at the end of their Wild Goose Room marathon, and just before Ford's actual shift, she began talking to him, and she had to admit that his slow-witted partner had made a good point about the Gryphon Gate Police and how well they knew the residents of the place.

Leland Ford, at least, definitely knew those people. And his insights into who among them might be most capable of murder had interested Diane very much.

But right now all she wanted to do was take a long, hot bath and go to bed.

Alone.

Maybe there'd be a horror movie marathon on one of the satellite channels (there usually was) that she could watch until she unwound and fell asleep. For some reason, horror movies had an effect on her that was directly opposite of the intended one. She was never scared, often amused, and always appreciative of style. She supposed it had something to do with the fun nature of fantasy bumping up against the grim reality of her job.

At any rate, when she unlocked her apartment door and went inside, that was all she had on her mind. She hadn't even planned on going into the little second bedroom office to check her messages, but found herself doing it out of habit.

That was when she saw that someone had sent her a fax, and she frowned as she crossed the room to the two-drawer filing cabinet under a window where the fax machine sat. Probably just some dumb ad. It was amazing how many companies managed to get their hands on confidential things like private fax numbers and send their garbage through so you *had* to deal with it whether you wanted to or not.

It wasn't an ad.

"What the hell?" she muttered, conscious of a peculiar, crawly sense of having something slimy too near for comfort.

In the center of the page, neatly typed, were a few words.

Be sure to go to church on Sunday, Diane. You won't regret it.

7

AT THE PRECISE MOMENT CAPT.
Diane Robards was relieving her fax of its mysterious message,
Aaron Kaplan was thrusting a fist into the air above his head.

"Yes!" The arm pistoned down.

"Moron," Aaron muttered, picking up his pen and returning to his
task.

Papers covered one corner of Rachel Vormeister's guest room,
some crumpled, others layered on the carpet or angled against chair
legs, bed skirts, and baseboards. A green hooded lamp bathed the
desk and its occupant in pale yellow light.

The victory arm pump was unusual for Aaron, a kid who rarely
showed emotion. More precisely, Aaron rarely *felt* emotion. The smiles
were there, of course—the frowns, the grief-puckered brows, each
response sending its proper social signal. But it was all for show. Real
feelings were much too risky.

Loving his grandfather had taught him that.

Grandpapa Kaplan had been the center of Aaron's boyhood universe. T-ball and swim coach, bubblegum smuggler and Popsicle con-
fidant, Grandpapa was always there. The two were inseparable. Ten
years ago the old man's death had shattered Aaron's six-year-old
world. Wounded, frightened, and confused, little Aaron closed all por-
tals. No love. No loss. No pain.

No one noticed.

Big Aaron was excited by just two things. Riding his skateboard down a handrail with the wind in his hair. And cryptography.

Aaron rarely thought of Grandpapa Kaplan anymore. But sometimes, lying awake at night, he allowed a tiny sliver. Always the same sliver.

Autumn cool. The smell of dead leaves in the gutter, dust, old wood. Aaron, age five, and Grandpapa cleaning the attic.

A cardboard carton. Grandpapa withdrawing an odd ring, laughing.

What, Grandpapa?

A cigar box relic.

What?

Trash.

Aaron had retrieved the thing, a Captain Midnight Decoder. Grandpapa had explained how to encode and decode messages by rotating the outer ring and substituting letters from the inner.

From the moment he set eyes on the strange gizmo, cryptography had been Aaron Kaplan's passion. Substitution ciphers. Shift ciphers. Transposition, polyalphabetic, digraphic. It didn't matter. The kid could crack most codes in an hour.

Thus, the disdain. The superior dismissal of yet another failed attempt at challenging him.

Wanting to make certain his notes were unreadable, Sigmond Vormeister had invented what he thought was a beauty of a code. Aaron considered it kindergarten crap.

Finding the coded journal hadn't been easy. Aaron would credit his brother-in-law on that. The search had required discipline. No wonder Robards's goons hadn't been able to find it. He'd had to wait until the house was empty, or until Rachel and his mother were asleep.

Late that afternoon his patience had paid off. He'd known at first tap. What else would be hidden in a false-bottomed drawer?

Aaron had worked nonstop since the discovery. Accustomed to her son's obsession with his hobby, Mrs. Kaplan hadn't questioned his seclusion. Rachel was too caught up in her grief to notice.

Ciphers can be categorized into a number of types: substitution, transposition, diagrammatic. Substitution ciphers replace letters with other letters or symbols, keeping the order unchanged. Transposition ciphers keep the original letters intact, but mix up the order. Diagrammatic ciphers substitute symbols for letters.

By eight o'clock, Aaron knew that his brother-in-law's algorithm was a hybrid. Vormeister had used the tired old standard of a tic-tac-toe board, two Xs, and dots, substituting the line shapes surrounding each letter, and adding dots where needed.

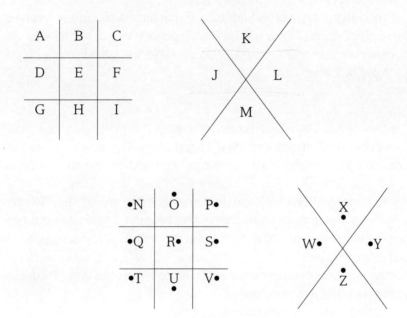

Though Vormeister had employed some sort of shift in assigning letters to his grid positions, he hadn't altered word lengths. That mistake was the cipher's undoing.

Of 612 characters on page one, Aaron calculated that the empty four-sided box appeared 116 times, representing almost 20 percent of the symbols.

Aaron checked page two. Similar frequency. Page three. Ditto.

The empty box had to represent *e*, the most frequently used letter in English. Aaron began a list.

The next most frequent symbols were the open-top dotted box and the inverted *v*. Aaron checked several pages, then jotted the letters *o* and *m* next to each.

When he'd identified as many single letters as he could, Aaron examined the order of frequency of digraphs, such as *er-, -on-, -an-, -he-*. Then the order of trigraphs, common doubles, initial letters, final letters, one-, two-, three-, and four-letter words.

About the time Robards was tiring of zombies on TV, Aaron was flying through Vormeister's journal.

About the time Robards was drifting off, a smile was crawling across Aaron's face, this one very real.

Though young, Aaron understood that most academics weren't in the AmEx Gold and Polo set. He'd occasionally wondered how his sociologist brother-in-law maintained the Gryphon Gate lifestyle.

Now he knew.

The tips of her Coco Beach Coral–lacquered acrylics dug four small crescents into Vanessa Drysdale's right palm. The newly arrived fax trembled in her left. Three readings, and still the words made no sense.

Vanessa glanced up, watched merlot ooze down the Bombay beige wall of her study. A mulberry mushroom was spreading on the carpet below the wall stain, darkening the shards of crystal glistening in the nap.

Vanessa was calmer now, beginning to regret the Waterford goblet the outburst had cost her.

But what did the message mean?

Again she read the quote. Again she felt anger rise like a hot, white flame in her chest.

> *"A talebearer revealeth secrets. . . ."*
> —*Proverbs 11:13.*
> Church tomorrow. Showtime!

Vanessa crumpled the fax and tossed it into the wastebasket. Taking a deep breath, she slowly, calmly, carefully picked up the basket, crossed the room, and began adding fragments of shattered crystal to the basket's contents.

* * *

Jerry Lynch spent a miserable night at the club on Friday, keeping up a facade of civility while inwardly fixated on his impending financial collapse. The moment Renée left for the stable on Saturday, he closeted himself in his office and began poring over the DOW and NASDAQ, the NYSE and AMEX, desperately seeking a path to salvation.

Jerry was still searching when Renée called to say that her horse had sustained an injury and that she would remain at the stable until very late. Jerry scarcely listened to his wife's directions concerning leftovers. His eyes never left the tiny figures scrolling across his computer screen.

Hours later Jerry barely noticed Anka's knock, paid no attention to the dinner tray she left on his credenza. He agreed to a request without hearing the maid's question.

The windows dimmed, grew dark. The monitor's glow became the only source of light in the study. At one point Jerry heard his fax connect, then print out a message. He ignored it.

Decades, millennia, eons later, Jerry slumped back into his state-of-the-ergonomic-art Relax Your Back executive chair and ran a hand across his balding crown. If anything, he felt more anxious than when he'd begun. Had the transactions made sense? Had he dug himself into a deeper hole?

Bloody hell. At least he'd taken action.

Jerry got up, scowled at Anka's tray, and headed for the kitchen. Passing the fax machine, he noticed the previously ignored communication. Ever hopeful of a business opportunity, he snatched up the paper.

> *"A talebearer revealeth secrets. . . ."*
> *—Proverbs 11:13.*
> Church tomorrow. Showtime!

Jerry's face went cranberry.

"Bloody hell!"

He looked for a return number or for some indication of the sender.

Zilch.

"Bloody hell," Jerry repeated, though this time less emphatically.

* * *

Feeling slightly confused after her unexpected meeting with the senator, Toni Sinclair spent all of Saturday with her daughter, feeding the deer, shopping, swimming, then dining at the marina restaurant. Miranda loved fried shrimp and picked the marina whenever given a choice.

Was that it? Toni had wondered, sliding into a booth opposite her daughter. Or was Mommy on some wild Freudian roller-coaster ride with her id?

After tucking Miranda into bed, Toni watched a series of sitcoms on The Comedy Channel. Gilligan and the captain were building a time machine. Lucy and Ethel were selling door-to-door. Barney and Gomer were bagging a skunk. Things went badly for all of them.

That's me, Toni thought, clicking off the TV. *I'm living a joke where nothing works out.*

Passing the open door to her office, Toni spotted a single fax lying on her machine. Her stomach knotted.

For a full ten seconds Toni simply stared at the thing, then her mouth contracted into a thin line of determination.

As she read, the line went slack, and the room receded around her.

> *"A talebearer revealeth secrets. . . ."*
> *—Proverbs 11:13.*
> Church tomorrow. Showtime!

After receiving her fax Diane Robards felt wired enough to put a double coat on Shea Stadium. She emptied every wastebasket in her apartment, took the trash to the dumpster, watered her potted cactus, changed the towels, fed her cockatiel, and mini-vacuumed the seed from around his cage.

Diane then showered, shaved her legs, and plucked her eyebrows. The bird watched without comment.

At eleven she crawled under the covers, clicked on the TV, surfed, and chose *Night of the Living Dead*.

No go. She was too distracted to concentrate.

Diane killed the TV and clicked off the light.

No go. She was too agitated to fall asleep.

After two hours of fighting her adrenaline, Diane drifted off. She slept like igneous rock, motionless and dreamless. By five she was up again.

By eight Sunday morning she was in her office at the precinct, peeling the lid from a plastic coffee cup. A donut oozed jelly onto a wax paper wrapper on her government-issue gray metal desk. Her booted heels rested crossed beside it.

On her way upstairs Diane had passed two uniforms relieving an intake of his shoelaces. Couldn't risk the village drunk hanging himself in a fit of remorse over his addiction to Thunderbird, she snorted to herself, reaching for the donut.

Diane blew across her coffee, took a bite of the pastry, glanced at her watch: 8:07.

Two minutes since she'd last checked. Three hours until church.

Down the hall a door opened. Some kind of hip-hop drifted out, was truncated.

Through her window Diane watched thick pewter clouds elbow for position in a pearl gray sky. Questions inside questions spun in her head.

What the hell did the fax mean? What could possibly take place at a boring, plain vanilla, nondenominational service? These people reeked civility. They hardly *sang* above a whisper.

Diane forced herself to sort through mail she'd been ignoring since Sigmond Vormeister's murder.

Eventually she heard a light tap.

"Captain Robards?"

Diane looked up.

A face was craning around her doorjamb. It looked uncertain.

Diane's eyes flicked to her watch, this time out of surprise.

"What are you doing in at eighty-twenty on a Sunday morning?"

The face was attached to Greg, the junior member of Diane's death investigation team.

"I—there's something I think I should show you." The young man shifted his feet. "I've been thinking about it and, yes, I think you should see it."

Greg sounded as though he were rehashing a dialogue he'd had with himself. Diane waited.

"It didn't mean much at the time, but later, well—"

The size-elevens shifted again, and the face went through a series of expressions, finally settling on determined.

"Jordan didn't think it was important, but I—"

"What is it?" Diane cut him off and immediately felt sorry for doing so.

"I didn't sleep worrying over this." Wounded. "Might be nothing, but at least I will know I did my job."

Greg stepped forward and placed a Ziploc baggie on Diane's desk. Inside were two pellets and approximately three ounces of crumbly brown matrix.

Diane looked at the bag.

"That came out of Sigmond Vormeister's right pants cuff. Jordan told me to toss it, but—" Greg shrugged. "I don't know. I just didn't. Bagged it, then tucked it in a cabinet and forgot about it."

Forgot about it! she fumed, saying nothing till he finished.

Greg placed a second baggie on the desktop. This one contained a single fragment no larger than a sunflower seed.

"I found that on the gurney we used to transport Lieutenant Colonel McClintock's body."

Same rusty brown. Same coarse texture.

"I think it's the same stuff."

Diane's heartbeat ratcheted up. She thought so too. What was Jordan thinking? She'd have his ass for throwing out forensic evidence.

"Do you know what it is?"

Greg nodded.

"That's why I thought it might be important." A pink patch was spreading across each cheek. "When this animal rights thing blew up, with the protest, and the swans, and the deer, and Lieutenant Colonel McClintock and all, well, I thought—"

"Just tell me what it is, Greg." Diane forced her voice calm.

"Deer chow."

"Deer chow?"

"Nuggets you set out for the deer to eat." Greg pointed to one of the pellets in the first baggie. "I recognized the whole ones right off, used to buy them on-line from Deer.com."

A billion info-bytes raced toward each other in Diane's mind, like particles of matter rushing together for the Big Bang. An idea struggled to take shape from the chaos.

Before the thought could congeal, the phone shrilled.

Diane picked it up.

"Captain Robards."

"Well, I'll be snookered. Caught you working on a Sunday. Doesn't say much for your social life, gal."

The medical examiner. It was a morning of surprises. Diane mouthed "thank you" to Greg and the young man left.

"I have no social life, you know that," she said.

"Tough on a lot of gals, now that George is dead and McCartney's married."

"There's always the mall. What can I do for you, Doc?"

"Got some news."

"And you say *I* have no social life?"

"After our talk my secretary waved a subpoena under my nose. Damn trial's gonna jam me up all week, so I decided to go ahead and finish up your Gryphon Gate boys."

Diane heard a squeak, pictured the pathologist in his big leather chair, cigarette burns dotting his shirt and tie, nicotine-yellowed fingers gripping the receiver.

"Found some mighty peculiar things."

"Oh?"

"Liver ain't right."

Diane understood dependent lividity, but knew the M.E. would explain it anyway. He did.

"Once the heart stops pumpin', the blood settles, due to gravity and dilation of the vessels. 'Cause of all that, the down side of a corpse turns purple."

"Vormeister died on his back," Diane guessed.

"Bingo."

"When we found him, he was sunny-side up, but his face and front were covered with sand. I suspected he'd been rolled."

"That's my thinking."

Diane was still following her own train of thought.

"So he died on his back, ended up in the sand trap facedown, then someone turned the body over."

The M.E. responded, but she didn't hear.

"So the body might have been placed in the sand trap after Vormeister was dead."

"Then rolled again," the M.E. agreed. "But it gets curiouser and curiouser. Because clotting takes place slowly after death, postmortem clots generally show settling and separation of the red cells from the liquid phase of the blood. Portions of the blood clot are cleared of red cells and come to look kinda like chicken fat. The portions into which these cells have sedimented look like blobs of currant jelly, and those blobs conform more or less to the shape of the vessel in which they're formed. You with me?"

"Yes." Diane pushed the remnants of her jelly donut aside.

"Antemortem clots don't show that sedimentation effect. The antemortem critters are more friable and granular, and they don't have the rubbery consistency of the postmortem type. And clots formed in a living person may have no resemblance at all to the vessel in which they're found. Most are discovered as emboli that took birth at some site distant from their final lodgment."

"And?"

"I found one whopper of a clot high up in Vormeister's left anterior descending artery."

"What are you saying?"

"I'm saying I found one whopper of a clot high up in Vormeister's left anterior descending artery."

"Antemortem?"

"Yes."

"Did it kill him?"

"Didn't see any indication of acute myocardial infarction or muscle damage, but his heart showed evidence of previous problems."

"And?"

"There's a good possibility the clot led to an arrhythmia and sudden death."

"Are you saying Vormeister died of natural causes?"

"I'm saying it's possible."

"What about the head wound?"

"Afraid I can't determine conclusively if the poor chap died from the clot or from the blow to his head. By the way, the injury on his forehead was no big deal. The one on the occiput was a humdinger.

If that didn't take him off, the thrombosis surely would have."

Diane's heart rate was cranking up again.

"Wounds don't bleed after the heart stops pumping," she said. "Vormeister's did."

"Almost true, young lady, but not quite. The lethal blow, if it was lethal, was to the back of Vormeister's head. The lividity pattern tells me he died faceup, so postmortem settling of blood into the area of the head trauma wouldn't be unusual."

Diane heard an expulsion of air and knew the M.E. had fired up one of his Camels.

"Bottom line. Vormeister could have been alive when someone took a swing at him, or he could have been dead. If he was dead, it hadn't been for long."

"How long?"

"Minutes."

Diane tried wrapping her mind around that.

"One last thing. I just finished my external on McClintock. Decided to call you before I made the Y."

The M.E. took a deep drag.

"McClintock was whacked with a cylindrical object, approximately one inch in diameter. Smooth, no grooves, threads, nothing like that."

"A lot of objects conform to that description."

"Yes, ma'am. But the injury pattern suggests this one had a notch at one end. I'll send over the pics."

"Thanks."

"One last observation."

Diane waited out another Camel intake.

"Vormeister's and McClintock's head wounds show identical patterning."

Leland Ford was tired to the marrow as he turned through the arch into Gryphon Gate. He'd worked Friday night and all day Saturday, having volunteered for a double shift. It had seemed like a good idea at the time, a move that would impress Diane Robards.

But Ford wasn't capable of running on adrenaline. Though young, he needed a solid eight hours. Always had. Ford's exhaustion was showing. His normally pink face had taken on a grayish cast, and the flesh under his eyes looked dark and puffy.

Like many in Gryphon Gate, Ford slept poorly Saturday night, dozing and waking, obsessed with the Vormeister and McClintock murders. Images haunted him, forming and reforming like colored crystals in a kaleidoscope.

Sigmond Vormeister, lying in the sixth hole sand trap. Had he known his killer? Had he noticed the weapon that split his head? Was he surprised to see the thing raised in anger? Terrified? Had those been the last sensations he felt?

Lance McClintock, sprawled on the clubhouse patio. Had the lieutenant colonel been attacked by the same man who killed Vormeister? *Was* it a man?

Why had the sociologist and the old marine been murdered?

Toni Sinclair disappearing below decks on the *Sans Sin.*

Roman Gervase streaking through the night, moon sparking his hair like cornsilk.

Diane Robards, dark curls framing her face, ass tight in her uniform pants.

Ford kept rehashing his partner's comments. Were the two deaths the work of a serial killer? A grudge killer? Fluke accident combined with impersonal coincidence?

Though nothing else added up, Ford was certain of one thing: Big, dumb John Carnegie was right. He and Carnegie knew the residents of their community better than anyone else on the planet. When it came to murder, no one was better positioned to fill in the motivational blanks.

That's why Ford was cruising Gryphon Gate at nine o'clock on a Sunday morning.

Clouds were gathering overhead, turning the morning dark and sluggish. The breeze carried a promise of rain.

As Ford cruised past the Sinclair home, he noticed Miranda sitting on the front steps, her attention focused on something in her hands. The little girl was wearing a green gingham dress with a white linen pinafore, lace-trimmed ankle socks, and black patent leather Mary Janes. Her hair was curled and bound into ponytails, each garnished with an enormous green bow.

Ford slid the cruiser to the curb. Miranda looked up and waved. Ford got out and strolled up the walk.

"You look beautiful today, Miss Miranda."

"Mama and I are going to church."

"That's a very nice thing, going to Sunday service. Used to do that with my mama and daddy."

"I usually go with Bertha and Bill. Mama doesn't like church too much."

"Something special happening today?"

Miranda shrugged and the ruffles on her pinafore brushed her curls.

"Well, you're a lucky girl to have friends like Bertha and Bill."

"They take me lots of places."

"Do they. What's your favorite?"

"My very favorite of all is the water slide, but Bertha and Bill won't go there."

"I guess they're a little too old for that."

"I guess." Miranda giggled.

"What's your favorite outing with Bertha and Bill?"

Miranda raised her chin and sucked her lower lip in behind her front teeth. "I think Santa's Village. You can buy lots of really cool ornaments and Christmas stuff. Even in the summer."

"Like elves?"

"You can't buy elves."

"I have one."

"That's not possible."

"He lives in a little house on my bedside table."

Miranda's eyes went wide, then Ford winked, and she giggled again.

"We went to Santa's Village last Thursday. And to the Dairy Queen. It was pretty cool."

Ford's radar sounded a beep.

"Thursday?"

"Uh-huh." Miranda looked down at the thing in her hands.

"Are you sure it was Thursday?"

"Yep. 'Cause I was on the news for the deer protest, then we went to Santa's Village; but we had to really hurry 'cause it was closing. Then I went to Bertha's house and watched *What About Bob?* That's a really funny movie. Bill rented it. Bertha said it was all right, even though it was late, 'cause the next day was Friday and no one had to get up early 'cause our teachers had a meeting."

Excitement gunned the engine in Leland Ford's mind.

"You're a very observant little girl."

"That's what Mama says."

Mama also says she spent that whole evening at home with you. Ford couldn't wait to call Robards.

"Where was your mama after the demonstration?"

Miranda shrugged again, her attention on the buttons she was pushing with her thumbs.

"That a Game Boy?"

"No." Miranda made a face as she raised her plaything to give Ford a better view. "Found it in the garden. It's boring."

The excitement spun a wheelie.

Miranda was holding up a Palm Pilot.

Lydia Upshaw crouched below the sill, watching the car with its three silhouettes. Only when the Volvo station wagon rounded the corner did she feel it safe to stand.

Two hours! Two full, wonderful hours! Lydia raised both arms above her head and stretched, slow, and lithe, and sinuous as a cat.

She was alone.

Gloriously alone.

As Lydia allowed the Sunday morning quiet to envelop her, she felt a tiny prick of conscience. She should have gone to church with Parker and the twins. She shouldn't have faked a migraine.

Forget it, her conscious mind countered. *You're doing them a favor. A sermon, then pancakes. It's a perfect opportunity for father-offspring bonding.*

Lydia dropped her arms and smiled. What to do with her mini-sabbatical?

Bubble bath? Sleep? Long, uninterrupted rendezvous with the Sunday *Times*? Mimosa with a little umbrella stuck in the glass? All of the above?

But first the chore.

Lydia hesitated. Why now? It can wait.

No. It has to be done.

Slipping on a robe, Lydia hurried down to the first floor. After retrieving the newspaper from the back stoop she stood in the kitchen, clutching the plastic-wrapped roll to her chest.

It has to be done.

Deep breath.

Lydia laid the paper on the counter and withdrew a key from the farthest recess of a kitchen drawer. Opening the basement door, she flicked on the light, stepped onto the top riser, and hesitated again.

Go.

Breathing deeply, Lydia crept down the stairs. At the bottom, the subterranean quiet seemed more threat than comfort.

Without hesitating, Lydia went straight to a door in the far wall, opened a padlock, and entered a small room lined with floor-to-ceiling shelves.

Propping a ladder against one end of the back wall, Lydia climbed the rungs and began checking labels on the top row of boxes. She was working her way along the shelf, her back to the door, when an odd rustling caught her attention.

Lydia froze. Had she locked the kitchen door? Any door? Was the security system on? People were being murdered in Gryphon Gate.

Lydia listened with every fiber of her being.

Nothing.

Find the damn thing and get on to the Mimosa.

Lydia resumed her search.

Seconds later, she heard more rustling. Louder. Nearer.

What the hell is that? Lydia thought.

Heart thudding, she scrambled down the ladder, scurried across the room, and threw open the door.

And stared into the greenest pair of eyes she had ever seen.

8

IT WAS NO ACCIDENT THAT
Peter's church was the most popular place of worship in Gryphon
Gate. There was a lot more to the Reverend Peter Armbruster than
most people thought.

At least in Peter's opinion.

With the possible exception of Mignon Gervase, just about everyone in the community thought him boring. Sanctimonious. But he
was actually a very learned man, with an undergraduate degree in
comparative religion underlying his seminary training. No one seemed
to appreciate the fact that it was he who had made St. Francis truly an
interfaith experience. He'd taken a cue from the Unitarians in provid-
ing something for everyone. And another from the great congrega-
tions of the 1970s in turning religion into entertainment.

It was a little hit or miss, of course. The zen roshi was definitely
a hit. He'd made everyone sit on the floor, taught them to sit zazen,
and rapped them authentically on the shoulders with wooden sticks
when their focus wandered. Mignon had particularly enjoyed that
service.

On the other hand, the neopagans, with their candles and robes
and pentagrams, got mixed reviews. The children loved them, but
some of the more conservative adults found them over-the-top.

Most notably Laura.

For today (purely by coincidence—even one so highly attuned

couldn't have predicted the murders) Peter had scheduled a scholar from Johns Hopkins to speak on the afterlife. The professor's subject was "Urban Myth or Muslim Heaven—the Twenty-Six Dark-Eyed Virgins," but at the last second Ahmed had been called to the White House for a briefing.

So Peter had to scramble. There was a Christian rock group he'd been thinking of scheduling.

But even as he reached for his card file, he knew it was hopeless. It was seven A.M. on Sunday morning. Anybody who wasn't already booked was sound asleep with the phone turned off.

Desultorily, he started to pick through the file, wondering if he knew anyone who owed him a favor, and his eye fell on the one card that was different from all the others. It was red.

And he knew just whose it was. He'd had it only a few days.

Excitedly, he grabbed for it, a voice, a sweet female voice, echoing in his ear: "Don't forget about me, Peter. I'd just *love* to give you a demonstration." The red card had been given to him by the owner of the voice, one Tiffany Turner, a waitress at the club.

Ms. Tiffany was full of surprises. It seemed she belonged to a group that did what she called "trance-drumming." Only a few nights ago, for the umpteenth time, she'd practically begged him to call "anytime" for a demonstration. Naturally, he'd thought she was just hitting on him.

Well, all the better, he thought now. If she had a thing for him— and obviously, she did—he of all people should be able to talk her into performing at the church on short notice. (No notice, actually, but there was also no choice.)

He plucked the card and dialed.

So here he was, standing up before the good people of Gryphon Gate with a motley crew of mixed racial and national origins, all dressed in white and placing offerings of rum and cigars on the altar. Peter was sweating; this was a bit more than he bargained for.

Crossing his fingers, he turned the pulpit over to Tiffany.

"Ladies and gentlemen," she began, "it's my pleasure this morning to introduce to you eight of the most gifted mediums at Umbanda House, where I live and worship."

The girl must be some kind of fanatic—she actually lived in a cult commune. Peter had had no idea. Laura was looking at him as if reconsidering the barbecue fork of two nights before.

But Tiffany was saying all the right things. "Afro-Amer-Indian" particularly caught his attention. How could you go wrong with that?

Diane Robards listened with half an ear, a lot more interested in her fellow churchgoers than in the musical program that was about to unfold. She'd slipped on heels and wriggled into a simple black dress for the occasion. Looking around her, she decided the pain of pantyhose was worth it. She blended rather well, so long as nobody checked her label. Some of the men were in golf clothes, but most had on jackets (though some wore them with deck shoes). The women were Ungaro'd and Buchman'd and Karan'd as usual—probably going on to lunch at the club.

The truth was, black was Diane's least flattering color. She knew she looked awful, and for more than one reason. She'd been up half the night and spent the early morning hours surfing databases available only to P.I.s and law enforcement personnel. She'd spent a good amount of time Googling, too. It was surprising how many people had an Internet presence, whether they knew it or not. Even more surprising, some had none—some who you'd expect to have high profiles. What she'd learned made her look at her fellow worshippers with a new and suspicious eye.

Jerry Lynch, Wall Street honcho, for instance. You'd think he was a nobody if you went on-line.

And Toni Sinclair. Funny, her interest in animals seemed of pretty recent vintage.

Then there was Vanessa Smart (before she got hyphenated). Vanessa had quite a little history behind her, including a jacket that wasn't Armani.

And there were others.

Diane had gleaned more tasty tidbits than Toni's herd of deer at feeding time.

Anka thought her head was going to split. That drumming! Ow!

What was the point?

Sweet little Tiffany had said something about calling on the spirits. Was this a séance or what? Anka really had no patience with it.

She was here for one reason and one reason only—to see and be seen. She'd be history soon, and good riddance to Gryphon Gate.

The gated communities of the world were lovely places for a while, delicious treasure troves of jewelry and cash and bearer bonds, maybe the occasional portable artwork. She loved them, she really did. But now and then you hit a snag.

Jerry Lynch was a big fat mistake. Or, more properly, Renée Lynch was. What was up with a woman who kept her jewelry locked in a safe deposit box? Never left so much as a tennis bracelet lying around? Anka had had to make other plans, and fast.

Worse, there was another complication—one so annoying there might be another murder before she left. She and her partner had worked this con at least five times, and Anka was gathering quite a little nest egg when suddenly her dear partner quit on her. Chucked the whole thing for a bigger score, just when Anka was floundering over at the Lynch mausoleum. She'd really had to scrounge around, but when you looked like Anka, it wasn't that hard. She'd found exactly the right person, too.

Having just lost her husband, Rachel Vormeister came to church looking for solace (though her mother was there for something else).

And what was she getting? Drums.

It wasn't what she had in mind, but it brought back memories of another life—the fulfilling one she'd had before she married. When she thought about it, life in Gryphon Gate was going to be pretty empty without Sigmond. She wasn't at all sure she wanted her unborn child to grow up in this expensive vipers' nest. In fact, if she weren't so sad, she could be pretty amused about what was happening here.

Rachel figured what Tiffany said went over most people's heads, but she knew the name for what they were about to witness—and she was pretty sure this was one church service they'd be talking about for the rest of their lives.

Some might find the drums compelling in ways they never dreamed.

Rachel knew enough to see that what Tiff and her buds were doing was calling the "entities" or "spirits" of their faith, sometimes called "saints" and "orishas" in Santeria, "loa" in a certain sect that was probably too much, even for Peter Armbruster.

"The belief," Tiffany was saying in that sweet voice of hers, "is that the entity can actually enter the body of a trance medium, and then that person is no longer himself, but literally becomes the saint during the ritual."

Rachel doubted a single person there—except herself—had a clue what that cute blonde kid was talking about. She leaned back to enjoy the show.

"As our custom dictates," Tiffany continued, "first we'll call Eleggua. He's sort of a gatekeeper to the other side, sometimes associated with the Christian Satan. But, of course, there's really no comparison."

Tiffany didn't seem to hear the collective gasp that ricocheted round the sanctuary.

The drumbeat changed, grew more intense. The earnest, white-robed Umbandans were already dancing at the front of the sanctuary. They began to chant something in another language.

As they chanted, the dancing grew more and more ecstatic, until one young man reeled abruptly, his eyes rolling back in his head. He struggled to keep his balance; immediately a cadre of dancers rushed to his side, some holding him up, one shaking a rattle at him.

Suddenly the young man—a cherubic redhead—stood erect, seeming to have grown a good six inches. His eyes bugged out. He picked up one foot and began to dance again.

On one leg only.

"Eleggua has arrived!" Tiffany pronounced, obviously thrilled to pieces. She resumed her commentary as if she were narrating a documentary. "Note the bugging eyes—this is often the case with spirit possession. It's said that the body is really too small to contain the orisha, and the bugging eyes indicate the strain.

"When the entity takes over the body, the 'horse,' or human host, channels the spirit. If we're lucky, Eleggua may speak to us through Danny."

Vanessa didn't like the sound of that at all. *A talebearer revealeth secrets . . .*

But neither Danny the horse nor his captured Eleggua showed any sign of speaking. The horse galumphed to the altar, seized the bottle of rum, and chugalugged mightily, after which he belched with enthusiasm. Then he began dancing again, seemingly oblivious of the chaos around him.

A willowy Hispanic girl, not even needing the rattle inducement, began to dance on one leg.

The rest of the Umbandans continued on two legs, ardently entreating Eleggua to claim their bodies as well, circling and weaving in delight.

The drums pounded.

Vanessa was still thinking of the fax. *Showtime?* she wondered. Surely this wasn't all for her. She glanced nervously at Peter, who was watching his tight-assed wife. Never in the history of Gryphon Gate had such a spectacle occurred. This had to be way, way out of line for Laura. Vanessa's eyes followed Peter's.

Laura was about to pop an artery. She leapt to her feet, obviously furious, and teetered for a moment on her Bruno Maglis. Her arm shot out, finger pointing at Peter, about to make him put a stop to it, and then the same arm rose slowly above her head, briefly circled, and, picking up her right leg, she began dancing on her left.

Peter rose in horror. "Laura! Are you all right?"

Laura didn't answer, only danced one-legged to the altar, plucked a cigar, lit it, and whooshed out a great stream of smoke. "Ahhhh!" she sighed, patting her stomach in a thoroughly unladylike way.

Miranda whispered loudly, "Mommy! Mrs. Armbruster's smoking!"

In Gryphon Gate, you could be forgiven for sleeping with your next-door neighbor—and usually were—but never for smoking. This was an ironclad no-no (unless you were Lance McClintock, of course—*expensive* cigars were exempt from derision).

Laura gulped down a huge swig of rum, the jacket of her green silk suit riding up to reveal orchid underclothing. Then she turned around to face the congregation. Her eyes bugged like tennis balls. As she danced, she whipped her arms about as if she'd just learned how to use them, and she laughed often, producing a deep, throaty rumble as much like Laura Armbruster's laugh as a dog's bark. (Or so it seemed at the time—actually, no one could remember ever hearing her laugh.)

No one moved. Peter turned the color of his affected clerical collar. Laura jumped and stomped and pirouetted in masculine abandon, clearly having the time of her life. Vanessa feared for the delicate heels on the fabulous shoes. Laura was practically Imelda Marcos when it came to footwear.

Finally, landing heavily after a particularly high leap, Laura swiveled to face the congregation, and once more she pointed. She spoke directly to the assembly, her bugging eyes as terrifying as they were green: "I need to talk to the werewolf."

The collective gasp echoed again, this time more like a scream. The voice was raspy and deep, and unmistakably male.

"It's a trick," someone whispered.

Laura set down her right foot and stood hips out, feet wide apart like a lumberjack. "Werewolf, stand!" she commanded.

Roman Gervase stood.

Laura pointed. "All bets are off," she announced. "You will cease and desist your absurd behavior."

Sweat poured down Roman's face. "Thank you," he whispered, sitting down hard, apparently overcome with fear and awe.

Vanessa noticed suddenly that the music had changed. "We're bringing in Oggun," Tiffany said. "The warrior god."

Laura raised her left leg and began to dance on her right, once again laughing her deep, throaty laugh, alternately puffing her cigar and swigging from the rum bottle.

Almost immediately a young black Umbandan reeled, received encouraging rattling, and stood up straight like Danny. Only this one seemed not merely taller, but suddenly giantlike. With august, noble strides, he approached the altar, jerked a candelabrum, fire and all, from its perch, and shouldered it like a rifle. Hot wax dripped on the crimson carpet. Laura would have a fit if she ever came to her senses.

The flames bloomed dangerously close to the young man's dreads.

Peter had gone from dead white to a frightening watermelon hue. Again he rose as if to halt the debacle, but Tiffany stopped him. "It's his machete," she said. "Oggun clears paths."

"He'll burn the place down!"

"Dr. Armbruster, you can't argue with the divine; I really can't be responsible if you try."

Nervously, Peter glanced at Oggun's pacing mount. He was about five ten and slight, but right now he looked as if he could take every man in the church—all at once.

The as-yet-unridden Umbandans and the three Elegguas (Laura included) danced merrily on. Oggun's horse—Tyrone, according to Tiffany—marched down the aisle, bugging eyes straight ahead, apparently seeing nothing until he came to the row where Toni was quaking with a very excited Miranda. He unshouldered the makeshift machete. "Lady of the deer," he intoned, his voice ringing with a metallic timbre, as if a great bell had been struck.

Toni hid her face with her hands.

"Look at me!"

"Mommy, look at him," Miranda echoed.

Toni dropped her hands.

"You have an enemy."

No kidding, Vanessa thought. *Lots of them.*

"You have a very dangerous enemy. Lies will be spread about you."

The church was full of talebearers, all right. But, so far as Vanessa could see, no real secrets had been revealed. Still, anybody in church was a sitting duck.

She was thinking of fleeing when suddenly a loud thump elicited more gasps. Momentarily distracted from her own pressing needs, she saw that Danny, the first Eleggua, had fallen flat on his face.

His comrades rushed forward with water.

"The orisha has left," Tiffany explained, still in *National Geographic* mode.

Once again the drumming changed. "Ah, time for Oshun, the spirit of the river, of beauty, of fertility—and lovely, lovely money."

The Umbandans were in a frenzy. Two succumbed simultaneously to Oshun, suddenly graceful as a river in Africa—no small feat considering that one was a 250-pound man.

No more than thirty seconds had passed before Parker Upshaw, cutthroat turnaround man and president of the homeowners association, got up, leaving the twins strapped in their toddler seats, and began to mince toward the front of the sanctuary, his walk somehow causing his Brooks Brothers suit to flow as gracefully as a sari.

Parker waved his closed hand in front of his face, as if wielding a fan, much as the other Oshuns did. He pantomimed primping at a mirror.

Vanessa thought she'd keel over.

When he reached center stage, he danced prettily for a few moments, as dainty as Toni's Bambis, but suddenly he stopped and shrieked, a high feminine wail debouching from his six-foot frame. "Eeeek! There's a bug in here!"

Just what we need, Vanessa thought. *Someone spying on us.* And then she saw something almost as unnerving: cute Ray Flynt, the webmaster, snapping away with his digital camera.

But she'd misunderstood. Electronic bugs weren't the kind Parker's Oshun had in mind. "Oshun hates roaches!" Parker screeched. "Won't someone kill the bug for Her Loveliness?"

Peter seemed about to expel bricks.

Vanessa squirmed.

The congregation sat transfixed as Parker flounced purposefully down the aisle, seized Jerry by the ear like an outraged schoolmarm, and squealed, "Out, roach!"

Off the hook, Vanessa thought. *For the moment.*

And there was a deliciously bright side. Laura was still dancing on one leg, Tyrone still marching with the lit candelabrum, and Parker-the-pillar had developed multiple personality disorder. Peter had to be desperate. She half expected the hypocrite to break down and pray.

But before Peter could get around to it, the door of the church flew open.

Lydia had always prided herself on her quick thinking. The green eyes she was looking at peered from a ski mask, never a good sign. Without a second thought she went for them with her key.

The man—if it was a man—stepped back to avoid her lunge, and she kneed him in the chicken tenders.

Unfortunately, she missed.

She fisted her hand and crammed it into his nose.

He reached for her flying fists, but she feinted and butted him in the chest, which caused him to double over, catching the sash of her robe.

She kneed him again, this time connecting. He fell backward, still clutching the sash, and Lydia seized her opportunity. She whirled and ran—through the house, out the door, all the way to the church screaming—*"Rape! Murder! Fire!"*—with equal insistence.

Not until she'd actually flung open the door did it occur to her that she'd left the robe behind.

Since Vanessa happened to be in church, it seemed perfectly appropriate to thank God she'd been spared Lydia's cellulite, which was jiggling quite literally in front of God and everybody. Her neighbor wore only a pair of Calvin Klein jockey shorts and a tiny cotton camisole, undoubtedly her sleeping outfit.

However, since she was screaming for help, it did stand to reason she'd left home in a hurry. But the moment Lydia exploded into the church, she shut up. Her mouth froze in an O of astonishment at the sight of her husband doing a fair impersonation of RuPaul.

Or perhaps she was even more riveted by the fact that Jerry Lynch seemed about to slug him.

Doubtless, the drums, the incense, the rapturous dancers, and Laura's baritone laughter all contributed.

Not to mention the cigar smoke.

Whatever the cause, Lydia sank to the floor in a dead faint.

Diane Robards stood. "That's enough!" she shouted. "Church is out."

Her command broke the spell. The possessed dancers started to fall like bowling pins.

Diane raced to Lydia's aid, Peter to Laura's.

It was Laura who came around first. "Whash that awful tashte?" she slurred.

Never had the club bartenders been called upon to concoct so many lunchtime drinks in so short a time. Mojitos, the drink of the moment, were going down like lemonade. Daiquiris, Bloodies, mimosas, Long Island iced teas, and the occasional Bellini were also being consumed in quantities usually reserved for New Year's Eve.

Since Laura was presumably home sleeping it off, somebody had to play her part. Henry Drysdale slipped into the role like a favorite sweater. "What the hell was Peter Armbruster thinking? Voodoo! In Gryphon Gate! God, I hope the papers don't get wind of it."

Rachel Vormeister, sipping a Diet Coke, took issue. "It wasn't voodoo. Umbanda is quite a different syncretic religion—meaning a mixture of Catholicism and various folk beliefs. Voodoo is Haitian, Umbanda is Brazilian. And here's a question for you, Henry—can seventy million Brazilians be wrong?"

"I didn't know there *were* seventy million Brazilians."

Rachel shrugged. She was enjoying this. "Well, that's what Umbandans claim," she said.

Mignon Gervase was pale and drawn, her hair damp around her face. "But what *was* that? It was like they turned into somebody else."

Well, duhh was not what Rachel answered, though she had to bite her tongue.

Henry took advantage of the pause to override Mignon. "How do you know so much about this, Rachel?"

Rachel gave him a winsome smile. "You didn't know about my sordid past, Henry? I'm a Jungian therapist. You may have heard that we Jungians are into archetypes."

"Uh—archetypes?"

"That's what those entities are—*ideas* of powerful beings. Gods, if you will. I did my thesis on Afro-Caribbean religion. It's a particular interest of mine."

Mignon's hands were shaking.

"What we saw, Mignon, was something called spirit possession."

"Yes, yes, we all heard Tiffany," Ned Carbury interjected. "But what was it, *really?*"

Rachel smiled again, rather smugly. "It looked pretty real to me."

The senator set down his glass so hard his gin and tonic splashed. "Come on, you're an intelligent woman. Is it some kind of mass hypnosis, or what?"

"Well, those drums are pretty hypnotic. But *you* weren't affected, were you?"

"I was scared out of my shoes," Mignon said. She was on her third mojito.

Silas Macgruder had bellied up with a Bloody Mary in hand and a broad smile on his face. "Laura Armbruster smoking a cigar! Parker Upshaw flapping his wrists! God, I'm glad I lived long enough to see it."

"Well, they were . . ." Rachel searched for a phrase these people had a prayer of understanding, ". . . under a spell, you might say."

She let them chew on it a moment. "Or maybe they were faking."

Her mother seemed to be thinking something over. "Well, it was a fascinating event, to say the least," Mrs. Kaplan said. "But tell me something—is it the custom in Gryphon Gate to advertise church services like plays or movies?"

The assembled group stared blankly, all except one. Anka—who'd been dispatched to the club for emergency takeout—knew exactly what she meant.

"Those 'Showtime!' faxes," Mrs. Kaplan explained. "Didn't everybody get one?"

Such a buzzing ensued you would have thought she'd reported seeing a spaceship.

Diane Robards had buttonholed Peter as he was trying to stuff his drunken wife into the family Volvo. Then she'd followed up by questioning Tiffany and placing a call to Ahmed, the no-show professor.

She'd been forced to come to a puzzling conclusion—no one could have predicted the scene in the church.

So, what was the fax all about?

She had a sinking feeling she knew the answer when the first call came in.

She'd described the scene to Leland, who met her over at the Upshaws, where, predictably, they found no one in a ski mask clutching his wounded privates.

What they did find, however, was a prodigious mess in Lydia's subterranean record room; but Lydia had been too distraught to figure out right away whether anything was missing.

Or so she said.

After calming the Upshaws, she and Leland picked up sandwiches and retired to her office. "I've been thinking," Diane said, "about what you said about Roman Gervase being disturbed."

"Yes?"

"Suppose he isn't."

Leland stared. "Can you give me one good reason why a sane man would behave like a werewolf?"

"Three." Diane replied. "I started thinking about what Laura said to him."

Leland considered. " 'All bets are off.' Ah. A bet."

"Uh-huh. Or maybe a promise."

" 'Be mine and I'll howl at the moon.' That kind of thing?"

Diane nodded, stretching long legs now clad in tight black pants. She'd ripped off her pantyhose the minute she got to the office, where she always kept emergency clothing. "Or a vow maybe." She nodded again as if talking to herself. "Could be a vow."

Leland was fast losing interest. "What do you make of that roach action?"

Diane frowned. "Hard to know. But I'll tell you one thing. I researched Jerry Lynch on the Internet last night, and, strangely enough, he hardly seems to exist." Abruptly, she changed the subject. "I've been in his office, have you?"

Leland shook his handsome head.

"Well, he's got this big fat diploma from Harvard Business School hanging on his wall. So I checked that out, too."

"You're some whiz with the databases."

As a matter of fact, she was proud of her electronic prowess. She wondered if Leland had figured that out. He certainly knew how to get to her. But the jury was still out on what was calculated and what was genuine where he was concerned.

"Just part of the job," she said.

"Well, let me guess," offered Leland. "Jerry didn't go to Harvard."

"Not the year he's supposed to have graduated. I checked the five years before and the five after, just to make sure."

"Still wasn't there?"

"No, but a funny thing—a certain Ronald Roach was. I remembered the name because it's so . . ."

"Repulsive?"

They were giggling when the first of the calls came in. It was Babs Blackburn. "My ring," she sobbed. "I've been robbed."

Toni had taken Miranda home immediately after the service, foregoing the bar like the good mother she was. The poor kid was just about freaked out of her mind.

Exactly how was Toni supposed to explain fainting ladies in their skivvies? Laura Armbruster turning into a gross old man with a double habit? Crazy adults running around in robes?

"It's was just a game, darling. You know how silly grown-ups can be."

"But, Mommy, Mrs. Upshaw seemed really scared. And so did Mr. Lynch."

"Mr. Lynch?"

"You know—when Mr. Upshaw called him a bug. Was he afraid of getting stomped?"

Hmmm, thought Toni. *Could be. You might have something, kid.*

For some reason, the part about her mother having an enemy hadn't spooked the child at all. But it was working Toni's nerves pretty hard.

It required a Haagen-Dazs lunch—strictly against Toni's principles—but eventually Miranda was calm enough to watch *101 Dalmatians* for the hundredth time. (It cracked Toni up, remembering the first time the kid had watched it. She was four at the time. Innocent little face turned up, freckles arrayed on her tiny nose, Miranda had pointed excitedly at the wide screen. "Mommy, Mommy, is that Mrs. Smart-Drysdale?" She meant Cruella de Vil, of course.)

Finally having a moment to herself, Toni retired to change out of her church clothes. She had worn a silk pullover and Michael Kors slacks, set off with a pearl-trimmed antique watch on a chain around her neck, a pair of simple pearl earrings, and her favorite ring— rubies set in a star surrounded by diamonds.

A gift from Lincoln, of course.

She stripped off the jewelry, hung up her clothes, and then opened her top bureau drawer to put the ring away. Her ring box was wide open—and empty.

Toni felt the blood rush to her face. Her heart pounded furiously. It wasn't fair!

You lived in a place like Gryphon Gate because it was safe. So you didn't have to keep everything under lock and key.

Frantically, she opened all her jewelry cases, some on top of the bureau, some in drawers like the ring box.

Not a single one contained so much as an earring.

9

TO SHARE OR NOT TO SHARE?

That was indeed the question.

Aaron Kaplan stood at the window, gazing out at the rich expanse of Gryphon Gate. He scratched his blond head and for a moment sucked in his gut. Pacing, he came to the free-standing mirror that stood near the door of the huge walk-in closet of the guest room he occupied in his sister's house. Really, really, sucking in, he wasn't all that bad. Weeks of daily crunches had added definition to his abs—not a six-pack yet, but a four-pack for sure. Aaron turned sideways to consider his glutes, lats, and delts. Not bad. Not at a distance. Still, there was the acne thing. Maybe if he laid off the Milky Ways.

Real exercise, that's what you need, young man! Discipline! Or so Lieutenant Colonel McClintock had told him on occasion. On occasion? Hell! On every occasion that he'd seen the old buzzard. In fact, McClintock had suggested to Rachel and his mother that he join the army—that would whip him into shape, not this sissy skateboarding stuff. Fat lot of good it did McClintock. Discipline or not, the colonel was dead.

Aaron turned away from the mirror. Maybe he wasn't an Adonis, and maybe he would never be.

Being smart was better.

All of them running around like confused ants. Even the cops. He, a teenager with acne, now held power over the lot of them, and he planned to use it.

Such a rich victory was something to be savored. Should he cast out a few clues? Scare the hell out of a few folks? Make some of the high and mighty itch and scratch until they were begging to know just where he got his information? If they only knew!

Smiling, Aaron returned to the window. Gryphon Gate was a rich and beautiful place. His sister's house alone was testament to that fact. Aaron loved his sister, but, really, it was all such a sham! What Rachel spent on Persian carpets could feed an army of immigrants for a year.

Outside a pair of blackbirds quarreled over the carcass of a dead squirrel like hungry jackals. Jackals, he thought, just like his sister's neighbors, living here together, enjoying the wealth.

Aaron knew he should run straight to the police. At the very least, he should tell his sister what he knew. Poor Rachel. She was truly upset over the death of old Siggy. Aaron had always considered his brother-in-law something of a weirdo, but Rachel had loved him. And now she was pregnant and Siggy was dead.

Siggy had never paid Aaron much attention. Funny how grownups always overlooked young people. If anyone but he had studied Siggy's notes, though, those notes never would have meant anything. But not to Aaron. Now he knew.

Aaron stared out the window for a long time, expecting Rachel and his Mom to return any moment from church. In point of fact, he was amazed that they had gone. Siggy was barely cold and still at the morgue. There would be a funeral to plan, and if his mother had anything to say about it, they'd have to sit shivah.

And now that old bag of critical wind, Lt. Col. Lance McClintock, was dead as well. That was a shocker. He'd been such a tough old bird. But even the mighty could fall to the low, especially when taken completely by surprise. Surely McClintock never saw it coming.

Aaron smiled slowly.

Hell, he was no lawbreaker. Eventually, he'd go to the police with everything he knew—and what that knowledge led him to suspect.

Eventually.

But first he was going to make the mighty squirm.

Aaron started downstairs, his footfalls silent on the carpeted treads. As he wandered through the quiet living room, a sudden shudder raked him.

What if . . . ?

What if by holding onto the information he caused someone else to die?

And what if that someone was him?

Dr. Charles Jefferson was no longer limping by the time he arrived at the clubhouse, and he headed straight for the bar. He planned to order something, anything, to dull the throbbing in his nose.

To his amazement, the barroom was empty, except for a few busy bartenders trying to pick up the place. It was a shambles—empty glasses everywhere, cocktail napkins and trail mix littering the floor.

"Hello!" a young woman said perkily, three empty highball glasses in each hand. She stared at him with a strange curiosity, as if she should know him but wasn't sure why, then set the glasses down on a tray.

Although Jefferson wasn't a man for false modesty, he felt himself puff up a bit. He'd been in the clubhouse before, of course, though he wasn't a resident. And, even if he did acknowledge it himself, he was an exceptionally good-looking man with ink dark hair—the peppering of gray adding a distinguished air—and his excellent green eyes. He was tall, and again, if he did say so himself, in damned incredibly good shape.

But that wasn't why she should recognize him; it was because his face had been on almost every magazine cover in the country.

"Is there something going on here?" he asked. Then, before she could answer, he remembered and added solemnly, "Besides the death of poor Sigmond Vormeister? Naturally, I read about it in the paper. I'm so sorry, of course." And then he added rather recklessly, "He was— or I should say his wife is—a patient of mine."

The girl gasped. "Of course! You're Dr. Charles Jefferson!" She set her tray down, miraculously not breaking any glasses, and rushed over to him. "I saw you on the cover of *Time*! They call you the genius of procreation!"

"Yes, that's me." He was about to say more, but he hesitated. He had come to Gryphon Gate for an important meeting, but as he neared the gate, the hordes of hovering journalists and a pair of well-armed guards had scared him off. Swearing under his breath, he'd pulled a U-ey and parked his car a half a mile away along the gravel road that led to Vanessa Smart-Drysdale's Forest Glen development. From there it was a short, soggy trek through the underbrush until he reached the water. A quick rinse of his shoes, a casual stroll along the beach, and he was in.

He was late, of course; and, to add to his annoyance, his appointment hadn't waited. As he stood in the cul-de-sac wondering what to do, a blond youth flew around the corner, jumped the curb, and ground his skateboard to a halt on the pavement a few yards away. "Looking for somebody, dude?"

"No thanks," Jefferson said, thinking quickly, pointing to the Upshaw house. "It's just there."

He knew the Upshaws well, of course, having managed their fertility plan. No harm in dropping in. No one had answered his knock, however, so he'd gingerly stepped into the entrance hall, calling out. Noise from below had drawn him to the basement, but before he'd had a chance to greet her, Lydia Upshaw had attacked him, then run away, God knew where.

He'd intended to find her—once he'd been able to stand again—and explain himself. Now, with all that had happened, he wasn't so sure he wanted to admit to anything. The place had him spooked. He was no longer wearing the ski cap he had donned against the chill of the morning, and he had shed the turtleneck sweater that had crawled halfway up his chin, but he didn't think that he wanted to explain himself to the police. They might think it was an odd way for a doctor to dress while paying a call on a patient, and he had walked into her house unbidden.

"I've been looking for some friends," he told the bartender at last, "but nobody seems to be at home. I realize, of course, that it's Sunday, but you've usually got quite a houseful in here on Sunday afternoons, so I thought—"

"Oh, they *were* all here," the girl said. "You just missed them." She stuck her hand forward again, pumping his. "I'm Tiffany Turner. Rev. Peter Armbruster allowed me to bring a very special ceremony to church this morning and—well, it was delightful, a true triumph of the spirits. But everybody went a bit mad! You would have thought

Satan incarnate came down!" She shook her head. "I'm afraid they're not a group that's used to being so in touch with the spirits."

"You're not a member, so I know I shouldn't," Tiffany said with a wink, "but what can I get you?"

Jefferson ordered a beer.

"I wasn't supposed to have worked today," Tiffany told him, centering a glass on a cocktail napkin in front of the doctor. "But after the rites they all rushed over from church and began drinking as if they'd been stranded in the desert for decades! But then, so much has happened! We've had two murders. Can you imagine? The police have been here roping off everything, asking all kinds of questions. . . ." Her eyes widened suddenly. "Hey, how did you get in here? No one is supposed to be coming in or out, except for residents and employees!"

"No one was at the gate," he lied smoothly, "so I couldn't get through. Had to leave my car outside and walk in. And it was surprisingly chilly, I can tell you."

He remembered the warm knit cap he had been wearing and the turtleneck sweater. Of course! That's why Lydia hadn't recognized him! Damn the woman! He'd be sore for a month.

"How strange," Tiffany said.

Jefferson smiled at her disarmingly over the rim of his glass. She was really a pretty girl. Tousled hair. Wide, innocent eyes. He found himself hoping that one day she'd have trouble conceiving a child and come to him.

"So much for our police protection," Tiffany shrugged. "Ah, well, even the best of things can go sour, right, Doctor?" She leaned forward and whisked a damp rag across the table, and he caught a flash of creamy breasts. "This did seem like such a dream place. Now two people are dead and everyone is squabbling. Over deer, and property, and developments—it's *so* sad, really."

"Terribly sad," he agreed. He felt a cold sweat coming on. He definitely didn't want to talk to the police.

Jefferson forced an easy smile and rose to his feet. Standing there with the little beauty in front of him, he realized that he didn't want anything more to do with Gryphon Gate. He should never have come.

Something akin to panic seized him. "Well, Tiffany, it was a pleasure to meet you. I think I'll just bow out of here quickly and let everyone deal with their grief in their own way. Take care, dear girl. Ah! And if you ever need a . . . I'm in the book."

The police. She had to call the police. She had been robbed, horribly violated, her precious jewels taken from her.

Yet, staring at her empty jewel boxes with tears in her eyes, Toni hesitated.

The police had been there too many times already.

Still, her jewels!

The police already suspected her of having murdered Sigmond. And now they might suspect her of killing the colonel, too.

But she had been violated!

A mother, with many secrets, and a child. A beautiful child. A beautiful, green-eyed little girl who must be given love and warmth and all the good things in life. No matter what.

The past be damned!

No one really knew.

Oh, yes they did. She'd received those faxes, and two men were dead, and the police were after her and . . .

She sank into a fit of hysterical tears. *It's so unfair!*

Her tears gave way to a cry of rage. Her jewels were gone. She was going to the police!

But again, she wavered.

You have an enemy.

A vision of Tiffany and her crazed acolytes shimmered in her brain.

People will spread lies about you.

She shook her head to clear it. It had just been a ridiculous facade of a church service, for heaven's sake.

But the police already thought that she might be guilty of the murders. And, yes, she had an enemy. Maybe the jewels had been stolen just so that she would go to the police. Maybe some kind of evidence had been planted that would incriminate her.

She wasn't the murderess! All right, so she might be considered *a* murderess, but she wasn't *the* murderess. And you couldn't really consider Lincoln's death a murder. It had been an act of mercy. Mercy for her, of course, but still . . .

Toni couldn't think straight. She needed a drink, time to sort it all out, make a plan.

She had just opened the liquor cabinet when the telephone started to ring.

Roach, roach, roach! No, Roach, Roach, Roach, capital R.

Jerry Lynch was beside himself. The service had been absurd. The silly hopping people had gone on and on disturbingly, and yet—ridiculous as it was—too much had come out.

He could still feel the drums beating in his head.

He needed to be by himself, to have time to think. Before he eluded his wife at the bar, Renée had said something about making sure Rachel was doing all right, so he was certain he'd have the house to himself.

But as he crossed the magnificent lawn that sloped gently away from his house toward the marina, he saw Anka closing the front door behind her. She was something, in a skintight synthetic pantsuit and with a briefcase in her hands. She didn't look like a maid at all, oh, no. She was exotic. Beautifully so. A temptress.

Suddenly it seemed that the drumbeats were no longer in his head. They had transferred to his groin.

Yes. Yes. Yes.

That was what he needed. Exactly what he needed.

He strode quickly up the walk, grabbing Anka's free hand. "Come back inside. Quickly. We've got some time alone."

Anka resisted. "I can't. I'm sorry, Mr. Lynch, I have to—I have to leave for a few days. My sister is ill. I've got to go right away."

"Your sister? You told us you were an only child," Jerry said.

"I—I only said that so you would hire me, so you wouldn't be afraid that I'd have to—well, that I'd have to run out like this," Anka explained.

Damn, her eyes were soulful. Huge, dark. Jerry felt the drumbeats in him again. Hell, he felt like a caveman. "Your sister will wait. I'll make it worth your while." He curled his fingers strongly around her arm, dragging her back into the house.

"Look, Mr. Lynch, I've got to get going, I must, it's a life-or-death situation."

"I'm a life-or-death situation at this moment!" he whispered passionately into her glorious hair.

He wasn't going to be able to keep her, he knew, but suddenly he felt more vital than he had in his entire life. Like a prize racing stud about to explode.

The nanny was upstairs with the baby, he reminded himself. But then, if the baby was sleeping, the nanny would be watching TV. It would take her time to come downstairs, even if she heard noises from the nursery.

The danger made it all the more exciting.

It was the drums.

It was the fear.

It was that damned spirit being calling out about Roach.

Whatever, he was feeling desperate.

He'd dragged her as far as the hallway—the marble-covered hallway just inside the front door. With the mirror at the entrance reflecting their every move, it would be ungodly sensual. Just what he needed. Right in Renée's beautifully designed, Louis Quatorze entryway.

"Quickly!" he urged.

Anka held the briefcase between them as if it were a lifesaver. Strange, he thought vaguely, that she was leaving with a briefcase, not a suitcase. But he was so enamored of her scent and hair and the rise of her breasts against the polyester that he couldn't concentrate on any such oddity. "Give me that!" he demanded.

A little cry tore from her lips as he grasped the case and sent it flying across the white marble. He was vaguely aware that it struck a wall. But his eyes were only for her.

"Mr. Lynch, honestly, I've got to go. . . ."

"I won't be but a second," Jerry moaned.

No, that's true, you won't be! Anka thought.

She couldn't see her precious briefcase anymore. Jerry was strong. And in some kind of a state. It must have been that stupid church service.

Great, fine, just do it! Then I can go!

Jerry didn't seem to know whether to claw at his own zipper or her pantsuit. Anka took over, sliding out of the garment—she had learned to disrobe very quickly in her business—and moved like lightning to help him as well.

The best-looking man in the world would seem ridiculous with his BVDs and trousers wound around his ankles. And though not bad, Jerry certainly wasn't the *best*-looking man in the world.

Just get to it! She told herself.

And so, there they were, she naked, Jerry all knotted up in his boxers and trousers, abandoned to passion on the white marble floor when the door flew open.

Anka looked over his shoulder and froze. She slammed a fist against Jerry's shoulder.

"Your wife!" she whispered.

"What? What?" Jerry demanded, panting hard.

Smart, clicking footsteps moved over the marble. Renée was above them now, staring down, oddly detached, a smile of amusement on her face. But her eyes cut like razors.

"She said, 'Your wife,' *darling*," Renée crooned.

Jerry went limp. He tried to rise and tripped over his BVDs. It was actually quite comical, Anka thought, or it would have been, had the situation not been so dire.

Surely, it was only seconds, but those seconds seemed like hours, as Jerry careened backwards and forwards, trying to catch his balance. He never succeeded. Jerry Lynch went down with a bang, moaning slightly as his head struck the marble.

"I thought you were comforting Rachel," Jerry complained, as if he were the one betrayed.

"She only needed so much comforting," Renée said crisply. "Jerry, for the love of God, get up and fix yourself!" Renee commanded. "And Anka . . . well, well. Actually, I imagined you'd look better naked. Maybe our next maid will be an improvement. Because you, of course, are fired."

"Yes, absolutely! She's fired," Jerry agreed, desperately searching his wife's face. "You've got to understand, Renée. I've had a few drinks. I didn't mean to . . . she was just here, naked in the hall, trying to seduce me. It was the drums. It was that ridiculous church service. It's as if I were . . . possessed."

"Um, right," Renée murmured.

"You, you're fired," Jerry repeated to Anka.

Anka didn't give a damn about being fired. All the better to get out of there quickly. Just as she knew how to strip, she knew how to dress in the blink of an eye. She kept her lashes lowered as she slipped back into her clothing.

Her eyes were still downcast as she spoke. "Yes, Jerry, I deserve to be fired, I'm so evil, it was all my fault. I agree, it was that church service." She turned to Renée, suddenly demure. "Mrs. Lynch, believe me, I'm so sorry. I understand, I don't protest your decision in the least. I'm getting out of here immediately. You'll never have to see my face again."

She looked up, amazed at the sound of the laughter that followed her humble admission of guilt.

Renée Lynch stood blocking the doorway, her arms folded over her chest. "I don't think you'll be leaving so quickly."

"But—but—you want me gone, of course."

Next to his wife, Jerry nodded vigorously and struggled with his pants.

"I think we have something to discuss," Renée said.

"I don't want a divorce," Jerry said dully.

"Of course not, dear," Renée reassured her husband, not sending so much as a flicker of a glance his way. She was staring at Anka. "I am sure, however, that you, like me, would love to have an explanation for all the jewelry spilling out of that briefcase over there. I know it's not *mine*. Thankfully, I keep mine locked away. You never know when someone might attend one of those spirit services and become possessed by a thieving Umbandan," she added wryly. "But for now, Anka, dear, an explanation would be in order."

The three of them were frozen there—Jerry, not fully recovered, still tangled in his pant legs, leaning bare ding-donged against the wall, Anka, dressed, but pale and feeling like a caged rat, and Renée, totally regal and bitchy, blocking the door like a sentinel, arms still crossed over her chest—when the phone began to ring.

Toni was seated on her bed mired in a true dilemma, when Miranda walked into the room. Her precious daughter crawled up on the bed beside her and cradled her mother's face between her two chubby hands. Miranda stared at Toni with beautiful, sorrowful eyes. Eyes far too grave, serious, and concerned for those of a child.

"Mommy, are you all right? They were wrong in church. You're sweet and good, and you love the deer and the other animals. You don't have any enemies."

So, she thought, quickly cuddling Miranda to her, her daughter was aware of far more than she had realized.

"Oh, my darling!" Toni murmured, so sorry for the all the evils in her life. "Please don't worry. It was just a silly happening at the church. Reverend Armbruster tries hard, but sometimes, he brings in people who are not quite right."

Not quite right. Like everyone living in Gryphon Gate, Toni mused with a weary philosophy that was unusual for her. "Don't be upset, Miranda. It's all right. Mommy's enemies are not going to get to her."

"I love you, Mommy."

"I love you, too, precious." And she did. Toni loved her daughter more than anything in the world.

More than her jewels.

She suddenly wished that Peter Armbruster was more of a priest. She could use some easement of her soul. Sitting there, holding her daughter, she tried to convince herself that what she had done was right. The state should have arrested Lincoln and executed him. The things he had done to young children had certainly been far more horrible than what she had conspired to do to him.

But it wasn't her right to take his life. And with Miranda at her side, the guilt of it weighed heavily on her. She didn't want to leave her daughter without a mother.

First, there had been the fax and the awful discovery of Sigmond's body. Then, the police—believing that she might have done it! Then, another murder and the horrible church service.

And now the call from Lydia. She sighed, ruffled her daughter's hair, and said, "Sweetheart, later we're going to do something fun. Together. You and I. Mother and daughter. But I have to leave you with Bertha for a bit."

"Why, Mommy?"

"Mrs. Upshaw is upset about something. I have to go see her."

"But you're upset."

Upset? The understatement of the year, Toni thought.

"No, darling, I'm all right."

"What are we going to do that's fun?"

"I . . . I don't know," Toni said distractedly. "We'll make cookies together, how's that?"

"Cookies?"

"Sure."

"You can bake, Mommy?"

"Yes, I can." She could have told her daughter that, once upon a time, before Lincoln, she had done many things for herself. She refrained.

"Cookies! We're going to bake cookies!"

Toni smiled as Miranda bounced away from her, twirling around the room with delight. Miranda stopped suddenly though, before the window, staring down.

"What is it, dear?" Toni asked.

"Oh, the nice security man is downstairs again."

Panic seized Toni. Irrational, she thought. With everything going on, thank God security men were around.

Except, *where the hell were they when her jewels were being stolen?*

Unless . . .

One of the security men had stolen her jewels?

Toni forced herself to be calm as she rose and walked to the window. It was Leland, the young good-looking one. He wasn't on her property, though. He had parked on the road and was just standing in front of her house.

"I wonder if he wants to give me back my toy," Miranda said.

Toni frowned instantly.

"What toy?"

"Oh, just a little black toy I found in the bushes," Miranda said briefly.

Still desperately trying for calm, she walked to her daughter and took her by the shoulders, crouching down beside her. "Miranda, could you describe this little black toy for me?"

Miranda nodded enthusiastically. "It was kind of like a Game Boy, but it was just black, and it didn't do anything fun."

Little, black, like a Game Boy. A Palm Pilot? Hadn't Sigmond had a Palm Pilot?

Toni reeled, wondering what information Sigmond might have collected. She closed her eyes, fighting another wave of panic. No. Sigmond had known nothing about her.

But somebody did.

She stood quickly. "I'll just get your toy back," she told Miranda. Toni raced out of the house, moving faster than she had in years.

But it was no good. Leland had gone by the time she reached the front yard.

Toni stood shivering on the lawn, wondering if she could get a lawyer good enough to convince a jury that killing Lincoln had been an act of both personal and national defense.

At last she stopped herself from shaking. She wasn't going to lose Miranda. She turned resolutely, calling to Bertha that she was going out.

Lydia had sounded as if a secret tête-à-tête between them was the most important thing in the universe at the moment.

The Palm Pilot was a maybe.

Lydia was a definite. And it wouldn't do to keep her waiting.

Lydia noticed Renée's agitation the minute she walked into the club room. Sleek, together, beautiful as Renée always was, today she was wound up tight as a violin string about to break.

Lydia wondered how such an incredible woman put up with her husband's philandering. There were many secrets at Gryphon Gate, as she was discovering. But it was no secret that Jerry Lynch always employed voluptuous maids.

Renée got right to the point. "Lydia, what is it? I have a situation at home with which I must deal, so I haven't much time. Whatever is going on, you must tell me instantly." She paused, lifting a hand to Tiffany. "God, I need a drink! And you—how is it that you're all so calm and pulled together now?" Being Renée, apparently, she couldn't quite help smiling. Or smirking. "Did the police find your attacker?"

Lydia realized that she was calm. Dead calm. She had reacted like an idiot in the basement; being alone and in the dark had fed her general state of paranoia.

"It's all part of the reason I called you," she said quietly. She was embarrassed that she had appeared in church practically in the altogether, but by now she had pulled herself together nicely. She, at least, had thought herself under attack, for heaven's sake; while they'd been acting like maniacs, prancing around the church without any such provocation!

"Okay, go on. Why did you call me?" Renée grew serious and whispered, "Does this have anything to do with the terrible things going on here—the murders, I mean?"

"No—well, I don't think so. Lord, who knows? It's all insane, isn't it?"

"You mean it could have something to do with the murders?" Renée squeaked.

"I mean I don't know. Probably not, but then again, who knows? What I have to say is quite personal."

"To the victim, murder is always personal," mused Renée.

"You're right, of course. Tiffany," Lydia called, "please get Mrs. Lynch a very big drink!"

"Lydia, talk."

"I will—just a minute. Ah, here comes Toni." She raised her voice again. "And a drink for Mrs. Sinclair, too, please."

Toni sidled through the tables to join them. "Thanks, I needed that!" she murmured, slipping into one of the chairs.

Renée squirmed in her chair. "All right, I don't begin to understand what's going on here, but I haven't much time," she warned.

"We've one more coming." Lydia said, sensing her friend's growing agitation.

Tiffany arrived with the drinks. Both Toni and Renée instantly picked up their glasses and downed them in a swallow. Lydia felt a strange and supreme sense of power.

"I believe the ladies need another," she said pleasantly to Tiffany.

"Certainly, it's been that kind of day!" Tiffany said cheerfully.

"Think *you* might have had something to do with that, dear?" Renée inquired of the bartender politely, the slightest edge to her voice.

Tiffany took no offense, merely laughing delightedly as she walked away to procure another round of drinks.

"Lydia!" Renée warned again.

"Wait. We've one more coming."

"Who now?" Toni demanded.

"Rachel."

"Rachel?" Renée protested. "The poor dear is still in mourning. She hasn't even buried her husband yet."

"Being out and about has been good for her, I think," Lydia said. "I understand that she was here earlier and seemed quite able to discuss everything that went on in church. Ah, and there we are. She's just walked in."

The three women watched as Rachel Vormeister made her way to them. As Lydia had predicted, she seemed amazingly calm, completely pulled together.

"How are you doing, dear?" Toni asked, showing her concern. Lydia had noticed that Toni hadn't stayed for coffee hour after church. But she'd had her daughter to deal with, of course.

"I think I'm still in denial, actually," Rachel said, sitting. She smiled. "My brother is here, and my mother is visiting, of course, and that helps. Although, God knows, it seems to me that Aaron is acting as strangely as everyone else! The young are usually so resilient, but a murder in the family . . ." She swallowed hard.

"Rachel, I'm so sorry." Renée patted her hand. "As I told you earlier, you know that my sympathies are with you." Renée turned to Lydia. "But now I've got a situation, and I can't deal with it until I find out what has Lydia all knotted up!"

"What situation?" Toni asked sharply.

Renée waved a hand in the air. "Nothing I can talk about right now."

"Difficulties with Jerry?" Toni suggested, watching Renée intently.

"Good heavens, no!" Renée protested, blushing profusely.

Thou dost protest too much! Lydia thought.

But Toni seemed intent on getting to the reason. "Is there something wrong at your house?" she demanded.

"Wrong? Like what?"

"I don't know. Poor Lydia was attacked. Maybe somebody broke in? To steal something?"

Renée lowered her head, setting her empty glass clumsily on the table. Suddenly the ever-efficient Tiffany appeared with the next round.

Reaching for a fresh drink, Renée nearly toppled Tiffany's tray.

"Oh, my God! You *were* robbed!" Toni declared.

"No!" Renée protested. She stared at Toni. "Why? Were *you* robbed?"

Toni took her drink, staring suspiciously at Lydia. "I—I don't know. Perhaps I'll have to go home and find out."

"Robbed! *Here*—at Gryphon Gate!" Tiffany cried with horror. Then, staring at Rachel, she seemed chagrined. "Of course, murder is far, far worse. So, I suppose, if there can be murder, there can be robbery," she finished lamely.

Rachel Vormeister stared blankly at the girl for a few seconds, shook her head, then smiled at Tiffany. "Thank you so much, dear. I think that will be all for the moment." She pointedly sipped her drink. Tiffany, abashed, awkwardly departed.

"Okay," Renée said. "Jerry and I are as happy as clams, and no one was robbed."

"So what is the problem?" Toni persisted.

"If you must know, girls, I'm firing the maid!" Renée said impatiently. "I need to get back to the house and make sure she's cleared out. So, Lydia, *please*, out with it!"

Lydia leaned over the table. "I know who attacked me."

"You do?" Rachel said.

"Have him arrested!" Toni interrupted. Then she hesitated. "Maybe he's the murderer, too." She glanced unhappily at Rachel.

"I don't think he came to attack me," Lydia said. "I think I overreacted," she admitted.

Renée leaned back, shaking her head. "Lydia, for the love of God, will you get to the point?"

"There was something, you see, that I remembered afterwards. Eyes. Eyes staring at me—from what I *thought* was a ski mask. It's May, of course. Nobody'd be wearing a ski mask in May. Silly of me to think so."

"Lydia, is your runaway imagination part of this?" Renée demanded.

"In a way, yes."

"Eyes," Toni murmured.

"Good lord!" Renée exclaimed. "What do eyes have to do with anything? Will someone please make sense of this!"

"Well," Lydia continued, "when I thought about the eyes I had seen, after I calmed down, had a few drinks . . . ."

"Great!" Renée groaned. "You've called us here because you had too many drinks."

"She's getting to the point," Toni said. "Listen to her."

"It was the doctor. Dr. Charles Jefferson."

"What?" Renée said incredulously. "Lydia, why on earth would your gynecologist break into your house to attack you?"

"Besides, nobody's supposed to be allowed in the gates," Rachel added.

"Right. Well, he got in somehow."

"Great security," Renée muttered.

"The best," Toni said, her tone hollow.

"I'm totally lost," Rachel said.

Renée stared at Rachel then. "He's your doctor, too, isn't he? And . . ."

"And I'm pregnant, yes. I was so delighted, but now . . ." Her voice broke. "Sigmond will never see his baby."

"He wouldn't have seen *his* baby in any case," Lydia said in a whisper.

"What?" Rachel looked up, confused.

Toni was staring at Lydia. *"That's* why she's called us all here?" She gaped at the other two women. "Once, I mentioned the extraordinary and beautiful eyes of some of our children," she said, looking to Lydia once again. *"Green* eyes."

"Green eyes. Like those of the man I had assumed to be my attacker," Lydia said.

Renée suddenly turned pale. "What are you getting at?"

"I'm getting at the fact that too many children in Gryphon Gate have extraordinarily beautiful green eyes," Lydia said.

Renée gasped. "You mean—are you trying to say—no, that's not possible."

"I'm trying to say that all our children apparently are related to our 'miraculous' doctor, the good Charles Jefferson. And I'm willing to bet that when Rachel's baby is born, it will have the same green eyes."

Rachel gasped, a horrible sound.

"What—what—do you think he did?" Renée asked, her voice trembling. She seemed to have forgotten her urgent situation at home for the moment. "You mean that, in the artificial insemination thing he—he substituted his own...? How could this have happened?"

Toni let out a sound. Dry, deep, and incredibly scornful. They all stared at her.

She lifted her glass. "Well, ladies, I'm not sure how it worked with you. But when I was desperate for a child and went to his office, well, I just decided to solve it the simple way the doctor suggested."

"Charles Jefferson was your OB-GYN when you had Miranda?" Rachel said slowly.

Toni nodded. "He was younger then—not such a hotshot as he is now."

"And what, pray tell, was your simple way? The way the doctor suggested?" Renée demanded.

Toni smiled then, honestly amused. "Ladies, I simply screwed the man." She leaned forward again. "Why don't we be honest here? Share and share alike, that's what I always say."

Rachel fell back in her chair as if she'd been slapped. "Oh, how could you even *suggest* such a thing?" she wailed.

Lydia shot to her feet and wrapped her arms around her sobbing friend. She glared at Toni. "That was cruel."

Toni lowered her eyes. "I know. I'm sorry. I don't know what came over me. It's just that you're all so *serious* about this foolishness. Surely you can't believe that a prominent doctor like . . ."

But the three women would never learn what Toni thought of the prominent Doctor Jefferson because suddenly, from the area of the bar, came a bloodcurdling scream.

10

TIFFANY SAT ON THE CHEST freezer in the storeroom behind the clubhouse bar and watched Danny lean closer to her, his red hair bright in the dim light. "Damn, that was funny," he said, and put his hand on her thigh.

Clearly, the light wasn't the only dim thing in the storeroom. Tiffany smacked him hard on the back of the head.

"Hey!" he said, ducking away.

"You know, Danny," Tiffany said, "I don't ask for much. Just that you do what I tell you to when I tell you to do it. And, yet, here we are with this mess."

"I did too do what you told me." Danny rubbed his head. "Hell, we all did."

"At what point did I tell you to dope the congregation?"

"Oh, come on." Danny grinned at her. "That Laura woman acted like she had God on speed dial, and then she kept a flask in the choir stall. Did you see her go for the rum on the altar? It was a no-brainer."

"Which explains your participation. Give it." Tiffany held out her hand and Danny passed over a small brown bottle. "This," she said, holding it up, "is a controlled substance. It is illegal. You could get busted for this, Danny. That would be bad."

"You don't need to act like I'm dumb," Danny said. "Tell you what, I've got a joint, let's . . ."

"Yeah, that's exactly what I need," Tiffany said. "Because the loons that populate this place aren't weird enough already, I should get stoned to improve the experience. No." She took a deep breath to get the irritation out of her voice. "Now explain to me why Tyrone went mental on Toni Sinclair and Parker Upshaw yelled at Jerry Lynch."

Danny frowned. "Toni who? The hottie with the kid?" He shrugged. "Tyrone said somebody paid him to spook her. I don't know about the other guy."

Tiffany grew still. "Somebody paid him? Who did he tell about the service?"

Danny shrugged. "Nobody. The guy must have known we were coming, because Tyrone found a fifty dollar bill in his costume pocket and a note telling him what she looked like and to say something about people being out to get her."

Which meant, Tiffany knew, that "the guy" had to be one of two people: the Reverend Peter Armbruster, who'd called her at the crack of dawn and asked her to provide emergency religion for his congregation, or the man she'd been in bed with when Armbruster called. *Jason, you opportunistic rat,* she thought, not without admiration. "And do we still have this note, Danny?"

"No," Danny said. "At least I don't."

"Okay." Tiffany took a deep breath. "Okay." She slid off the freezer, trying to look bright and cheerful. "I appreciate the favor you and the rest of the troupe did for me, great job. Now it's time you left."

"Left?" Danny looked even more cluelessly cherubic than usual.

"Departed. Went elsewhere. Became absent."

Danny's face darkened. "Hey, wait a minute, I thought that you and me . . ."

"You keep making that mistake, Danny," Tiffany said. "Don't think. It's not your area of expertise."

"Hey," Danny said.

Tiffany waited for a moment and then realized that that was his entire comeback. Right. This was Danny she was talking to, not Jason. "Look, honey, your performance was great. You have a huge future; I thought so when I saw you at the comedy club in Annapolis, that's why I hired you for this gig, and you were so amazing this morning that I think it's time you went to Chicago."

"Chicago?" Danny said, still not following, but visibly perked up by the "your performance was great."

"Second City," Tiffany said. "You're ready to leave this two-bit coast and head west." She reached up on the shelf over the freezer and took down her purse. "Go to Chicago and audition. It's time. I even have your ticket." She pulled the airline folder out and gave it to him. He opened it, still looking confused, so she gave him a hint. "It's your ticket to the big time, Danny."

"Wow," Danny said. Then he looked closer. "This is for today. This is for *this afternoon.*"

"Tomorrow's Monday," Tiffany said. "You want to be there bright and early to audition, right? You fly in tonight, get some sleep, plan your strategy."

Danny frowned.

"*Rehearse,*" Tiffany said, "and you'll be in. When opportunity knocks, Danny, you open the door."

"Right," Danny said.

The next job I do, Tiffany told herself, *I'm going to work with people who can understand words of more than one syllable.*

"But what about us?" Danny said. "You and me? We never—"

"I'll wait for you, Danny," Tiffany said, putting a thrill in her voice.

"Yeah." Danny moved toward her.

"No." Tiffany stepped back, one hand blocking him, the other over her heart. "I can't bear it. Just go, and leave me with my memories." *Like, you kiss like a fish.*

"I'll be back." Danny saluted her and went out the back door.

"God, I hope not," Tiffany said, and was considering ways to worm the information she needed out of Jason when she heard the scream.

Across town at the police station, Diane Robards tossed the file on the desk in front of Leland Ford and said, "We're missing the big picture here."

"Okay." Leland leaned back and put his hands behind his head. It did nice things for his black T-shirt, which Diane was pretty sure he knew. "What's the big picture?"

"Vormeister was killed and dumped in the sand trap," Diane said. "Who benefits?"

"Anybody who told Vormeister a secret and regretted it later." Leland yawned. "We did this. You're just pissed because somebody cleared his Palm Pilot."

"That hasn't made my day any better," Diane said, sinking into her desk chair. "But they'd been telling him secrets for years. Why kill him now? What suddenly made him dangerous? Was he threatening them? You knew him. Did he change suddenly?"

"No. He was talking about writing a book, but he wasn't threatening anybody."

Leland stretched again and Diane thought, *He's not showing off, he's tired.* This case was probably the biggest thing he'd ever been involved with. He'd probably been working round the clock, trying to make it his big break. *I'd have done the same thing at his age,* she thought. "Tell me about Vormeister," she said, to give him an in. "What was he like?"

Leland stifled a yawn. "Well, he wasn't the kind of guy who hurt people. He was like one of those guys who takes cars apart just to see how they work. He'd talk to you, and you'd tell him everything because he really wanted to know. And as long as I've known him, he never told me anything about anybody here."

"He has all this information, he's practically the father confessor of Gryphon Gate, and he never tells anybody?" Diane shook her head. "He must have told his wife."

"Nah," Leland said. "Nice woman, but she's one of the biggest gossips we've got. Anything he told her would have been all over the place. That's probably why he kept his notebooks in code."

"Did we get anything from those notebooks?" Diane said.

"You left them at the house," Leland said, rubbing the back of his head.

Diane sat up. "What?"

Leland shrugged. "I thought it was dumb, but the techs left the notebooks at the house."

"Oh, for crying out loud," Diane said and picked up the phone. When she hung up a few minutes later, she said, "They didn't take them because they couldn't read them. Idiots. We're going to have to go get them."

"Well, it's a fair bet nobody else can read them either," Leland shrugged. "We're at a dead end."

"No, we're not. Send them over to the Defense Intelligence Agency at Fort Meade. It might take awhile, but if DIA can't decipher them, nobody can." Diane took a paper out of the file. "And we've got this: Jordan found a handkerchief at the scene with an *A* monogram."

"We don't have anybody—"

"Anka, Aaron, or either of the Armbrusters," Diane said, "but they don't strike me as the monogrammed-handkerchief type. My money's on Toni Sinclair. Toni, short for Antoinette. Toni, who is also blocking the development, which is the only money I see in this picture. Toni, who also was singled out in that ridiculous church service this morning."

Leland began to look more wide-awake. "I don't think Toni Sinclair would—"

"Three of them," Diane said, overriding him so she wouldn't have to hear him defend that label-flaunting twit. "Gervase, Jerry, and Toni. Why those three?"

"You think God is trying to tell us something?" Leland said. "Maybe you shouldn't work on Sundays."

"I think somebody is trying to tell them something," Diane said. "Maybe not Gervase, since it's long past time somebody told him to keep his pants on. But the other two? I think they told Vormeister something they regretted."

"Okay, say that's true," Leland said. "What was Lance McClintock doing in this mess?"

"My favorite part." Diane picked up another folder and took out a fax. "Jordan found this in his desk." She passed the fax across to Leland and watched while he read it.

"Barbi in San Diego?" he said, handing it back. "I don't—"

"McClintock married a Barbara Clegg in San Diego forty years ago," Diane said. "That's the only marriage he has on record."

"So he's not married to Camille? I can't see him killing over that."

"It's not addressed to him," Diane said. "It's addressed to Barbi at his and Camille's fax number. And I don't think *he* was Barbi."

"Camille got the fax?" Leland began to look less skeptical. "And the colonel intercepted it. He was definitely the kind of man who'd protect his wife at all costs. And the guy served tours in every war in the last half century, so he'd know how to do it. But I don't see him dumping Vormeister's body in a sand trap."

"Big picture," Diane said. "Here's what I think. Camille tells Vormeister her secret, whatever it is. Vormeister passes it on to X. Then X sends Camille a poison-pen fax just to watch her squirm, the same thing he or she did with the others. But this time McClintock gets it, knows that the only person Camille would talk to is the person everybody talks to, and confronts Vormeister. Vormeister is appalled, tells McClintock he wouldn't do that, which McClintock already knows. So, he says, who did you tell? Vormeister goes to confront X, X knows Gryphon Gate would never forgive a poison-pen, so X kills Vormeister to keep the whole thing from blowing up in his or her face. Then he or she waits for McClintock by the pool, since that's where McClintock always goes to smoke, hits him with a taser, beats him to death, and walks off into the dark."

"A taser?" Leland said.

"The autopsies showed identical marks on the bodies, small puncture wounds about four inches apart. Whoever killed them stunned them with a taser first and then smashed in their skulls while they were helpless."

"No." Leland looked ill. "We have a real assortment of wackos here, but nobody that nuts."

Diane shook her head. "I don't think whoever did this is nuts. I think she is just very determined to protect her secret."

"She?" Leland said.

Diane shrugged. "Or he."

Leland looked at the fax again. "Why didn't McClintock tell us about this? Oh. Right. Protecting his wife." He pushed himself out of his chair. "Okay, let's go talk to Camille McClintock."

"Not just Camille," Diane said. "Those three who were targeted in the church? What do you want to bet those weren't just public faxes?"

"Four poison-pen victims?" Leland nodded. "Those nuts don't usually stop with just one, do they?"

"They usually don't stop with just four." Diane got up and grabbed her suede jacket from the back of her desk chair. It had been her favorite until Toni Sinclair had looked at it with such contempt. Diane shook the jacket out and could almost hear Toni sneering, "Off the rack."

"Something wrong with your jacket?" Leland said.

"No," Diane said and shrugged it on. "This is a great jacket. Let's go get those notebooks."

And after that they were going to go make Toni Sinclair's Sunday even more miserable than it already was.

When Tiffany got to the bar, Babs Blackburn had stopped screaming and was pointing to the pretzel dish in horror.

"Oh, jeez, Ms. Blackburn, what's wrong?" Tiffany said, back in bubblehead mode.

"That," Babs said, looking like an expensive deer caught in headlights.

Beside the pretzel dish sat a little green frog, its red toes gripping the bar, paralyzed with terror. Its eyes bugged out, giving it a striking resemblance to Babs.

"Oh, that's just a tree frog," Tiffany said. "They're all over out here." She went over to the bar, scooped the little thing up, and took it to the terrace doors to set it free. *Wrong wetlands, frog,* she thought as she goosed it in the direction of the golf course.

"That's the scariest thing I've ever seen," Babs said, easing her way back to the bar and to Vanessa, which proved Babs had no sense of self-preservation, since the tree frog couldn't hurt her, but Vanessa had been known to make grown men weep with terror.

"You and me both," Vanessa said, not looking scared at all. "Little bastards are making my life hell. Tell me you killed it."

"Sure," Tiffany lied. "Now, how about another martini?"

"We'll have our next one at dinner." Vanessa slid off her bar stool. "Ready, Babs?"

Babs had evidently unearthed a buried instinct, because she was now looking at Vanessa as though she were another, bigger red-toed frog, but she nodded and followed her fiancé's ex-wife into the dining room and certain disaster.

Always go with your instincts, Babs, Tiffany thought. *Aside from your boobs, they're pretty much all you've got.* When Babs and Vanessa were safely out of sight, Tiffany looked around the bar and saw only a threesome at a table across the room—Toni Sinclair, Renée Lynch, and Rachel Vormeister—completely absorbed in their conversation, now that Babs wasn't screaming anymore.

Tiffany took out her cell phone and hit her least-favorite number on her speed dial. "It's me," she said when the ringing stopped.

"Interesting morning." The voice on the other end was dry, low, and disinterested.

"One of my freelancers got creative," Tiffany said.

"Explain."

"Danny doped Laura Armbruster, who then took it upon herself to bust Roman Gervase's chops."

"Why?"

Tiffany leaned on the shelf behind the bar, keeping a wary eye on the threesome. "My guess is Laura was either trying to cure him of his werewolfism, or trying to get him to stay home with his wife so she'll stop boffing Laura's husband. It's hard to tell with Laura."

"And Toni Sinclair?"

Tiffany stifled the urge to ask, "How did you know that?" Her client always knew everything. "She was set up. Either Peter Armbruster wanted her warned, or my buddy Jason is jerking her chain. One of them paid that idiot Tyrone to scare her. But that doesn't explain why Parker Upshaw would go ape and bust Jerry Lynch."

"Jason. That would be your book-editing friend, Mr. Salinger."

"If Jason Salinger is a book editor," Tiffany said, "I'm a virgin."

"We believe Mr. Salinger placed a call to Mr. Upshaw this morning shortly after the reverend called you."

"He did?" Tiffany faked a heartbroken sigh. "Here I've given him all my trust and devotion for two whole months, and this is how he repays me. Romance is dead."

"So are Doctor Vormeister and Colonel McClintock. Do you have any information that ties those deaths to our problem?"

"Not directly, no," Tiffany said. "The waters here are murky, so it's hard to tell. But Parker Upshaw is Senator Carbury's best buddy. I wonder what Jason has on Upshaw that could make him threaten Toni Sinclair?"

"Perhaps you could ask him."

"Sure. Then you can pull my body out of the Potomac. Do you

think Jason sent those faxes inviting people to the church? Because, if so, I'm impressed with his ability to see into the future. Nobody knew we were doing the service until Armbruster called me this morning."

"We believe that your new friend Anka sent the invitation faxes in order to have access to the empty houses."

"Well, that would explain why she slipped out the back when the fun started. She must have thought that mess was a gift from God. How many houses did she hit?"

"We believe three."

"We believe." Tiffany's exasperated sigh went straight into the phone. "Do we *know* anything?"

"Mr. Salinger sent a message to Senator Carbury asking him to meet Mrs. Sinclair on her boat yesterday, and he signed her name to it, then alerted Detective Robards that there would be an assignation."

Tiffany straightened. "Carbury again."

"Yes. It is gratifying to finally draw close to our problem, isn't it?"

"Why would Jason want Carbury caught by the cops on Toni's boat?"

"Exactly. And why would your Mayor Drysdale be so interested in Senator Carbury that he'd watch from a helicopter with a surveillance expert by his side?"

Tiffany rolled her eyes. "Don't read too much into that. He was probably hoping Carbury was meeting Vanessa there so he could catch her bribing a politician and have her executed. Honest to God, these people are—" She broke off as Roman Gervase came in from the golf course. "Well, hi there, Mr. Gervase!" she said, letting the hand with the cell fall behind the bar.

"Set me up a whiskey sour, Tiffany," Roman said, passing by her on his way to the bathroom. "I'll be right out."

"That would be our surveillance expert?" the dry voice on the phone said when Tiffany picked up the phone again.

"And local werewolf," Tiffany said, keeping an eye on the door. "You know, it occurs to me that being thought of as the local nutcase would not necessarily be a bad thing for a surveillance expert. He could go anywhere he wanted at night, and, as long as he howled, people might not see what he was up to."

"People see what they want to see."

"Not me," Tiffany said as the rest of Roman's foursome staggered in. "I see dull people." She beamed at the newcomers, uniformly covered in plaid and sweat. "Gee, you guys look like you played hard!" *And got put away wet.* "I have to go, Mom," she said into the phone as they settled in at the bar.

"Do not call me 'Mom.'"

"And give little Bobby and Gail big hugs for me."

"Tiffany."

"Yes?"

"Be very, very careful with Jason Salinger."

"I will," she said and made a kissing noise into the phone. "Bye now."

"That's really nice," one of Roman's golf buddies said to her as he looked at her T-shirt. "Calling your mother."

"Well, I'm an old-fashioned girl," Tiffany said and picked up the martini shaker ready to pour.

And listen.

When Toni got home, she dropped her purse on the hall table and went out to the kitchen to see if she had chocolate chips. Of course she had chocolate chips. She had a Viking range, she had a Sub-Zero refrigerator, she fed endangered deer, she entertained senators to save the wildlife and her lifestyle, so she sure as hell had chocolate chips somewhere. She was rummaging through Bertha's baking cupboard when she noticed the back door was ajar and heard a chair scrape behind her.

She turned and saw Jason Salinger sitting at the granite-topped island and screamed before she could stop herself.

"Hi, Toni," he said, smiling at her, his deep, rich voice going straight to her bones. "Got your message."

"How'd you get in here?" she said, trying not to shriek at him again.

"Your security stinks," he said. "But then, it always did. What do you want?"

He looked the same as he had two years ago, maybe a little heavier, but his dark hair still fell over his forehead, his eyes were still hot behind his wire-rimmed glasses, and he could still turn her on even while he terrified her. Which meant he was probably still the same immoral opportunist who'd do anything and anybody to get his way.

Thank God. Now all she had to do was convince him he was in danger, too, and he'd take care of the bastard with the fax machine. She leaned across the island, trying to look earnest and appealing. "Somebody's sending me threatening faxes. Saying they know about you. About *us*. You're in danger, Jason. That's why I wanted you to meet me at the boat where it's private, so we could figure out a way to fix this. I know you can fix this."

"Well, honey, I went to the boat, but when I got there, you were entertaining a branch of the legislature." Jason grinned at her and she lost her breath. The bastard still had it. "Good to know you've become politically active," he said.

Toni narrowed her eyes. Hot or not, he was up to something. In fact, she was pretty sure he'd sent Carbury that invitation to the boat and signed her name instead of coming himself. *Don't accuse him,* she told herself. *You need him.*

"I try to do my part to protect the environment," she said. "Just like *we* did two years ago, protecting the helpless. Lincoln was a pervert. He targeted children on the Internet. You were right to kill him, it was a duty as a human being—"

Jason's face hardened, and Toni realized how much he'd changed. *Not a boy anymore,* she thought, and wondered what he'd learned since the last time she'd been with him.

"Tell me," Jason said softly, "that you haven't said that to anybody else."

"*Of course not,*" Toni came around the island and grabbed his arm and felt the muscle there tighten under her grip. That hadn't changed either. "But it's a defense for both of us. If this—"

"Okay." Jason detached her hand from his arm, and she stepped back, stung as much by the flat tone in his voice as by his rejection of her touch. "First, talking dirty to cheerleaders on the Internet is not a death penalty offense, especially since most of the cheerleaders he was talking to were probably other middle-aged men."

Toni blinked at him. "Jason, I—"

"It amazes me how delusional people are about things like that," Jason went on, looking at her with barely disguised contempt. "It never occurs to them that, since they're lying about who they are, the person on the other end is probably lying, too. Or that since they're cheating, their spouses are probably cheating, too."

Toni stepped back again. *"Jason—"*

"Or that meeting senators for trysts on their boats while the cops watch leaves them vulnerable to gossip, or even prosecution, for bribing with sexual favors."

Toni froze. The bastard *had* set her up.

Jason leaned closer. "Or that the people they're warning about danger might be the people they should be afraid of. So, I repeat, I don't know what you're talking about, but I suspect that you're trying to implicate me in something you did long ago. Are you taping this, Toni? Are you admitting to your husband's murder?"

Toni took another step back and hit the counter behind her. "I'm telling you, *somebody knows about us.* Not me, *us,* Jason."

"Then you're in trouble." Jason stood up. "I'm really sorry, Toni, you seem upset, but there is no us and this has nothing to do with me. I came out here for old time's sake, but with you raving like this, I'm afraid I'm going to have to ask you not to call me again." His voice softened. "You really should get professional help, Toni. I know you've been through a lot, but if you keep sharing these paranoid delusions with people, you could lose everything."

"You could take care of whoever it is," Toni said, making one last desperate play on his vanity. "You can find out who he is and take care of him. You took care of Lincoln. You can do *anything.*" She leaned closer to him and then heard footsteps in the hall.

"I can leave." Jason stepped away from her. "And I can tell you that if you ever call me again, you'll be sorry."

"Jason—"

"Mommy!" Miranda threw herself through the door of the kitchen, a picture in starched green gingham and perky grosgrain bows. "Are we going to make cookies now?" She stopped, her perfect little mouth open, when she saw Jason. "Hello."

"Hello," Jason said, smiling at her. "You must be Miranda."

"Yep." Miranda hopped to the island on one foot, clearly scarred by her experience in church that morning. "Are you going to make cookies?"

"I've made enough cookies in my life," Jason said, looking at Toni.

"After a while you want something a little more substantial. Which I now have. And which I am keeping." His eyes narrowed at Toni. "I mean it. If you'd like to keep what you have, don't call again."

"What are you—"

"You have as much to lose as I do, and I'm not just talking about your reputation in the community." Jason nodded at Miranda and Toni felt her breath go.

"You wouldn't," Toni said.

"Of course I wouldn't," he said. "I would never hurt anybody. I never have. Have I?"

The silence stretched out between them as he stared into her eyes, paralyzing her, a rabbit to his snake.

"No," she said.

He patted Miranda on the head. "Your mommy's a smart woman." Then he walked past Toni to the open back door, leaving without another word.

"He didn't say good-bye," Miranda said. "That's not nice."

"He's not a nice man," Toni said, staring after him. *The bastard,* walking into her house uninvited, setting her up, turning her down.

"We're nice, aren't we?" Miranda said, hopping again. "People like us."

Miranda lived in such a simple world. *And it's going to stay that way,* Toni thought. She was not the kind of woman people suspected of paranoid delusions. She drove a Mercedes, she kept time with a Rolex, she wore Escada, damn it. He was not going to ruin her life. She'd do whatever it took to stop him, to protect her life, to . . .

Miranda said, "Mommy?"

To protect her child. She was a good mother. Any good mother would do anything to protect her child. Even if Jason Salinger was smart and tricky as hell, he wasn't immortal. And at this point nobody would be surprised if another body turned up in Gryphon Gate.

"People like us, don't they?" Miranda said, switching to the other foot.

"Yes, sweetie," Toni said. "We're popular."

And we're going to stay that way.

* * *

"I can't believe McClintock married a hooker," Diane said as they drove away from the Vormeister house. "I can't believe Camille McClintock *was* a hooker."

"Hey, she was sixteen; he was twenty, about to ship off for 'nam, I can see it," Leland said. "He was big on saving people, he saved her, she loved him for the rest of her life. I think it's romantic."

"Romantic," Diane said. "So how many times *did* you see *Pretty Woman?*"

"I'm just saying—"

"I know, he died trying to protect her," Diane said. "He's one of the good guys."

"He was," Leland said. "Let's get the guy who killed him."

Diane turned down Toni's street. "I wouldn't count on it being a guy."

"Somebody pretty hefty got Vormeister's body into that sand trap," Leland said. "And there were some strong guys on Aaron's list. Jerry Lynch could have done it."

"Aaron's list," Diane said. "There's another problem. I got the definite feeling that Aaron might have thoughts of turning a profit on those notebooks."

"Blackmail?" Leland said. "Is he that dumb, to try blackmail when somebody is killing to keep a secret?"

"Money makes people stupid," Diane said as she pulled into Toni's driveway. "And once they've got it, they'll do a lot to keep it." She waved her hand at Toni's mansion. "Mrs. Sinclair does not strike me as the type to willingly downgrade to smaller quarters."

"Boy, you've really got it in for her," Leland said.

Diane opened her door and got out, trying to loathe Toni Sinclair for her many deficiencies and not because Leland was defending her.

Leland got out and slammed his door. "You know, we have no evidence she's guilty of anything."

"Sure we do," Diane said as she headed for the house. "The way she dresses her kid is a crime."

Tiffany hit the fourth-floor landing of her fifth-floor walk-up and saw Jason sitting on the top step by her apartment, his trademark lock of dark brown hair falling over his brow, his eyes deceptively sweet behind his wire-rimmed glasses. "Jason!" she said, and went to him wondering if he'd killed anybody lately.

He leaned down and kissed her firmly, his hand light on her cheek. He definitely kissed better than Danny. Of course, carp kissed better than Danny. "You rat," she said against his mouth. "You told me you had to leave and wouldn't be back until next weekend."

"I couldn't leave you," he said, that rich, dark voice oozing over her. He shifted on the stair, and she sat beside him as he slid a warm arm around her. "Besides, I wanted to know how it went this morning. It sounded like it was going to be a hoot."

"Oh, that's romantic." Tiffany pouted. "You only come to me for laughs."

"I come to you because you're irresistible," Jason said, his eyes fixed on her lower lip. "Can we go inside? Your stairwell smells like garbage."

Imagine how bad it'd be if I really lived in a place called Umbanda House, she thought, but she kept the pout in her voice as she said, "You'll have to do better than that. I've had a very hard day."

"Really." Jason grinned an invitation at her. "Let me in and make me a drink, and you can tell me what happened in the land of the rich and ridiculous."

That's what you really want, Tiffany thought, and then he leaned in and kissed her again, and she thought, *Well, that and sex.*

Fifteen minutes later she was settled in her chair with an orange juice laced with water that Jason thought was vodka. He, on the other hand, was drinking real bourbon.

"So," he said, sitting down on her dilapidated couch across from her. "What happened at the church? Did the comedy group do their thing?"

"Oh, they just beat some drums and danced around and said stupid things." Tiffany bent over to put her drink on the floor and waited to see whether the church or her cleavage would get his attention.

Jason raised an eyebrow. "Stupid things?"

So much for cleavage. Tiffany got up and moved to the couch. If he wanted information, he was going to have to work for it. "I don't want to talk about them, Jason. Tell me I'm beautiful and I'll forgive you."

"You're beautiful," Jason said and kissed her. "So what did they say?"

"Hmmm?" Tiffany smiled up at him, projecting inanity. "Oh, Parker Upshaw yelled at Jerry Lynch that the church had a bug in it."

"A bug?" Jason said, looking innocent.

"A roach," Tiffany said, and Jason started to laugh. "Hey, roaches aren't funny. They're really hard to get rid of."

"Oh, just call them something else and they go away," Jason said, clearly amusing himself. "What else?"

"One of the guys said something to that nice Mrs. Sinclair," Tiffany said. "Which is ridiculous, because she's so good that she's all right-to-life for animals and save the whales. Or at least the deer and the swans." Tiffany smiled at him and then sat up, galvanized by an idea. "Oh. Wait. Those PETA people do terrible things sometimes. Do you suppose she's the murderer?"

"I don't know." Jason sat back. "She'd have to be unbalanced."

"I bet she would to save the deer," Tiffany said, working dumb blondity with everything she had. "The colonel was going to shoot the deer and drown the swans or something. Maybe she thought it was her duty to kill him."

Jason shrugged. "She must be nuts. Better keep an eye on her. Those kind will do anything."

Tiffany let her shoulders slump. *Boy, you* are *out to get her.* "That wouldn't explain Mr. Vormeister though. So I guess not. He was always taking notes on people, but Toni doesn't have any secrets, she's all perfect mother and citizen of the year." She smiled at him. "Which is a good thing, because otherwise she'd be really suspicious, don't you think?"

"I think I don't care." He pulled her back to him and kissed her.

"Oh, Jason, you're so good at this," she whispered in his ear, telling him the truth for the first time that day.

The phone rang and she started to get up, but Jason caught her. "Let the machine get it," he said, and she giggled and let him pull her back down onto the couch. Behind them the phone rang again and again while Jason's hands moved over her. The machine clicked on, her message played, and then she heard a no-nonsense voice say, "Tiffany, this is Detective Diane Robards."

Tiffany jerked away and sat up as Robards gave her contact

information and asked her to call. She met Jason's eyes and he nodded, so she picked up the phone.

"Detective Robards, it's Tiffany," she said. "What's up?"

"I understand you were friends with Anka Kovacik?"

Were? *And another one bites the dust.* If somebody didn't quit killing off all her leads, she was never going to finish the job. "I just met her a couple of days ago," she said, and then paused, pretending that the verb tense was just sinking in. "What do you mean, were? I still am. I mean, I still know her."

"We just found her in Toni Sinclair's koi pond," Diane said. "Weighted down by a lot of jewelry and a bag of deer chow. She floated to the top when the deer chow dissolved. I'm at the Sinclair house now, so if you could—"

"I'll be right there," Tiffany said and hung up. She sniffed once and turned back to Jason, her face crumpling in grief. "A friend of mine was just *murdered,*" she told him, and he stood up and put his arms around her. "It's so *awful.*"

"I'll wait here for you," he said and kissed her cheek. "You go find out what happened." His warm eyes smiled into hers, and she thought, *You are good, sonny, but you're not asking any questions, which is just not human nature. What do you know about a drowned bimbo thief?*

"Thank you, Jason," she said, letting her lip tremble. "It means a lot to me to know you'll be here." *And not out murdering any more of the population.*

"I'll always be here for you, honey," Jason said. "You go find out what's happening and then come back and tell me all about it."

"All right," Tiffany said, pretty sure she wouldn't be reporting anything he didn't already know. *Men,* she thought, *you can't trust any of them.*

Then she went out to the Sinclair house to lie to the police.

11

WOULD SOMEONE *PLEASE* GET
the fish away from the body?" Diane said, exasperation showing in
her voice. She was too damned tired to care.

The photographer was capturing Anka in all of her dead glory. Or
at least trying, but the fish kept swimming over the woman's face.
Mostly they were interested in the globs of soggy deer chow floating
on the surface of the water. A leather briefcase was tied haphazardly
to Anka's chest, but it had popped open, possibly in the struggle with
her killer. Jewels winked from rocks, and gold glimmered in the clear
water.

One of two large bags of Purina Mills Deer Chow floated on the
surface, nearly empty. As pellets had spilled from a large split in its
side, it grew too light to keep Anka's lower body pinned down. Her
legs had floated to the surface while the briefcase and a full bag of
congealed pellets still held her face beneath the water.

Diane's team awaited, ready to descend on the scene and find the
tiniest clue to nail the son of a bitch—or just plain bitch—who'd done
this. Diane glanced across the pond at Leland, who was questioning
Bertha, Toni's maid. As though he sensed Diane's gaze, he looked up
and gave her a quick, sympathetic smile before returning his attention to Bertha.

Diane felt a thrill like a shot of espresso dart through her veins. She
touched her hair self-consciously, painfully aware that she probably

looked like she'd been to hell and back. Leland had the nerve to look good, even when he looked tired. She knew she just looked haggard. Damn men.

She steered her thoughts back to the scene. Jordan, her longtime associate, was taking a sample of the water. "What's it look like?" she asked, kneeling beside him.

"At this point, death by drowning. My guess is someone slammed her in the head with a heavy object and rendered her unconscious. There's bruising around her right temple, see?" He pointed to the dollar-size mark. Then he gestured at the many statues around the pool. "Maybe with one of these, which we will determine. Then he— or she—pushed her in the pond, weighed her down with the brief-case, and dragged the bags of chow over for extra insurance." He pointed. Bits of the paper bag on the concrete bore him out. "I suspect she was unconscious until she took her first breath of water," Jordan continued. "We won't be sure until we can get her out of there."

Diane could well imagine the horror of that kind of death. The look on Anka's face didn't help. The photographer signaled that he was done and Diane's team moved in to claim the body. As the body bag zipper slid closed over the victim's blank, sightless eyes, Diane tried to piece together what she knew.

Bertha and Miranda had been making cookies in the kitchen when Bertha heard the pump in the koi pond making strange gur-gling sounds. Luckily, she'd left Miranda in the kitchen while she in-vestigated. The deer chow had been sucked into the pump's intake, jamming the valve. Bertha had noticed the lumps floating on the sur-face seconds before taking in Anka floating just below. After regurgi-tating the cookie dough she'd been nipping from the bowl, she'd returned to the kitchen and called the police. No one had heard a thing, of course. No one had seen a thing.

Diana's headache had increased tenfold. The good thing about another murder, she supposed, was that she had another opportunity to find a clue. Her mother had always taught her to look at the bright side.

Clouds had been building up all day, and now they scooted across the sky with alarming speed. So far, only two waves of light rain had fallen, each lasting a few minutes. More would come, Diane was sure of it.

"Captain Robards," Carnegie said, bringing an older man over to her. She recognized him as Silas Macgruder, neighborhood busybody. A cop loved busybodies.

"I saw a man hanging around here an hour ago," Silas said without preamble. "Young feller, probably in his twenties, medium build, dark hair falling in his face. He knocked on the front door, and when no one answered, walked around to the side. I didn't see him come out."

Diane stemmed her impatience. "Did you think to alert the authorities?"

He nodded toward Carnegie. "I called the security office, left a message. Nobody was there."

Carnegie's face flamed red. "I've been on patrol! You've taken Leland, and that rookie's more interested in checking his profile in the mirror than patrolling. It's put a lot of pressure on me."

Pressure. He didn't know from pressure. Diane ignored Carnegie and turned her steely gaze on Silas. "Did you recognize him at all?" When Silas shook his head, she asked, "Did you see a vehicle?"

"None. Security around here is getting downright lax. Frightening, I'll tell you." He shot a contemptuous look at Carnegie. "Might as well move to a *middle-class* neighborhood."

Diane stemmed an outburst from Carnegie by quickly saying, "Mr. Macgruder, I'll need you to accompany this officer down to the station to give us a description for our sketch artist. You may very well have seen the murderer." *Maybe a triple murderer,* she thought hopefully. Would it be that easy? She was willing to bet that Silas's description would match the one Miranda had given them of the "rude man in the kitchen who didn't say good-bye."

Carnegie was still choking on excuses when Diane rejoined Leland and Bertha.

"I should be inside with Miranda," Bertha complained, wringing her hands. "I'm sure she knows *something's* going on."

The look Leland shot Diane was subtle, but she read him instantly, with a certainty that longtime partners develop. He'd gotten everything he could from Bertha, the look said. She could go inside now.

"Wait," Diane said as soon as Bertha had turned. "One more question. According to your statement, you found the woman in the pond and immediately went back inside to call police. Didn't you check to see if she was still alive?"

Bertha stopped short for a moment, but recovered quickly. "I knew she was dead. I could tell jes' by lookin' at her." She quickly slipped into the house.

Once she was gone, Leland said, "Interesting observation. I would have dragged her out, checked her pulse . . ." He smiled ruefully. ". . . and thoroughly compromised the crime scene."

"Life is more important than evidence," Diane said. "Still, I have to wonder if Bertha simply *knew* she was dead. We never found anything incriminating in her past. Maybe it's time to check deeper. And where is her husband?"

"On a gambling junket in Atlantic City."

"Let's make sure of that. What else did you find out?"

"Ms. Sinclair was home baking cookies with Miranda when Mrs. Upshaw stopped by and said something about seeing Doctor Jefferson in Gryphon Gate. Mrs. Upshaw urged Ms. Sinclair to leave with her. The maid reports that Ms. Sinclair said something to the effect of"—he consulted his notes—"'I have no problem with Doctor Jefferson, other than he was a hotshot and had very little bedside manner, if you know what I mean.' But Mrs. Upshaw said they had to all band together, that he'd taken advantage of her, too, and then she practically dragged Ms. Sinclair out of the house. I sent a couple of men out to look for them. They just spotted Mrs. Upshaw's car at the clubhouse."

"What does Doctor Jefferson have to do with this? How had he taken advantage of Toni and Lydia?"

Leland lifted an eyebrow. "The plot thickens."

"The plot is already as thick as peanut butter. He's not a resident, is he?"

Leland shook his head.

"Then how did he get into Gryphon Gate?"

"We'll have to ask the good doctor ourselves."

"Captain Robards," Carnegie interrupted, apparently over his embarrassment. "Tiffany Turner is here to see you."

Diane shot Leland a look. "Let's see what Tiffany has to say about her new gal pal."

* * *

Dr. Charles Jefferson would never forget the sight of that lifeless woman being shoved beneath the water.

He had seen her murderer.

Now Charles skulked around the edge of the golf course trying to stay out of sight. Damn those faxes! The first one had been a bust, bringing him to Gryphon Gate on a cold blustery morning, only to be stood up. The fax that had come this morning, though, was more specific: *I know about the green-eyed children of Gryphon Gate. It's going to cost you. Meet me by the koi pond in Toni Sinclair's backyard. 2 P.M.*

He almost hadn't gone. What had he gotten out of the first visit, after all, other than a swift kick in the nuts? But then, he'd relented. He'd been amazed, really, that no one had connected the dots on the green eyes before. His best feature, but alas, a giveaway. So he decided to meet with the person, see what they wanted, and figure out how to deal with it.

Once again Charles had parked on Vanessa Smart-Drysdale's property and slogged through underbrush and along the shoreline to Gryphon Gate.

Charles prided himself on being early; he was that rare physician who took his appointments on time, instead of making patients wait— one of the many reasons his patients loved him so. That had probably saved his life. Perhaps it had been *he* the murderer had intended to do away with, and the hapless woman had stumbled into the trap instead. He'd thwarted death, but she'd paid the price.

Yet, he was a skilled professional, far more valuable than any young woman could be. He brought people into the world. He, in fact, helped to create them. Why, he was almost a god!

At the koi pond Charles had had only an instant to weigh his options. Should he pursue the murderer, or try to help the poor victim?

Hippocrates won out.

Charles had rushed to the edge of the pond, but he was too late. The woman was clearly dead. So, Dr. Charles T. Jefferson, M.D., OB-GYN, A.R.T., had turned, and run the other way.

Even now her eyes stared sightlessly, seeming to accuse him.

He needed a drink. Or five. The thought of slogging back through the woods didn't appeal. The nearby clubhouse did. He made his way there, hoping to procure a drink and find a quiet, out-of-the-way table where he could think things through. *Of course* he would go to the police. He was a law-abiding citizen. Well, mostly. But what was his story? He needed to get everything absolutely straight, to think through what he'd seen—and who he'd seen doing it.

The pretty, perky bartender wasn't there to slip him a drink. Pity. Charles ordered something stronger than beer this time—a bourbon straight up, and he brazenly signed the chit with Laura Armbruster's membership number. *It's the least Laura can do,* Charles thought, sipping his drink gratefully, *for a* relative.

Thankfully, there weren't many people in the bar. He recognized two of his patients huddled at a corner table deep in conversation. Luckily they hadn't spotted him. Charles slipped around the corner to a quiet alcove, where he plopped himself down on a plump, upholstered bench, stared out the window at the approaching storm, and considered his options.

Aaron Kaplan was going to take a chance. Just one chance. He deserved it. Ever since old Siggy'd done that faceplant in the sand, Aaron had cooperated with the police. He'd given them Siggy's precious notebook, for heaven's sake.

But Aaron didn't need the notebook for this particular victim, Dr. Charles Jefferson. Maybe he was no Sigmond Vormeister, Ph.D., but Aaron was pretty good at assessing people. Jefferson was a poseur— Aaron hated poseurs—and he was confident the doc wouldn't have the balls to whack him back. He'd probably chew his manicured nails down to the quick, but he'd pay up.

Aaron wasn't greedy. Twenty-five thou for his silence—barely one year's college tuition—and he'd even make up some green-eyed uncle to dash rumors, should there be any, when Rachel had her child. Her pretty little green-eyed child.

Hell, it was a bargain!

Aaron left a message with the doctor's answering service and, hoping that the rain would hold off a bit longer, took a victory skateboard ride through Gryphon Gate. As the wheels on his deck turned, so did the wheels of his mind. His very excellent, devious mind, he amended as he ollied over a curb. He'd hacked into Gryphon Gate's Web site. He could have a lot of fun with what he knew. Oh, yeah, a *lot* of fun.

With his right foot, Aaron pushed his deck up the driveway, then turned, riding backward under the portico. Whoa! Doctor Jefferson was walking into the clubhouse. He nearly collided with the dude! With a practiced move, Aaron kickflipped his deck and caught it with one hand. He tucked it under his arm and headed toward the door.

Laura Armbruster was also heading for the front door, with the determination of a torpedo. Come to think of it, she kind of looked like a torpedo. A hungover torpedo.

Forget manners, he thought as they reached the entrance simultaneously. He straight-armed the door and started through—except he was no longer walking forward.

Mrs. Armbruster had pinched the back of his shirt and was pulling him backward. "Ladies first," she said, pushing her way ahead of him and into the lobby.

"Hang on to your flip-flops," Aaron muttered. Man, she hadn't even noticed his T-shirt—stick figures on decks saying "Don't Bust a Nut." Mrs. A. hated that shirt. She regularly inspected the graphics on his apparel. But not today. Bad vibes! What was going on?

Aaron smoothed out his shirt and followed the club manager inside. Mrs. A. cruised through the bar like a shark on patrol. When her bloodshot eyes lit on the doctor, she made a beeline in his direction. Whoa, dude! The doctor was his. Aaron set his deck on the carpet and tried to skate past her, but the wheels wouldn't budge in the plush pile. He abandoned his deck and raced toward her, aiming to cut her off.

"There he is!" Lydia Upshaw's voice sounded from behind him. She was dragging Toni Sinclair by her striped Missoni sleeve while gesturing to Renée and Rachel, who were sitting at a table in a corner of the bar. The two women jumped up and headed toward the doctor, who was wide-eyed, just realizing he was about to be ambushed.

"I was here first," Laura Armbruster said. "We have, er, church business to discuss."

Aaron nudged her aside. "Take a chilly pilly, Mrs. A. I was here first. I've got . . . a condition I need to talk to him about."

All five women turned toward him. Lydia said, "You have a condition? A condition? He's a *gynecologist!*"

Aaron knew he'd lost this round. Laura rolled her eyes and relieved Charles of his drink. Lydia seized his other arm and began tugging the doctor away. "Ladies, I don't have time right now—"

"I'm next!" Renée said, waving her hand like an eager schoolgirl.

Aaron decided to get urgently scarce. Those women had something pretty serious on their mind. Perhaps even murder, by the glint in their eyes. For another thing, he studied the club manager, who watched the circus for a moment with a tense expression on her face, then turned on her heel and retreated to a nearby bar stool. What exactly did *Mrs. Armbruster* want from the doc?

On second thought, maybe he'd stick around the bar and find out.

Dr. Charles Jefferson didn't like it, not one little bit. His terror grew as his four former patients dragged him out the back door and around the pool, to a table that was blocked from view of the clubhouse by an ornamental stand of bushes. He was sure—at least, mostly sure—he could overpower these women, but he didn't want to. Think of the publicity!

Renée shoved him down into one of the chairs. "We know."

Rachel placed a hand on her small belly and tears filled her eyes. "How could you *do* this to us?"

"We trusted you!" Lydia added, poking her finger into his exceptionally hard chest. Her acrylic nail scraped at his skin.

Toni crossed her arms and said, "You're a very unprofessional man."

"Ladies, what are you talking about?" Charles tried. He was seriously outnumbered, and they knew it.

Lydia and Renée pulled out their wallets and, one by one, tossed photographs at him. From where they landed on the tabletop, three sets of green eyes peered out at him. "And the Anderson boys!" Renée cried. "Thank god they've moved to California!"

"And Rachel's baby, too!" added Lydia.

Rachel burst into tears.

Charles did his best to look contrite. Not an easy task for a man like himself. "All right, so you've figured it out. But why are you all so mad?"

That shut them up—for a few seconds anyway. Rage suffused their faces with color, and they started moving toward him stiffly, like characters in a monster movie. For one insane moment, he tried to stand, but Lydia shoved him back down. "We should report you to the AMA," she snarled.

Renée stared at Lydia as if Lydia's law degree were printed on her forehead. "We could sue," she suggested.

Charles held up a hand. "Ladies, ladies. I've given you beautiful children who may someday grow up to become famous! Doctors and scientists! Politicians! Your children have *excellent* bloodlines, you know. They're related to *the* Thomas Jefferson. Think of it!" He added, "Not that you can actually claim that, of course, but, you'll know in your hearts. You must admit, we all make gorgeous babies together. Right? They are gorgeous, right?"

This wasn't working. Even Rachel looked enraged. Her arm shot out and shoved his chair backward. Luckily the clubhouse used tall-backed, padded chairs, or Charles might have cracked his skull open. Still, he felt less than dignified lying on his back with his legs flailing in the air.

"All right, all right. It was wrong. It was . . . ." Time to drag out his dirty laundry. Perhaps it would save his reputation, if not his life. "My wife will not have my children." When that caught their attention—at least they weren't looking quite as murderous—he continued on in a soft voice full of humility and shame. "It's true. When we married, she said she wanted children. But afterward she refused. She didn't want to ruin her figure or be tied down. Can you understand what that did to me? A man as beautiful as myself, as intelligent . . ."

Toni's eyes narrowed, and he thought steam would shoot out of her ears, so he switched his tack. ". . . as loving and . . . giving, yes giving, as myself, not able to share that with offspring. It broke my heart."

"Why couldn't you just divorce her?" Renée asked, her voice dripping with skepticism.

"She funded my research, my office building—even me. If I left her, she'd have destroyed me." Was he getting through? He couldn't tell.

Lydia's voice was cool, controlled. "Well, now *we're* going to destroy you. DNA tests will prove just who fathered our children."

Rachel was rubbing her belly again. "Is my baby . . . *yours?*"

He couldn't remember. Dammit, he'd gone overboard. He knew that now, but the rush of power must have overtaken him.

"He doesn't even know!" Renée shouted. "His sperm's probably everywhere. We'll get an investigative reporter, the police—the FBI!"

Charles's mind was spinning at a hundred miles per hour. "Wait,

wait! If you expose me, your own families will be hurt. What will your husbands think? Will they love your children the same way if they know the truth? And the children! What will you tell *them?*"

The women looked at each other, fear and puzzlement in their eyes. Charles tried to get up, but Lydia pressed her open-toed Fendi sandal hard against his chest.

"He's right," she said, addressing her cohorts. "We can't let this hurt our families."

Rachel said, "But we can't let him get away with this!"

Lydia chuckled, glancing down at him with a devious gleam in her eyes. "Oh, he won't get away with it. Toni, go check out the gardener's toolshed. What we need is a nice long length of rope."

Laura Armbruster gulped her Bloody Mary, hoping to ease her pounding headache. "Where did they go? What could they be talking about for so long?" She eyed the sulky teenager with the obnoxious T-shirt. "I'm next, Aaron," she reminded him. "Ladies first."

She had moved with Aaron to an intimate table that overlooked the pool outside, where the wind was drawing little eddies on the surface of the water. Laura had long ago lost sight of the doctor and his gaggle of admirers.

"Youth before beauty, isn't that what they say?" Aaron responded, tipping back his Dr. Pepper.

"What could you possibly have to talk to Doctor Jefferson about? Certainly not a *condition?*"

He snorted. "It's a condition all right. He owes me some money." He tilted his head and studied her, making her nervous enough to tap her nails against her glass. "You're a wild woman, Mrs. A. Never would have figured you for it."

She lifted her chin in an automatic gesture. "I'm not wild. My bloodlines go back a long and distinguished way."

He only laughed and flopped his gray and red-sneaker-clad feet up on a nearby chair. The hems of his jeans were worn to a frazzle. "I saw you at church, guzzling rum and dancing like a stripper on speed."

Her stomach churned, as it did every time she got flashbacks of the horrible scene. "You were there?"

"Nah. Saw it on Gryphon Gate's Web site."

She would have thrown up right then if it hadn't been such an undignified thing to do in public. Or even in private. "I'm on the Web site?"

"Yep. Maybe you should check into that. Like right now." He pointed at his blue plastic watch for emphasis. "You still have time to get the pictures removed before *everyone* sees them."

She would check into it immediately. She'd tear that Web site down. Wait! Doctor Jefferson should be back any minute, and she wasn't going to let this snot-faced teen beat her to the punch. Laura settled back in her chair and imagined firing whoever had posted those pictures. And she had a very good idea who.

"Ah, don't worry, Mrs. A.," Aaron soothed. "What you did is no worse than what some of the people around here have done. And are doing."

She picked up on the tantalizing tone in his voice. "What do you mean?"

"Oh, just that there are lots of secrets around here. Lots and lots. Even you have a few secrets, don't you, Mrs. A.?"

She shifted uncomfortably. "What do you know?"

He gave a coy shrug.

She decided to appeal to his teenage ego. "You're a very intelligent young man, aren't you? I'll bet you know a lot."

His face lit up at her compliment, and he pulled his feet off the chair and faced her. "Sigmond knew everyone's secrets, right? And he was very careful to keep them secret. He coded all of his notes. But I found the notes—and cracked the code."

He was smarter than she gave him credit for. She leaned closer. "So now you know what Sigmond knew. What do you intend to do with the information?"

"I don't intend to blackmail anyone, if that's what you're thinking. That's a dangerous business, don't you think?" He acted as though her opinion really mattered.

"Blackmail isn't such a bad thing in certain cases," she suggested carefully, feeling her way. "For a good cause, I mean. I don't think God would frown on it then. That's—well, that's why I need to talk to Doctor Jefferson. I know a secret about him."

Aaron's eyebrows bobbed conspiratorially. "That he's, like, the father of several of the children here at Gryphon Gate?"

She felt the air rush from her sails. So he knew that, too. "Is that why you're here to talk to him?"

He started to give one of his noncommittal shrugs. "Whoa! That's why *you're* here to talk to him, right?"

She had a sudden urge for a cigar. Wait a minute. *A cigar?* She shrugged it off. "I just want what's rightfully mine."

Aaron's smile was smug. "You want to be buried in the Jefferson family plot. I read about it in the notes."

Those notes! She decided not to get indignant. She knew a lot of secrets, too, after all. Everyone thought she was a gossip, but she knew how to keep the important secrets. "Not just me," she said. "I want my relatives buried there, too. It's only right. I—we're related to Thomas Jefferson, too. I plan to appeal to Doctor Jefferson to, shall I say, *persuade* his family to let us in. And I don't mind using a little genetic pressure to get my way, if you know what I mean."

"I guess that's fair. Me, I only want a little money out of the deal. There's enough of it to go around, don't you think?"

"I thought you weren't going to blackmail anyone."

"I meant, I'm not going to blackmail *everyone*. One's enough."

She was studying Aaron now, wondering how she could use his intelligence and ambition for her own purposes. That he looked so unassuming, so nerdy, could only work in his favor. When he caught her staring at him, she glanced at her watch. "What can be keeping them this long? Should we go out and see if we can extricate the good doctor?"

Aaron jumped to his feet. "We'll work as a team."

"Have you seen Toni Sinclair anywhere around here?" Carnegie, the older security guard, had entered the bar so quietly that Laura dropped her celery stick on the carpet. "There's been another murder," he announced.

"My god!" said Laura.

"Bummer," said Aaron.

Behind them there was a gasp, and the trio turned just in time to see the door close silently over the back of Lydia Upshaw's unmistakable electric blue Roberto Cavalli blouse.

* * *

Lydia rushed back to join her friends. "I was just coming out of the ladies' when I heard voices. Carnegie's inside looking for Toni! There's been another murder!"

Toni shot to her feet, her eyes as bugged out as her precious frog's had been earlier. "He's looking for me? Why? Why me? Did he say? Why would he be looking for me?"

"I don't know, but we've got to scram. We don't want to be caught here with *him*."

They all looked down at Doctor Jefferson, who was trussed like a Christmas goose, bound securely to his chair. Renée said, "What are we going to do about him?"

"This table's pretty hidden. He's not going anywhere. We'll come back and deal with him later."

All four women scattered.

It hadn't taken Carnegie long to round up Toni Sinclair—skulking down the driveway toward the rec center—and deliver her to Diane Robards in the Wild Goose Room for questioning. It hadn't gone well. Toni expressed shock and surprise at the body in her koi pond, then clammed up.

After Toni left, Diane laid her head on the desk and squeezed her eyes shut. "Something's rotten in Gryphon Gate and I intend to find out what it is. If only people would start telling the truth."

Leland replied with a snort. When Diane met his gaze, his smile vanished. "I only meant that these folks wouldn't know how to tell the truth if God Himself asked." He walked up behind Diane and slid his hands across her shoulders. He began kneading her knotted muscles.

If she'd been a lesser woman, she would have melted all over the desktop. Surprise at the familiarity turned into reluctant acceptance and then relief. And then her eyes rolled backward and she accidentally let out a low moan. Oh, jeez, she *was* a lesser woman!

Shocked at her lack of self-control, Diane quickly turned around to face him. "We know Tiffany is lying. What did you think of Toni's story?"

"It sounded just like Mrs. Upshaw's story. And Mrs. Lynch's story. And Mrs. Vormeister's story."

Diane was glad they were back on track, even as her gaze rested on his strong, masculine hands. "Exactly. It sounded rehearsed. While Anka was being murdered, they ran into Doctor Jefferson—who, I might add, had no business being in Gryphon Gate in the first place. They needed to talk to him urgently about"—she checked her notes—"overcharges on their bills, some of which occurred years ago. Yeah, right. Then he blew them off and left. And not a one of them saw where he was headed."

"Sounds fishy to me. Oh, sorry." After the koi pond, fish were still a sore subject. "Mrs. Vormeister was really nervous, too. Did you notice how she kept tapping her fingers against the side of the chair?"

Diane tilted her head. "Leland, why aren't you a real cop? You've got the brains and you've got the brawn. You're being wasted here in LaLa Land."

Her bluntness seemed to take him off guard, but she only knew blunt. Who had time to beat around bushes?

"It's . . . well, my father was a cop. A real cop." He began to pace back and forth in front of the fireplace. Carved duck decoys stared at him from their perches on the elaborately carved mantel. "When I was growing up, I thought he was God. He was the fixer of all things, the champion of justice. I wanted to be just like him." Leland paused and turned to face her. "When I was sixteen, he was killed during a bank robbery. I still wanted to be like him, but I didn't want to be dead. His death broke my mother's heart and she begged me not to join the force. This seemed a good compromise." He lifted a shoulder. "It used to, anyway."

So he wasn't simply pretending interest in her as a toehold to get onto the force. He just didn't want to break his mama's heart. Was this guy for real? All Diane knew was she wanted him in her life, but she didn't know a thing about making that happen. She stood. "Let's get out of here, get some fresh air."

Although it was nearly nine o'clock, the bar was empty, the residents safe and sound in their homes. Well, she hoped they were, anyway. Probably, they were in somebody else's homes, somebody else's beds. As long as they weren't out killing anyone. She just couldn't take another dead body.

As they walked through the dimly lit room, Diane radioed one of her officers. "Found Doctor Jefferson yet?"

"Negative. Left his office after lunch and hasn't been there or at his home since. Hasn't answered his pager either. We'll keep looking."

Diane shook her head as they walked through the quiet hallway and out the back door to the pool area. The night air was fat with impending rain, and she inhaled deeply. Thunder rumbled overhead, seeming to echo for miles. "He's been seen in Gryphon Gate twice now without having any business here. Maybe it's as simple as him being our man."

"But you think it's a woman," Leland said with a hint of a teasing smile.

"Or her accomplice, of course."

"Of course. The question is, was Anka's murder related to the first two? She wasn't killed like the others. And there's the jewelry to consider."

"It wouldn't be the first time a maid lifted her employer's jewels. Wouldn't be the first time an employer killed a pilfering servant either. But why would she—or he—not recover the jewels? Why leave them there like a statement?"

Her cell phone chirped. Cause of death had been confirmed. Anka had been drowned, pinned beneath the water until her lungs were full. Diane closed her eyes. How awful it must have been to see daylight and oxygen only two feet above you and not be able to breathe. She shook off the thought, and when she opened her eyes again, she was surprised to be gazing on more water.

The pool was lit like a gemstone. You couldn't tell a man had been murdered there only days before. They still hadn't figured out why there had been no blood beneath McClintock's body. They still hadn't figured out a lot of things. She let out an exasperated sigh.

"You should get some sleep," Leland said as they skirted the pool. "You'll probably figure it out in your dreams."

She smiled, touched that he cared about her well-being and that he had faith in her abilities. Unfortunately, all she could think about was falling asleep with Leland wrapped around her. Just sleep, just his warm body snuggled against hers, hearing him breathe in the darkened room. It had been a long time since anybody cared about her. When she looked up at him, he was watching her. How much had he read on her face?

Too much, evidently. Leland cupped her cheek and rubbed his

thumb across her lower lip. And then he leaned down and kissed her. His mouth moved across hers in a feather-light whisper, and her heartbeat pounded in her throat. When she opened instinctually to him, he deepened the kiss.

"Let's get you home," he said in a husky voice. He took her hand and without saying a word led her toward the parking lot and the waiting cruiser.

Diane wondered what he meant by getting her home. With him? To sleep? Or more? Her head swam with moral dilemmas. Oh, the way his hand felt as he decisively led her around a clump of manicured bushes!

She would never know what Leland's intentions were. She tripped over something in the dark and fell against him. Her instincts went on alert as Leland reached to his holster and his flashlight.

"I believe we found the elusive Doctor Jefferson," he said, still holding protectively onto her arm.

She pulled away and followed the beam of light to the scene before them. The doctor was tied to one of the pool chairs, lashed to the arms and legs of the chair with rope. He lay on his back, his legs in the air. His formerly handsome face had been bashed in. She recognized the wound pattern. Unless she missed her guess, the M.E. would find it had been caused by the same smooth, cylindrical weapon used on Sigmond Vormeister and Lt. Col. Lance McClintock. Only this time the killer had gone overboard.

"My team should be about finished with the body over at the Sinclair place," she said. "At least they won't have far to drive." She sighed, exhausted. Could it get any worse?

Leland knelt down next to Doctor Jefferson, shining the beam of light on the wreck of his face. "Oh, God, look at this. Someone's gouged out his eyes."

And then it started to rain.

12

TONI SINCLAIR WAS fLOUNDER-
ing in a nightmare from which she struggled to awaken, but no amount
of pinching herself or trying to force her eyelids wider open would
bring her out of it. No comforting hand reached across to her, no voice
said soothingly, *It isn't real, don't think of it anymore! Look, you're safe
in bed in your own room and everything is as it should be.*

On the contrary, nothing was as it should be. There had been two
more murders, one of the bodies drowned in her koi pond! Thank
heaven, at least Miranda had not been the one to find it. That was
about the only mercy there was.

Now Charles Jefferson was dead too, and hideously. The thought
of what had been done to him made her sick. She could feel her stomach churning, as imagination of it touched the edge of her mind. She
refused to let it come closer; once inside she would never be able to
get rid of it. She would wake up sweating in the night with its horror
embedded in her memory.

She could control it! Of course she could. She had conquered the
memory of Lincoln, hadn't she? Well, almost. Surely if she could ban-
ish it altogether, she would be less than human. After all, Lincoln was
Miranda's father, and she had certainly loved him once.

Can you forgive anyone for causing you that much pain?

She sat huddled on the sofa, her knees drawn up as if she were
cold inside, shivering, although it was still mild enough, even if it was

189

getting oddly dark and there was a heaviness and an unease in the air.

Lincoln had told her that she was naïve, that she expected far too much. She had wanted a dream man, not a real one, and it was her unspoken demands, her inability to love him as he was, that had driven him to seek other women—other girls, to be precise—who knew how to give what she could not.

But that was not true. To begin with she had adored him, simply and naturally for who he was, his charm, his generosity, the way he made her laugh, the beliefs they shared. It had not fallen away bit by bit, but suddenly with a shattering pain. She had found the E-mails, the whole grubby truth spilling out in one drowning tide.

He was right about one thing, she had lived in a dream. The Lincoln she had loved had never existed. The outer man was the same— the manner, the face, the voice, even the jokes. But the mind was alien—and soiled with lies.

She had been so hurt she could not even remember all the things she had said and done in those first awful days, or had it been weeks? He had not even understood why she was furious. Then, when she could not be cajoled, charmed in the old ways, he had become angry, too, and blamed her. She could still see the bitterness in his face. How different he had looked. How could someone you had loved suddenly become completely hateful?

But she could remember Jason Salinger, no matter how hard she tried to forget. And she had tried! She had tried with sleeping pills, with alcohol, with wishing until she dropped, or partying until everything else was a blur. But still he remained as huge and real as the week it had happened.

He had found her when she was so vulnerable, when she had first discovered the truth. He had been a friend, listening, comforting, sympathizing. And of course, since he had worked for Lincoln in the business and even installed the security system here in the house, she had felt a unique kind of trust. He knew all about Lincoln and the girls; schoolgirls, only a few years older than Miranda was now! That thought woke a fury in her that could have killed Lincoln again, this time with her bare hands.

But she wouldn't have then! She wouldn't! She hadn't! They were just idle, stupid words, spoken in anger! She had NEVER meant it! Wasn't there something in English history? Some king or other had cried out, "Who will rid me of this meddlesome priest?" And someone listening had gone and murdered the archbishop. And the king got blamed for it! It wasn't his fault. He had not meant it any more than she had.

She had cried in Jason Salinger's arms, broken by disillusion and hurting more than she could bear, and she had said she wished Lincoln were dead!

Jason had listened. Then a few days later Lincoln was dead. It was not until after the funeral and the unquestioning verdict of accident that Jason had come back smiling and full of outward sympathy for the new widow. Then he had said how clever he had been, and wasn't she pleased? And he hoped she was going to honor her debt to him with suitable payment. They had not discussed money, but hadn't she said something about "give anything"? Well, he wasn't greedy, but a nice lump sum of fifty thousand dollars would enable him to start off his own business very well. If anyone asked, she could call it a loan; only he really did not think he would ever find it necessary to repay her. He was sure she understood.

She understood perfectly. There had been a few more "investments" in his business since then, made through an account she could not trace back to him. Wiser, he said, in case the weight of guilt for her husband's death ever grew too heavy for her and she chose to confess it all to some psychiatrist. He could not take that chance. Guilt was a funny thing. It made otherwise reliable people oddly self-destructive. She might even become so irrational and unlike her usual self as to forget the possible consequences to Miranda.

So, of course she had kept silent and paid him. It had made her isolated, unable even to look for any kind of further happiness, far less to accept it were it offered.

Was she guilty in some deep moral way? She had said the words. Did that make her to blame for what Jason had done? It had never crossed her mind that he would act on them; they were just words cried out in her pain. But he had believed her! He had done it, and Lincoln was dead.

Now, in spite of his earlier threats, Jason wanted to see her again privately, and she could think of no way at all to avoid it. She felt as if she were waiting for her own execution, and it was as inevitable as night falling.

* * *

Roman Gervase was sorry about the murders that had happened at Gryphon Gate. He certainly would not have wished them, but there were other things pressing on his mind far more importantly, such as at last resolving his own personal life, and equally importantly to him, doing something to help Toni Sinclair.

Evidence to solve the first had finally fallen into his hands. Mignon must go. Of course that had been obvious for a long time. How to achieve it without having her financially around his neck for the rest of his life was another matter. And he must be blunt about it. If he connived, used legal trading, then it would haunt him forever. There were no new starts even to dream about, however hard one tried, or with all the luck in the world, if one were still dragging behind old guilt and memories.

Which brought him to the second issue. How could he rid Toni of the demons that followed her and seemed to cloud every happiness she reached for? That mattered to him, it mattered intensely. Even the thought of her face, her laughter, her eyes when she spoke of the wild creatures made him smile as he waited to confront Mignon. They were so different, the two women. Mignon was beautiful. Every man he had known thought so. He could see it in their expressions, even if they had not said. But it was all on the outside. It was shape, hair, texture of the skin, color of the eyes. It was empty.

No, that was not true. There was greed in there, and vanity, and contempt for other people. There was mockery of mistakes, laughter at those who were weak or who failed. He was very tired of it.

She came into the room barely noticing him. Even in the sombre light of the heavy overcast and first beginning rain she looked perfect. It did not move him at all. It was as if something inside him had grown up, put away the illusions of the child, and accepted reality.

"What are you doing in here?" she said abruptly, irritated that for a moment she had been unaware of his presence.

"Waiting for you," he replied.

She did not catch the change in his voice. "I'm busy, Roman. I really haven't got time for talking now. There's been another murder. The police are all over the place." She was barely looking at him as she spoke.

"Yes, I know," he replied, moving to sit up a little straighter in the chair. "Doctor Jefferson. But it doesn't concern us. At least it doesn't concern me. And if you have something to do with it—"

"Of course I haven't!" she swung around, her eyes blazing. "Why would I have anything to do with murder? What are you accusing me of?"

"Well, murder would do very well," he said with the slightest smile. "But I haven't any proof, and, honestly, I haven't any reason to think you would." He saw the amazement in her face with pleasure. "Adultery is good. Serial adultery is better. But I'm not sure in a place like Gryphon Gate that it would count for a lot, even on your scale."

She was a little tense, but not badly jolted. She raised one exquisite eyebrow. "Wouldn't that make you look rather foolish, Roman? You could hardly claim to have just discovered. It would make you look like an idiot. Everyone else knows."

"You've probably *slept* with everyone else," he replied, now smiling broadly at her. "And if you are going to say that I was—I think 'complacent' is the word—then yes, I was. I really don't care who you sleep with, as long as is doesn't have to be me."

"Then you should be very happy!" she snapped. "Because there isn't a snowball's chance in hell that it will be!"

"How about theft?" he said gently.

She went white.

"A little dipping into the trust fund here and there?" he went on. "Did you sleep with Arthur to persuade him to do it for you?" He was referring to the lawyer who was the fund's trustee. "Of course, I have just discovered this." He pulled a slight face to let her know he was mocking her. "And I am horrified. I am suing you for divorce. If you agree to a very reasonable sum—well, reasonable to me—then I shall not press charges. I think that is very good of me. I am not a vindictive man."

She started to speak, but there was nothing to say. She could mock him about her affairs, his temporary lapses into highly eccentric behavior, and she had. But money was serious. Even in Gryphon Gate money was deadly serious. No one forgave crimes of property.

"Yes?" he said with raised eyebrows. "You have ten minutes to consider your answer. I rather think I have waited long enough. It feels as if there is a storm coming, which might put an end to things like telephone calls, e-mails, and so on. Let's get it over with."

"I'll . . . I'll find a way to put it back!" she spluttered.

He opened his eyes very wide. "Really? In ten minutes?"

She shook her head as if to focus her vision properly, and realized at last that something in him had changed. She was beaten.

He smiled. "A reasonable settlement," he promised. "And that's an end to it. You are free to go whenever you wish, and sleep with anyone you like. And so am I. I have things to do, important things. Be gone before the storm hits." He rose to his feet. "Take your things with you. And please be careful that it is only yours. The alternative would be most unpleasant for you. Good-bye, Mignon." And without turning around he walked outside into the rising wind.

Tiffany was in the bar, and at last it was empty, and she had an opportunity to use the telephone in private. She had been waiting for over two hours, but every time she crossed towards the office, someone came in gasping, demanding a drink. Now she intended to go, regardless. One offhanded remark about Toni Sinclair from the Reverend Armbruster, of all people, had given her the last piece of the puzzle.

She picked up the phone and dialed, keeping her eyes towards the open door and the bar. She could not afford to be overheard. It was ringing at the other end. Please, God, let her be at home! Answer! Answer, damn it!

Someone passed beyond the bar. Whoever it was, let them wait!

It was still ringing. Where was she?

The person moved back towards the bar. Damn! It was the guard, Leland Ford. Wish there was time so pursue him. All sorts of ideas were possible. He could be a good detective, without it being for the police. After all, wasn't she?

"Isobel Clancy," the familiar voice said on the line.

"Ah." Tiffany caught her breath. "Mrs. Clancy, this is Tiffany here." She heard the swift gasp, the controlled expectancy. This time she would fulfil it. "I'll have news for you tonight. I just need to know one more thing. Was Jason Salinger still working at the company offices the day before Lincoln died?"

There was silence on the other end of the line.

Tiffany waited.

"Yes," Mrs. Clancy said at last. "Yes, I know he was, because I saw him there myself. Why? Do you think he killed Lincoln?"

"Yes, I do. I have just a little more to prove, then I'll have it. Thank you." And she hung up and went to see what she could do for Leland Ford.

Toni had persuaded Bertha to take Miranda out, late as it was, and in spite of the weather, which was now gray and blustery. There was no rain yet, but it was coming.

There was a knock on the door and she winced as if she had been hit. Please, heaven, let it be Jason Salinger so she could get it over with. Funny how disadvantaged she felt with her jewelery gone. Every piece of it represented some event in her life. It was as if the thief had taken her past, as well as a great deal of money. If Jason wanted more, she might have to start converting a certain amount of principal to cash. That was her safety, her future. One thing Lincoln had done right. She wished he had not poisoned so much memory.

She opened the door. It was Jason looking smug and handsome. Nothing about him pleased her. She wanted this to be over as quickly as possible. "Come in," she ordered, stepping back to allow him to pass.

"Thank you," he accepted, swaggering a little as he went across the hallway and into the main room. He looked around appreciatively. "I like this house. It has an air to it. I could be happy here."

Toni felt as if she had swallowed ice. Fear churned in her stomach, nauseating her. "No you couldn't," she contradicted him. "This is my home."

He looked at her with a wide, leering smile. "Oh, I wouldn't dream of putting you out. Last thing on my mind. I was thinking how good it all is. I've come to like Gryphon Gate altogether. It's a great life: golf, swimming, a little bridge now and then, excellent bars, even horseback riding if you want. And the marina, of course, for those who have boats—as you do."

"Yes, it's good." Why couldn't she stop her voice from shaking? Could he hear it? "And I mean to keep it!" That was bravado. If he insisted, she would have to pay! She had told him to kill Lincoln, even if she hadn't meant to. Would any judge take that into account? He might have, in the beginning. She could have simply denied it. It was only her word against Jason's. Except that, as Jason had pointed out, he had no quarrel with Lincoln. Far from it, he admired him enormously, and they had been friends! And he had nothing to gain, whereas Toni had everything to gain. Which of them would anyone believe? No, she would have to pay.

"I mean for you to keep it," he said soothingly. "I expect you'll live here for the rest of your life. Miranda will grow up here, I dare say be married from here. Why not?"

She was feeling sicker. What did he want, with his soft voice and his obscene smile? "Probably," she agreed. Now her throat was so tight she could hardly force the words through.

"Oh, definitely, sweetheart," he answered her.

"Don't call me 'sweetheart,' you bastard!" she snarled.

"I think it's a very good idea," he continued. He looked around again, savoring the room and everything in it. He licked his lips. "Because I think you should marry me. Then we'll be a nice family, you, me, and Miranda. Of course, maybe a brother or sister for her in time, but let's not rush things. Three of us, to begin with."

She could not believe it. It was preposterous—and disgusting! She could not find a word violent enough to express her loathing. Now her whole body was trembling. "Never!" she said between her teeth. "I'd rather be dead!"

"If you want, I'm sure that can be arranged," he answered, still smiling at her. "But after we're married, not before. I'll look after Miranda, I promise you—sweetheart! Just as Lincoln would have!"

She threw herself at him, lashing out with her fists, wanting to strike his face, claw at his skin, tear him. But he saw her coming and caught her wrists, only very slightly staggering backwards under the onslaught of her weight. They struggled for a moment or two, breathing hard, muscles clenched. Then he twisted her arms and threw her back, letting her go.

She cried out in pain, and fell backwards, stumbling over the settee and collapsing onto it.

"Don't do that again," he warned. "There are laws against hitting your spouse, you know, husband or wife. Wouldn't want to end up in prison now, would you? Think of Miranda. Terrible to lose both parents, one way or another."

I won't! It beat in her head—*I won't* ever! But she did not say the words. The thought was unbearable. She really would rather be dead—except for Miranda. She had to stay alive for Miranda. She had to protect her. She said nothing. It choked her to give in, the words simply would not come.

He was waiting, watching her suffer.

"Get out!" she whispered. "Get out of my house!"

"All right." He looked annoyed, sulky, almost as if he thought that she might have agreed immediately. "But I'll be back—in fact I'll be back in a couple of hours, and you'd better have a different answer for me then. I'm not playing, Toni, I'm perfectly, deadly serious." And with that he swaggered past her to the door and out into the gloom under a heavy sky.

The lights had been on in Toni's house, and Roman Gervase saw Jason Salinger inside. Of course he could not hear what either of them had said, but he saw Salinger's sneer, and he saw very clearly the tension and the revulsion in Toni's face—the way she moved her body, as if the thought of Salinger touching her made her ill.

That thought made Roman ill as well. He was glad he had taken certain precautions. He had to muster all the forces of intelligence he possessed in order to conquer the emotion and instinct that urged him to storm in there, pick up a chair, and smash it over Salinger's head. But he knew that it would accomplish nothing, and make him look absurd. And surely he had done enough of that already. The thought of some of his escapades made him sweat with embarrassment. How on earth would he ever live them down?

Then he remembered the insane service at the church, and a great many people behaving in ways they would certainly not care to remember, still less to have anyone else remember. Of course it was induced by some substance that Tiffany had brought, or those friends of hers. No doubt she had a reason. She had been inquiring very discreetly into a lot of things since she had been here. He did not know for whom, but he had worked out why.

Naturally, everyone realized about the substance now, and excused themselves accordingly. But his bizarre behavior was substance-induced as well. The doctor had given him those pills to combat the headaches he still got now and then, left over from the accident and his head injury. Now his medication had been changed, and the whole world had righted itself, so at least he could see it clearly, even if he did not always like what he saw. Especially, he did not like Toni being frightened and obviously threatened in some way.

At first he had merely liked her. She was less critical than the others at Gryphon Gate, less intolerant, less prone to mock. The small kindness she had shown him had loomed large where he was concerned. Gradually, he had seen the beauty in her beneath the surface polish. Her hunger and her dreams made her vulnerable, human, able so often to think of others before herself. And he liked her anger as well, the way she leaped in to defend the deer and the swans without thinking of possible cost to herself. He loved enthusiasm—and someone who could make him laugh.

If only there were something he could do to rid her of Salinger. Of course she would not trust him. Whatever he did, he would have to do it without her help. Sympathy would be fine, all very sweet and friendly; but what she actually needed was intelligence, cool thinking, and decisive action. He knew exactly where to go to find an ally with those qualities.

He turned and walked away from his discreet watching place and made his way back toward the clubhouse and the bar.

He found two or three people there and was obliged to wait, shifting impatiently from foot to foot until Tiffany was free.

"Yes, Mr. Gervase?" she said pleasantly.

There was no time for finesse. He smiled and dropped his voice to the slightest murmur. "I know who you are, and why you are here, Miss Turner. I think you need to act very quickly, or the whole thing will slip beyond your control, or anybody's." He saw the denial in her face. "I'm perfectly serious! Jason Salinger has just been to Mrs. Sinclair's house and threatened her. I couldn't hear what with, but she attacked him and he threw her off. She looked very frightened, and he walked arrogantly, as if he knew he had won. It will be only a matter of time before she has to give in."

She was still uncertain, on the edge of speech and not daring to commit herself.

"I know you want to find out who killed Lincoln Sinclair," he said more urgently. "I just don't know why, or for whom. But I know Salinger is involved, and I think Toni could be next. Maybe . . ." He stopped. It was stupid. No one could mistake Anka for Toni. ". . . The jewelry was Toni's, even if she doesn't dare admit it to the police. Someone is after her."

Tiffany made her decision. "I'll get one of the other girls to cover for me. Meet me outside in ten minutes."

"I'll be there!" he said grimly. "And if I have to do this alone, I will. But I could spoil whatever you are here for!"

"You don't need to threaten me, Mr. Gervase," she replied. "I know that. I don't want her hurt any more than you do. And I'd love to catch Jason Salinger so far out on a limb he'd never crawl back again—to anything!"

Roman smiled. She was startled how it changed his face. It lit him from inside, and she realized how attractive he could be.

"Who for?" he asked her the moment they met outside. The air was colder and fat drops of rain splattered on the concrete. Out in the bay there were broad wind patterns spreading across the water and here and there white crests.

"Mrs. Clancy," she answered. She might as well tell the whole truth now. Time was getting short, and she had a strong conviction that Roman Gervase had both seen and understood a lot more than most people imagined. "She's Lincoln Sinclair's sister. She knows he was murdered, but she doesn't know by whom. She does know that whoever it is is blackmailing Toni, and what she is terrified of is that Toni will pay them and lose all the money Lincoln left her. But what she's most afraid of is that it will come out why Toni would have wanted to kill Lincoln, apart from money, which she had anyway."

"Toni wouldn't kill him!" he said instantly, anger and defiance sharp in his eyes and his voice.

Tiffany smiled. So Roman was at least a little in love with her. Why not? His wife was a tart, albeit an expensive one, and Toni Sinclair had a gentleness about her that would last far longer than a good figure or flashing eyes. And she could be funny and brave as well—more than could be said of most of the women here. They were like expensive collectors' eggs—perfect to look at, very brittle, and totally empty inside. Maybe Toni went a little overboard about the deer, but it was a good eccentricity. Everyone needs a little madness to be perfectly sane.

"No, Mrs. Clancy knows that," she soothed. "But she had plenty of cause, and that's what she wants to hide."

"Cause?"

"Lincoln was rather heavily into schoolgirls," she said patiently. "On the Net, but he'd begun practising a little 'in the flesh' as well, so to speak. It was only a matter of time before it got extremely ugly. Toni was pretty broken up when she found out. It shattered her world. That was about the time Salinger showed up rather a lot." She glanced over her shoulder to where Vanessa Smart-Drysdale had come out of the club door and was looking at them.

Roman saw her, too, and started to walk away. Tiffany lengthened her stride to keep up with him.

"Poisonous woman," he said between his teeth. "Reminds me of my wife—my ex-wife, as soon as it can be arranged! Sorry—I shouldn't have told you that—it's just such a relief." He looked relieved as he said it; there was a weight gone from him, he stood straighter, there was more color in his face, and he walked with a certain new grace.

But he was still anxious. "Why?" he asked. "What has Salinger to do with it? Did he kill Lincoln? Why would he do that?"

"Yes. I'm pretty sure he did," she answered, regretting the next bit. "I think Toni asked him to."

"That's a lie!" he said immediately, anger rising in his voice.

"It's a good one," she pointed out. "He's been blackmailing her ever since, and she's been paying him nice big slices of all that nice big inheritance she got from Lincoln's death. Not that Lincoln wasn't a thorough turd," she added. "He was. Unfortunately, that doesn't give anyone a license to electrocute him on the john, more's the pity. I could think of a few for whom that fate would be particularly fitting—starting with Jason Salinger himself."

"What does Mrs. Clancy want?" he demanded. "Justice, I suppose?!"

"Certainly not," she answered decisively. "I think she's not convinced that he hasn't already got it. She wants silence. She's older than he was. Got a couple of children herself, with big ambitions socially. Ivy League, good marriages, all that sort of thing. Tend to find a few doors closed if uncle was a bit of a pedophile."

"So she doesn't want Toni prosecuted for it?" He turned to look at her hopefully.

"Last thing she wants," Tiffany agreed. "She wants her protected."

"Then we need to get rid of Salinger quickly. He's closing in for a kill of some kind," he urged. "And if he murdered Lincoln, then if it suited him, he'd murder Toni, if he thought he'd get away with it." Now he was afraid. She could see it naked in his eyes.

"I know," she agreed. "I've finally got the proof that he killed Lincoln."

"Then use it! We don't want him tried, but wouldn't it be enough to make him go away?" he asked. "Lodge it somewhere safe and say that if he ever comes anywhere near Toni again, even writes to her or calls her, it goes straight to the D.A."

She hesitated. "He would say he did it for her. He thinks he's been terribly clever hiding it, but there's ample proof she paid him and is still paying him. If she wasn't involved, then why doesn't she tell him to go to hell?"

"To protect Lincoln's family?" he suggested. "Miranda? She'd do anything to protect her."

"Not pay Salinger and let him go on bleeding her—and hanging around," she answered. "No, there's something else we still don't know. But I'm going to find out." Unconsciously, she increased her stride. It would give her intense pleasure to fix Jason Salinger—permanently. She just needed the one final card, then she would be ready to play her hand. And Toni Sinclair had that; it would just be a matter of persuading her that it was in her interest to give it to Tiffany. After all, they wanted the same thing, just for different reasons.

"I'm coming with you," Roman stated.

"No you're not! I've a much better chance alone."

He said nothing, but kept pace with her.

"No, you're not," she repeated.

Again he ignored her. They were moving swiftly towards Toni Sinclair's house. There was not much time left for argument, and she had no authority to make him go away. She stopped abruptly.

"Look, Roman, this has got to succeed. If we make a mess of it this time, we won't get another chance. You like her, yes? In fact, you more than like her."

He colored faintly.

"Maybe she likes you," she went on. It was ruthless. Toni Sinclair probably didn't even know he was alive, but there was no time to be delicate. "Just get out, and leave me to do this! Please!"

Reluctantly, he stood still. He nodded, unhappy, embarrassed.

"Sorry," she added, then walked away, leaving him standing there. She almost ran the last fifty yards to the door and beat on it hard until Toni opened it. Tiffany pushed her way in without asking.

"Look. I don't know—" Toni began.

"There's no time," Tiffany dismissed her protests. "I'm a private detective. I work for Isobel Clancy, your sister-in-law. She knows Lincoln was murdered."

Toni was pale already; now she grew white as a sheet. What on earth did Tiffany mean?

Tiffany took her by the shoulders and guided her backwards to the sofa. "If you're going to faint, do it there. It'll hurt less. Mrs. Clancy doesn't think you did it, certainly not personally. She isn't looking for revenge. She'd much rather it was all hushed up, primarily because she doesn't want anyone knowing the very good reason you had for suddenly wanting your husband dead."

Toni said nothing, just collapsed and sat blinking—numb.

"The schoolgirls?" Tiffany prompted, just to make sure Toni was following. "Was it Jason Salinger who actually killed him?"

Toni nodded again, slowly.

"And you've been paying him blackmail ever since?"

Toni's voice was hoarse, as if she could barely breathe. "He wants me to marry him. I don't know what to do!"

Tiffany had not thought anything could shock her, but the thought of this woman's predicament was enough to chill her to the bone. She imagined being in the same position and it made her stomach heave.

"For God's sake, don't!" she said.

Toni whispered. "If I don't, he'll—he'll tell the police I asked him to kill Lincoln—and paid him. I didn't! I just said I wished he was dead! I didn't mean anyone to do it! But I paid him to keep quiet. It's too late now." She gulped. "Nobody would believe me. I hated Lincoln for what he did to me. He destroyed what I thought I had! He smashed it all. I *loved* who I thought he was, who he pretended

202

to be." She leaned forward and buried her face in her hands.

Tiffany was desperately sorry for her, but she could not afford to stop now to offer comfort. That would have to come later, when she had dealt with Jason Salinger. Now at last she knew how it had happened. Poor, stupid Toni! And yet, who hasn't ever said they wished someone would fall under a bus or drop dead? They didn't mean it!

"Just hang in there," she said in a loud, clear voice. "It'll be sorted out. Don't do anything stupid. Lock the door, take a hot shower, and look after yourself. Don't get drunk! I might have something good to tell you."

And she went out, leaving Toni still sitting with her head bowed.

The wind was gusting harder, and it was nearly dark when she faced Jason Salinger in one of the private rooms in the club. No one felt like having a party tonight and there were plenty of places to choose from. This one served her purpose very well. She put on only one small light, and it gave the place an eerie quality, with the wind rattling the awnings outside and moaning around the eaves.

"It was very cleverly done," she said with mock admiration. "All-around a good plan—nice mixture of opportunism and preparation. You discover Lincoln Sinclair has a taste for young girls and his wife knows about it." She looked at his face in the lamplight. "You go and comfort her distress," she went on. "She says she wishes Lincoln were dead. So you oblige. You were the one who had designed that very special headset for him, and you knew he wore it all the time when he was listening to one of his favorite tunes. Sooner or later he was bound to go and sit on the john with it, plug it in to the amplifier you hot-wired. And then . . ." she clapped her hands together, "no more Lincoln. What a ludicrous end for a man of his talent, eh? Electrocuted with his pants down! Ironically satisfying."

"You can't prove I tampered with that amp," he said calmly.

"I know you did," she replied. "The unit was perfectly all right when it left the bench where the last technician upgraded it according to your instructions, because he tested it himself."

"It needs grounding to electrocute someone, sweetheart!" he said with a sneer.

203

"I know that!" she snapped. "Perhaps you've forgotten, but they have sophisticated testing equipment in the workrooms! The technician checked it out thoroughly. And he'll swear to that. He gave it to you to take and pack up for Lincoln. It wasn't unwrapped until Lincoln had it installed."

He looked paler, but not pale enough. He wasn't frightened—not really. She had just proven him guilty of murder, and he wasn't sweating.

"Except, I didn't touch it," he said with a slow smile. "I took it straight to the delivery room. Five minutes tops. And I can prove that. It would take half an hour for the sort of modification that killed him. Sorry, angel, but I didn't kill him. I couldn't have. I may be a computer whiz, but I'm not a master electrician. I just let Toni think so because she feels as guilty as hell, and she'll pay me for it very nicely. Maybe she did it herself? Ever thought of that?"

"I don't believe you!" she said, but there was no conviction in her voice. She did believe him, that was the sickening thing. He was a total opportunist, but perhaps he didn't have the nerve or the skill to have killed Lincoln. Anyway, why would he? Simply to blackmail Toni? Too big a risk. No—she believed he had just taken his chance. "Who could prove you didn't have it for hours?" She needed to know. If he couldn't prove it, she might still break him.

"Gus Devon and Arnie Whyte," he answered without hesitation. "Sorry, sweetheart! You lose! Not very good, are you?" He straightened up from where he had been leaning against the mantel. "Is that all? Can't stay, I have an appointment to keep. I'm going to be married soon, and I have things to do. Good night! Take care, or you'll get wet. We're going to have a hell of a storm."

Tiffany was so furious her teeth were clenched till her jaw ached. She stood still in the half-light trying to marshal her thoughts, till she heard the door open and thought perhaps it was Jason come back again. But it was Roman Gervase.

"You lost," he said quietly, seeing it in her face. "What happened?"

She told him, trying to swallow the self-pity and disgust.

"It doesn't have to have been done before it was delivered," he said steadily, a tiny thread of excitement rising in his voice. "Lincoln took that headset with him everywhere in his briefcase. Jason could have come by afterwards, anytime, at Lincoln's home or at his office, and rigged the amplifier privately at his leisure!"

"How would he get in?" she asked.

"He was in control of the security of their house!" he replied. "I know that because Lincoln told me himself. Who better to break in and rewire the whole thing?"

She stared at him incredulously. "You mean . . . do you think he did it?"

"Who cares?" He shrugged. "He can't prove he didn't! Maybe he did? Maybe he killed Lincoln for his own reasons. Maybe he's been threatening Toni all this time, and that's why she paid him, so he wouldn't electrocute *her!* Or worse, *Miranda!* He's got the skills. He wants her, and he's obsessive."

"Hasn't he waited rather a long time for an obsession?" she said reluctantly.

"Building up the pressure." He dismissed the criticism. "He had to wait a decent interval, or she wouldn't marry him, and that's what he wants—the house, the money, the boat, and her—the whole lot. Worth waiting for, don't you think? Especially for a man like him, ambitious, clever—but not clever enough."

"Yes," she nodded, excitement and the taste of victory boiling up inside her. "Yes—exactly! Roman, you're brilliant!" She forbore from mentioning that he was also more than a little mad, but then maybe that was in the past. People should be allowed to get over their mistakes. Heaven knows she had a few to put behind her.

"Only if it works," he said guardedly. "We need to get him to threaten Toni again and tell her that he killed Lincoln for her, and that she has to marry him or else he'll tell the police the whole thing. Except he wouldn't, of course. He'd probably say she asked him enough questions to know how to wire it herself. He's not going to take the blame for anything. He wouldn't even admit the blackmail. He'd say she forced it on him to silence him."

"Right," she agreed. "But it doesn't matter now. We've got to get Toni to ask him back, and we'll tape it. Do you know how to do that?"

"*Do* it?" said Roman with a grin. "My dear girl, electronic surveillance is my specialty!" He pulled an audiotape from his pocket and tapped it. "I've already *done* it! This should be enough to persuade

Jason Salinger to go away—as far as possible—and stay there. All we need to do is confront him."

"You're on!" Tiffany said decisively. "Delivered, trussed, and ready—one turkey called Jason Salinger!"

It worked—it worked perfectly. There were a few agonizing moments when it seemed he might slip away, but Toni had gained a sudden hope, and with hope, a confidence. She played him perfectly. Everything he had said to her before was played back to him from the recording, in the living room of her house, as the three watched him squirm.

"I think you should leave Maryland," Tiffany said when they faced him. "California would be a good idea. It's another world, believe me."

"Alaska," Roman amended. "And don't come back. The case will remain open, and several copies of the tape will be available anytime. In the interests of your own safety, you should leave tonight. Like, right now."

Jason stood motionless. The seconds stretched out. He looked at Toni and saw that she was no longer afraid of him.

Roman moved a step closer to Toni.

She looked at him as if seeing him clearly, even recognizing him, for the first time.

Tiffany found herself smiling. She could be about to make a great report to Isobel Clancy—*and* get paid!

Jason Salinger knew when he was beaten. Better to escape while he could—and live to fight another battle, another day. He hadn't done badly out of this—considering he had not actually done anything, or run any risks.

"Thank you," Toni said with profound sincerity.

Salinger shrugged and walked away, tossing his last words over his shoulder at them. "But I didn't kill Lincoln, you know, I really didn't! Whoever did that is still here! And still killing! Good luck!" His laughter was hollow, and the wind tore it away.

13

THE WINDS WERE FROTHING THE
Truxton River into a frenzy of white, when Aaron stepped from the
house onto the bluff, holding his new skateboard gingerly in his finger-
tips. He was bundled against the coming storm in a slicker that read
EUPHORIC and a cap that screamed in red letters: SKATE TILL YOU BLEED!

He checked his screws, trucks, and deck, then he ollied up and
flossed a cool, one-footed, frontside boardslide down the iron railing
skirting the stone steps—a long, long downhill curve to the Gryphon
Gate forest. At bottom, where the rail leveled off, Aaron whipped a
"540 Air"—*Excellent!*—then he put the four down and slalomed off
into the deep, dark woods.

Whoa! Dude! Chomp on that! Anyone stupid enough to try pop-
ping *that* trick the first time out—especially on a brand-new deck—
would wind up squashed like your proverbial ramp pizza: trail mix,
dude! But not Aaron. Maybe he was a nerd at that snooty school
they'd stuck him in, but on his deck Aaron was a bird in flight.

A few more months of practice left until school started again
and—who knew?—if his plans took flight, too, by summer's end Aaron
would be executing a "900 Air"—two and a half turns in midair—like
the biggest name in vert skating, his idol, Tony Hawk. Aaron would
be a *real* pro—not one who needed photos to prove it. He'd have
tricks named after him and endorsement offers for glamorous boards
and barrel shoes. No more money spent on schoolyard protection for

him. That is, if he played his cards right—with *her*—when they met across the woods, as planned, this morning.

Aaron hadn't recalled how dense and dark the Gryphon Gate forest was. The approaching storm had already blackened the sky, but here in the woods the trees were so high, the canopy so broad, he couldn't even *see* the sky: twenty-two acres of ancient, virgin timber that went back to the days of the Indians who once lived in these parts. His late brother-in-law, Sigmond, had once told him these trees were under government protection; they would never be harvested or even thinned.

But right then Aaron could have used a little light—it was mandatory information for a dude to obtain, when plowing downhill at breakneck speed, hurtling between giant trees on a little chip of wood. But he didn't want to slow down if it rendered him late for this assignation with Destiny.

His blood was rushing, the wind cutting tears from his eyes as he hurtled downhill, so distracted by the trees that he was almost at the bottom of the glen before he saw the figure.

A tall, dark, broad-shouldered form stood in the middle of the trail at the very base of the gully, wrapped against the wind in a long black cloak, the face partly concealed by what looked like a hood—at least, as far as Aaron could tell at warp speed.

He didn't want to look like a twerp, slowing in fright, but his heart was pumping—and he was moving too fast to do a nose grind without flipping on his head. Then he heard that little inner voice saying, *Dude, what is wrong with this snapshot here?* And now the pounding moved to his ears. Had he overlooked anything?

Why would *she* be meeting him in an isolated glen inside the compound, when they'd arranged to meet at the far side of the woods—as far from Gryphon Gate as possible? Why was *she* suddenly rigged in what looked like druid camouflage gear? And, holy noggles! The thought occurred—about a billion light years too late to do him any good—that the police still had not figured out who had murdered those four inmates of Gryphon Gate!

Aaron felt like he was going down in a bad salad grind: This trail was the only way in or out, and it was all uphill either way—which would call for him to run flat-out for maybe three hundred yards on a grade to escape. Aaron was a skateboarder, not a pentathlon star. If he knew any prayers for winged feet, he would have said them right now.

Then the figure on the trail tossed back the hood, and raised one hand to halt him. It was not the person he was expecting—but at this moment, in this precise situation, it *was* the very last person on the planet he wanted to see!

"Roman," said Toni, watching the mist rise from the bottle of champagne she had just opened, "I hope you understand that you've saved my life? Not to mention my sanity! When I married Lincoln, I was just a kid fresh out of high school. He was older, wealthy, brilliant. When I realized what he had found so attractive in me—what he really was. . . ." She turned her face away and poured the wine into two chilled glasses, then blotted her eyes. "There were times when I think I truly hated him. But I never wanted him dead."

"Antoinette," said Roman, coming up to take the champagne flutes, "I never doubted for a moment that you were the one completely innocent person in all this mess. I've watched you from afar, you know, almost from the moment you moved here. As you probably know, I spend a lot of time on my own, outside—late at night."

"Roman, maybe this isn't the right time, but I feel so close to you after what's happened. What did Laura Armbruster mean, when she said in church that you could drop the act now—that the 'bets' were off?"

Roman threw his head back, and for an instant, she was afraid he would start howling like a wolf—but it was broad daylight, and there was no full moon. Instead, he laughed uproariously.

"Listen," he said, handing Toni her glass, "Laura and I knew that her husband, Peter, and my wife, Mignon, were having an affair. We discussed it and I gave Laura the money to hire detectives. In the course of our cooperation I shared some of my own angst with her. Years ago, I had suffered a head injury in an accident and my medication made me hallucinate badly. It made me imagine I had fur sprouting all over. I would rip my clothes off, run through the woods naked, and howl at the moon. I still have lapses, though the medication has been cut back. I actually bet Laura a pittance that I could observe more from my wolf's-eye view, by night, than her costly private eye could, using more traditional methods.

"The point is, my darling," he added, "after being suffocated throughout childhood in European prep schools and military academies, I found the ability to live as a wild animal—even briefly—to be exhilarating. It's that same feeling for nature, for the swans and deer, that I recognized in you and your daughter, that brought me to want to come to your aid." He added, "I would love to have children."

Toni didn't miss the fact that Roman had called her "my darling." She couldn't help wondering what it would feel like to strip naked and run through the woods by his side, drenched in the light of the full moon—free as a white-tailed deer.

Without thinking, Toni said, "Oh, Roman, I wish you weren't married!" No sooner had she spoken than the blood drained from her face and she bit her knuckle. "Oh God, how could I? The last time I wished for something, Lincoln ended up dead."

"No, sweetheart," said Roman, putting his hand on her shoulder, "I think you realize that neither Laura Armbruster nor I will remain married to our respective spouses very long. But a wish can't kill someone. Your husband was murdered—and, as we have just learned, it wasn't the result of your thoughts or your words."

"But he *was* murdered—even if Jason didn't do it," insisted Toni. "That stereo system was tampered with—and by someone who must have known that he had stainless steel fixtures in his private office bathroom. So who could have done it?"

"Whoever it was, he's still at large," agreed Roman. "Dearest, now that you're in the clear, I think we should notify the police. How do we know that Lincoln's death isn't somehow connected with these recent murders? After all, he *was* a resident of Gryphon Gate." Then he added, "Too bad Tiffany had to rush off so fast with those tapes for Mrs. Clancy, or we might have learned what else they had gleaned by spying on you and Jason." When he saw that Toni had paled again, he said, "What's wrong?"

"Roman, I'm afraid I may have made a terrible mistake," Toni told him. "Things were so confusing when Tiffany came barging in here today. She's so commanding I felt exactly like those people she said her friends drugged during the church service—I felt that I had to do whatever she said because she knew everything about me!"

Roman had set down his glass and grasped her by the wrists. "*What* mistake?"

"I thought she knew everything, Roman," Toni said tearfully.

There was a brief moment when Roman felt the desire to lap the tears from her face with his wolfish tongue. He tried to focus.

"She knew my innermost thoughts," Toni was going on. "She knew all Lincoln's perversions and Jason's deceptions. Lincoln had already concealed so much from me, so I assumed that whatever Tiffany said about Mrs. Clancy must be right, too."

"Your sister-in-law?" said Roman. When Toni said nothing, he added, "You mean Lincoln's sister?—Mrs. Clancy, who hired Tiffany to learn the truth?"

"Roman," said Toni, "Lincoln never had a sister. At least, not that I ever heard of. He was adopted from an orphanage; I can show you the papers. Miranda and I were the only ones mentioned in his will. When he died, no other relative came forward, despite the enormous press coverage—and Lincoln was a very wealthy man."

They stared at each other for a long, long moment, digesting just how this might fit into the larger picture. At last Roman cleared his throat and said, "Tiffany never met her client—Mrs. Clancy was just a voice on the phone."

"How do you know that?" asked Toni.

"Because when Tiffany left here just now, she told me she was going to meet her client, Mrs. Clancy, face-to-face for the first time—and receive her final payment."

Neither of them wanted to imagine just what that final payment might be.

"Roman, there is only one woman I know of who hates me enough to try to frame me for murder. And I don't even know what I might have done to deserve that. I'm sure she planted Sigmond Vormeister's Palm Pilot in my yard where Miranda would find it; she drowned Anka in my koi pond; and she has planted deer chow at the murders, when everyone knows I feed the deer! She has made her intentions so clear. I'm afraid for Tiffany, if there's even a chance my suspicions are right!"

"Darling," said Roman urgently, "we must go to the police at once!"

"That's the one place I absolutely cannot go," said Toni, tears welling up again. "Don't you see, Roman? The person I'm talking about—the one who's been trying to frame me all this time—is Captain Diane Robards of the metropolitan police!"

*　*　*

There was a tap on Capt. Diane Robards's door. She'd escaped there, going over papers in her temporary office at the security station. Her head hurt so much that she seriously contemplated crawling under the desk so they'd think she was out to lunch. *Well,* thought Robards, *I am out to lunch—at least in this cockeyed investigation.*

"Come in," she snarled as uninvitingly as possible. Leland Ford popped his head around the door. She was about to tell him to get lost—though she remembered his hands on her shoulders, his lips warm against hers—the only worthwhile input she'd received to date on this case.

Leland smiled, as if apologizing for not being able to deliver more of the same, and she started to melt down again—which infuriated her. God, she was confused.

"You have a visitor," he said. "Somebody who has new evidence, so she claims."

"She?" said Robards, nodding to wave the visitor in.

Great. It had to be a woman. Robards had never seen so many useless, sex-crazed bimbos as the ones they seemed to breed here at Gryphon Gate—she winced at her own double entendre.

She had hardly failed to notice the percentage of kids with green eyes, nor the fact that Doctor Jefferson, the breeding expert in more ways than one, had the same color eyes—eyes gouged out by the murderer only two days ago.

But when Robards saw who Leland was ushering in, she had to dig her fingernails into her palms to keep from groaning.

"Permit me to introduce myself officially," said the middle-aged woman as she reached across the desk to hand Robards an ID card the size of a passport, protected by a plastic wrapper.

"Of course I know who you are, Mrs. Kaplan," said Robards, motioning for both her visitor and Leland to take a seat.

"Not quite," said Mrs. Kaplan. Turning to Leland Ford, she added, "You will no longer be needed, and we will call for you if you are."

Robards started to object, but then she glanced at the card she'd been handed:

Cunegonde Schelling
Reuters News Service, Vienna
Official Press Pass, 1960–69

Beneath it was a photo of a young woman—striking, handsome, but not beautiful; short-cropped blonde hair with a small fringe of bang; prominent Roman nose. The perfect likeness, on an old coin, of young Caesar Augustus when he was still Octavian. And, as unmistakable as the rain that was now pounding against the windows, it was the portrait of the woman who stood before her—Mrs. Kaplan, some forty years ago.

Leland left the room and Mrs. Kaplan took a seat; Robards let her fingers drift over her computer keyboard as if she were playing a brief run of a Chopin *Fantasie*. Up popped the FBI profile screen:

Cunegonde "Cundy" Schelling; b. 1939, Vienna, Austria; parents d. WWII; award-winning career as investigative undercover journalist: Baader-Meinhhof gang in Germany, Daniel Cohn-Bendit and Red Brigades in France; Fulbright 1970 to Johns Hopkins School of Advanced International Studies; m. Pulitzer Prize–winning journalist Hiram Kaplan (1919–1983); 2 children—Rachel, 1972, Aaron, 1984

"You're actually Cundy Schelling?" Robards looked up at Kaplan in disbelief. A name legendary in journalism, like Margaret Bourke-White or Oriana Fallaci.

"In person," said the woman she'd regarded as a bumbling Jewish mom.

Robards felt sick. No *wonder* this investigation was going nowhere. She, Diane Robards, was being investigated by the suspects themselves! And their mothers! If Mrs. Kaplan's credits were any indication, they all probably had better credentials than her own staff.

"Captain Robards," said Mrs. Kaplan (despite her soft Viennese accent, she sounded impatient), "I think we have—shall I be polite and say *'procrastinated'?*—on this investigation long enough. As a journalist, I am obliged to relate to others, put myself in their shoes, sense what makes them tick. From the first, as I watched you conduct your inquiry, I knew you were handicapped in your job because you don't want to think of yourself as a woman. You lack compassion. You are so tied to the success of your career—your obsession with facts, figures, forensics—that you cannot see the people involved. My inside sources have confirmed these fears."

"Inside sources?" said Robards, digging her nails deeper. She wanted to pop star investigative journalist Cunegonde Schelling Kaplan right in her perfect white teeth. "Perhaps you could share those sources with me, Mrs. Kaplan? Or am I being too inquisitive? Maybe you require no help from the police? Let me guess: through compassion, you have already divined who the murderer is?"

"Yes, I do know who the murderer is, Captain Robards," Cundy said, not dropping a beat. "I believe we can lay all five murders at the same person's door. Though I can't prove it yet, I believe I know where the last piece of evidence can be found to help put this heinous killer behind bars for a long, long time."

Diane sighed. This couldn't be real. She *knew* who "the heinous killer" was? But she had noted that Mrs. Kaplan said five murders, not the four of record. Diane's headache seemed miraculously to have vanished. Maybe she was just delirious.

"Mrs. Kaplan," said Diane Robards, "I hope I may ask something, without your taking it the wrong way. But how long, would you say, has it been since you have done any real investigative journalism?"

"I've never stopped," said Cunegonde Schelling, her blue eyes like steel razors. "You see, Captain Robards, my late son-in-law, Sigmond, was working with me on the investigation of Gryphon Gate, long before any murders took place. I am convinced that our investigation was the direct cause of Sigmond Vormeister's death."

Kaplan and Vormeister were investigating Gryphon Gate? Could this be the missing button she'd been praying for in this button-down community?

"What piece of evidence are you missing?" Robards asked with excitement.

"Didn't you wonder how everyone in Gryphon Gate received faxes, demanding they come to Sunday's church service," said Cundy, "when Reverend Armbruster himself knew only hours earlier what the theme of the service would be?"

Robards was too humiliated to confess she had checked every possibility in her Rolodex for a preplanned scenario—and that she had come up with zip. She just nodded for Kaplan to continue. After all, the woman thought she knew something.

"Proverbs 11:13," said Cundy Kaplan. "'A talebearer revealeth secrets'—"

"Three secrets *were* revealed at the service," agreed Robards, privately chuckling to recall the zany occasion—the first levity in this whole dismal affair.

"But we've checked them all out," Robards added. "Laura Armbruster had some bet with Gervase, the werewolf, involving their faithless spouses. It's personal—unrelated to our case. Then 'Jerry Lynch,' aka 'Ronald Roach,' served time in Boston for a real estate scam at Harvard, selling dim-witted undergrads bogus historic titles to plots in the Harvard Yard. Jerry's still pulling the same crap now—on Wall Street, as I understand it. They never learn, but it doesn't add up to murder. Then we have Toni Sinclair—now there's a possibility for you!" Her eyes lit up. "Hubby Lincoln had just sold his high-tech business for gazillions, then accidentally electrocuted himself on the john. Rumors abound that Toni and her lover, Jason Salinger, 'arranged' a few things. . . ."

Robards stopped because Mrs. Kaplan was on her feet heading for the door.

"Captain Robards," said Kaplan, "regardless how despicable the dead may have been, they did little to deserve *you* as the only officer resolving their murders. Anyone who talks as much as you do could not possibly have time to learn anything new." Robards was rendered speechless—but Cundy hadn't quite finished.

"Proverbs 11:13," she reminded Robards. "Look it up. Then give me a call. I'll be at my daughter, Rachel's."

As Kaplan turned to go, Robards quickly tapped into her computer: BIBLE, OLD TESTAMENT, PROVERBS 11:13.

And the answer came back: "A talebearer revealeth secrets. But he that is of a faithful spirit concealeth the matter."

A faithful spirit? In this quagmire of greed, lust, and deception? Robards almost snorted. But when she looked up, she saw Cunegonde Schelling Kaplan, in her long black cape, sweep through the office door and shut it soundlessly behind her.

*   *   *

Vanessa Smart-Drysdale, wearing a chic, taupe suede pantsuit, paced restlessly before the floor-to-ceiling windows of her posh Alexandria high-rise. Her longtime trysting place with Sen. Edward "Ned" Carbury, the flat had been her best-kept secret.

Vanessa had purchased these executive suites overlooking the Potomac from Lincoln Sinclair when he'd wanted to cut a deal on her property at Forest Glen. Vanessa would never forget the terrified expression on the face of that idiotic wife of his—Toni—when she learned her husband had been fried like a frittata on his executive toilet—right here, downstairs in the business offices of the Sinclair Building. What a joke. As if Toni hadn't planned the whole thing herself, with Jason Salinger.

Vanessa watched with mounting tension as black rain clouds gathered, obliterating her view of the Maryland shore. Around the bend lay Gryphon Gate.

Vanessa had waited half the morning at her Forest Glen property for that little skateboarding twerp, Aaron Kaplan, to meet her. Now she was nervous beyond belief. The idiotic child had threatened to blackmail her with data he had *decrypted* (he'd actually used that Captain Marvel term) from Sigmond Vormeister's files—information about her "affair" with Ned Carbury!

Vanessa—never one to be taken unawares by a teenage boy—had immediately counter-offered with the proposal of building an $800,000 skate park at Forest Glen.

The park would be thirty thousand square feet—the largest in the state of Maryland, including seven-foot half pipes, eight-foot quarter pipes, fun boxes, spine runs, lumpy ramps, flat bars, and handrails—called "kinked hand-jobs" (she'd done her homework) by the incredibly stupid boys who had invented this incredibly stupid pastime.

Vanessa was in fact astonished to discover a cottage industry in the tacky, bowling-alley mentality of *skateboarding*—an industry that, upon research, proved to have more revenue-producing potential than the entire New Age. And Aaron, she'd assured him, would be her consultant and partner in crime.

They were scheduled to haggle terms this morning. But Aaron

had been a no-show. His news was *trop passé,* at any rate. It was somebody else's no-show that enraged her.

Vanessa picked up her glass of iced Lillet and took a sip.

Just who the fuck did Sen. Edward Carbury think *he* was—to tell her they should put their affair "on the back burner until the publicity died down"? That they should avoid even being seen together!

Yeah—like, these murders had anything to do with their relationship! Ned had been only a mediocre real estate lawyer when Vanessa found him, when she had browbeaten her then-husband, Henry Drysdale, into hiring him. Ned's negotiation—through all the foibles and tangles of the law—of Gryphon Gate, the first gated community completely orchestrated at all levels, had made Vanessa and Henry rich—and had bought Ned Carbury a seat in the United States Senate.

Vanessa threw her Baccarat goblet across the room and watched it smash against the far wall. With great pleasure. Luckily, she had cornered the market on crystal—and that wasn't all. Never let the bastards get you down.

Then she picked up her cell phone and punched "redial."

Camille McClintock watched from her enclosed veranda as the gusts of rain struck the glass panes in horizontal sheets, like a runaway locomotive, car after car. It should have been hypnotic, but the rhythm of wind and water on glass wasn't lulling her at all. Over and over, with each onslaught, she kept thinking about Lance.

Camille had never believed that the fax they'd received had anything to do with her own long-forgotten past as "Barbi" the call girl. It had to be something else—a kind of coded message that only Lance would understand. And that was what killed him.

Lance had been behaving strangely, ever since that awful night of confrontation in the club between the "Bambi huggers" and Lance's organized posse of deer hunters. He'd said something that made her uneasy. Maybe something he had said in the bar: "To bitches everywhere." Was that it? Or was it something else?

The wind had grown wilder now; Camille even imagined for a moment that she actually heard it *howling* like a human voice or an animal's. Good lord!—Roman Gervase wouldn't be out in this weather, would he? Even though he was crazy as a loon and wilder than a . . .

And then she got it! She recalled what Lance had said that night in the bar! It seemed like nothing then, but now it came together in a rush, like that wall of water, a deluge. Camille was on her feet—she had to notify the police at once!

She grabbed her cell phone, but the message said the lines were all jammed. So she reached for the house phone—but she found the line had gone dead. Oh God.

It was then that Camille heard the tapping on the French windows. There, just outside in the storm, stood a tall, hooded figure dressed all in black.

Renée Lynch was depressed. Really depressed. She had known for months that their house was bugged—she'd even tried to hire their neighbor, security expert Martin Herbert, to trace who did it, with a singular lack of success. But Renée had assumed it was due to Jerry's shenanigans involving the New York Stock Exchange. Now that Anka, their maid, had been brutally murdered in the Sinclair koi pond, Renée realized with an awful shudder that it might well have been due to Jerry's shenanigans with Anka instead!

It all made sense, now that she thought of it. Why had Anka "accidentally" knocked the phone off the hook whenever she and Jerry had sex? Renée couldn't count the number of times she'd found the receiver on the floor. Obviously, Anka was signaling someone that she and Jerry were occupied—which meant Renée must be out of the house, too—and the coast was clear. But for what?

Anka clearly had a partner—maybe more than one—or how could she have gained access to all those houses filled with jewelry? But Jerry couldn't be involved. Renée knew her husband too well— like that real estate scam when he was just a kid, which even Parker Upshaw seemed to have heard of, given his dancing act in church.

No, Jerry was too greedy, too sex-crazed, too into instant gratification ever to be involved in a long-term plot involving petty theft— much less murder! Renée shuddered again.

On the other hand, how could Anka have escaped without help? When Renée had responded to Lydia's urgent message to meet her at the club, Anka was already trussed in the entrance hall like a holiday turkey, Capt. Diane Robards was en route from the station, and Jerry was ensconced in his study, where he could keep an eye out from the upper window for the vice squad's arrival.

When they'd arrived, however, neither Anka nor the loot was to be found. It was only three hours later when they were discovered, dead weight, in Toni's pond. Since the jewels were there with the body, maybe the larceny had just been a front, thought Renée; maybe the killer had already gotten what he wanted from dear little Anka: information.

Jerry swore he'd heard nothing, that he'd seen no one enter or leave the house until the police.

But Renée knew it was only a matter of time before the autopsy results were in. Then everyone would learn that, even if Jerry Lynch had not been the last one to see Anka alive, he was certainly the last who had sex with her.

Only when Lydia Upshaw was absolutely positive that her husband Parker had left for his office in Georgetown did she put the twins into their padded playpen, check all the outside doors to be sure they were locked, and head downstairs to the cellar.

This time she'd make no mistakes, as with Charles Jefferson's unexpected arrival. Poor Charles—despicable though it was, what he had done to all the women—Lydia still felt guilty. If they hadn't tied him up near the pool, he might not be dead. And they might be one step closer to knowing who the murderer was.

Lydia felt guilty as well for sneaking behind her husband's back to check up on him like this. The whole spirit of their marriage had been one of openness, faithfulness.

But Lydia had been really worried, ever since Mignon Gervase told her about the fight she'd overheard on the golf course between Lance McClintock and Sen. Carbury—only hours before Lt. Col. McClintock was murdered.

Mignon and Silas MacGruder were held up for twenty minutes or more on the seventh hole. They couldn't play through: the two men were really going at it up on the next green. Silas, whose hearing wasn't great, kept asking Mignon what they were saying, but she didn't tell him.

She told Lydia instead.

Mignon thought Lydia had a right to know. After all, Ned Carbury was Parker Upshaw's best friend, so Lydia's husband might be tarred with the same brush Lance was using on Ned. The colonel accused the senator of "corrupt dealings" in the creation of the founding documents for Gryphon Gate.

"You've dragged us all into this quagmire," Mignon had heard McClintock say. "As of now, I've got the proof that will put you away. We're talking major class action lawsuit, buddy-o. Billions of dollars in fraud. How do you plan to wriggle out of this one?" And more of the same.

To make matters worse, Lydia herself had been on the greens with Sen. Ned Carbury, one day earlier, on Wednesday, the same evening that Sigmond Vormeister died. What was that cryptic remark Ned made to her?

"Just tell Parker that all his hard work is about to pay off, and big."

Everyone, including Mignon, knew that Parker Upshaw's firm had been key advisors on everything from the acquisition of property to the formation of Gryphon Gate as a legal entity—though Ned Carbury himself had done the legal work.

But there was something else, something *no* one knew. No one, that is, but the late Lt. Col. Lance McClintock. And Lydia herself.

Lydia thought back to that first night—the meeting at the clubhouse, where she and the McClintocks had each invited their own experts from the U.S. Department of Natural Resources and an assortment of other government agencies. It had likely taken Lance more than a swift glance through the boxes of contradictory reports supplied in anticipation of that meeting before the truth first leapt out at him.

But back then everybody, even Lydia, thought the deep issues had to do with mute swans, lyme-diseased deer, cute little endangered frogs. God, how she wished right now that it were really so.

Lydia swallowed her bitterness, switched on the dim cellar light, and went to the files she had carefully stored after the last meeting. Beyond the cellar door, she could see the rain slashing down along the gravel path that led to the woods. The twins always slept through storms. This one wouldn't let up for hours.

Lydia pulled six boxes of papers from the shelves and set them on the laundry table. She flipped carefully through the first five boxes, pulling out the reports, one by one, that she thought pertinent. She laid the reports side by side on the table; then she put those boxes back.

From the sixth box she extracted the massive incorporation documents for Gryphon Gate, along with the preliminary reports that were always required for a project of this magnitude: analyses of field, marshland, forest, watershed, and proposed golf course—the many environmental impact, historic preservation, title abstracts, and right-of-way studies. She laid them in a row beneath the first set of papers. Then she drew a stool up to the laundry table and started her painstaking legal review.

Lydia blocked out the sound of the wind howling beyond the cellar door. She focused on one thing only: when she left this cellar, she would either know that her husband, Parker, was indeed a criminal—or that she, Lydia Upshaw, could be the only person still alive who had the evidence to prove who the murderer was.

Tiffany Turner slogged through the puddles, her magenta poncho streaming with water, her Peruvian oiled wool socks soaking into her shoes. She squished with every step. To make matters worse, she really had to take a leak—of the powder room variety. But there was no public facility in sight. Indeed, there was *nothing* in sight, what with the rain socking in everything like the inside of a giant black compost bag.

What on *earth* was the story with Mrs. Clancy? On the phone she'd seemed to Tiffany like an upscale, uptown chick who was only concerned with her family's reputation. But to pay off her final bill, she wanted Tiffany to meet her on the gravel path *behind* the Upshaws' cellar door?—the remotest spot in all of Gryphon Gate.

Blaagh! A huge gust of rain-bearing wind grabbed Tiffany's poncho and nearly lifted her off the ground like a catamaran tacking on the bay.

Clients! Tiffany vowed that before she accepted any more assignments, she would get character references and a complete background composite sketch. As long as they didn't get the same thing on *her!*

Just then, through the pounding sheets of rain, Tiffany spied the gravel drive behind the Upshaw home. And there was her client, Mrs. Clancy, waiting in the rain—wrapped to the teeth in her long, black, hooded cape.

The windshield wipers of the periwinkle blue security car were slapping time futilely against the wall of rain, as Capt. Diane Robards struggled to see anything at all beyond the black-and-white hood decoration on the BMW. She found herself humming "Bobby McGee" to the slapping rhythm of the wipers, but she throttled the song before she got to the hand-holding part.

Leland Ford sat beside her, his computer resting on his lap.

"You sure you want to hear all this stuff I downloaded?" he asked. "Maybe we should drop back by the station so you can dry off; you got pretty wet on that last little foray across Camille McClintock's lawn."

"I can't believe it's almost June; I've never seen weather like this," Diane agreed, yanking back the hood from her soggy black rain slicker. Her hair underneath was just as wet. "But as for the station," she added, slipping the car into neutral and turning on the flashing side light, "I don't think we're going anywhere at all for the moment. I can't see to drive. So give me the goods on our little skateboarding perp and his sister."

"Okay," said Leland. He scrolled down the computer screen. "In 1971 Cunegonde Schelling married her professor, Hiram Kaplan, who was Andrew Mellon Professor of International Relations at the Johns Hopkins School of Advanced International Studies, or S.A.I.S., as they call it. You know what they do there, right?" Leland added.

"Think tank," Diane said. "Training for diplomatic corps and possibly CIA?"

"That's the buzz," said Leland. "Anyway, Kaplan was twenty years Schelling's senior; they had their first kid—the present widow Rachel Vormeister—when Schelling was thirty-three and her husband fifty-three. Then twelve years later Kaplan died, leaving his wife pregnant with little Aaron."

"Rachel told us during her interview with us that her mother didn't raise Aaron," Diane mentioned. "He was raised by his grandfather. When Grandpa died, Aaron went to live with Rachel."

She dumps her kid while she's studying with spies and schmoozing terrorists, Robards thought privately. *And I'm* the one who's supposed to be compassionless and career-obsessed?

"Grandfather: Spinoza 'Spin' Kaplan," Leland read on. "Basketball and swimming coach—but he was a mathematician before he fled Europe in the 1930s. He must be the one who taught Aaron about encryption. The kid won awards at school when he was only eight years old. Which explains how he learned enough to try blackmailing half the occupants here at Gryphon Gate. Five bucks says he deciphered Vormeister's notes."

"If those notebooks are really the reason people are getting killed—which I highly doubt," said Robards, "then the kid might actually be in danger. Anyway, since the phones aren't working, I thought we should head to the Vormeister place, as Cundy Kaplan recommended, just to check things out."

"Why do you doubt that Sigmond Vormeister's notebooks were the motive for his murder?" asked Leland.

"Because nobody has ever tried to steal them or destroy them," said Robards with a shrug. "But somebody *did* swipe-and-wipe Sigmond's Palm Pilot—and dump it on Toni Sinclair's lawn for her little daughter to find."

"So, the Palm Pilot had the real information the killer wanted?" Leland surmised.

"Nope," said Robards, "that was just a plant to incriminate Toni. So, now we ask ourselves: Who would want to focus suspicion on Ms. Sinclair? Who would send you and me to the Satterfields' empty boat just when Senator Carbury was arriving next door at Toni's? Who would sprinkle deer chow at the site of several murders?"

Leland Ford was mystified. "Who?" he finally said.

"The same person who wants us to believe that Toni murdered her husband, Lincoln Sinclair," said Robards.

Glancing at the brief break in the rain, she started the car up again.

"After my little chat a moment ago with Camille McClintock, I think I've figured out *who,*" she informed him. "Now, let's go talk with the person who sent those faxes and see if they can tell us *what, why, and how.*"

* * *

"Oh, hello, Captain Robards, Officer Ford," said Rachel with a smile as she opened the door of her Tudor manse and ushered them in. "We've been expecting you. But my mother isn't back yet. She told me to make you comfortable till she gets here, and to brew you up a nice pot of herbal tea. Can you believe this weather?"

"We wanted to speak with your brother, too; where are they?" asked Robards as she tried to peel her soaking-wet raincoat free of the soaking-wet clothes beneath. Damned government-issue rainwear. She should have joined the fire department—they knew how to keep their powder dry.

"Aaron's upstairs finishing some computer work that Mother asked him to do, and Mother had a meeting over at Lydia Upshaw's," said Rachel. "She'll be here soon. But there's someone waiting here now that my mother wanted you to meet. We're out in the kitchen— the only place that's warm—I hope you don't mind."

Ford and Robards followed Rachel to the kitchen, where a woman was sitting wrapped in a thick-knit pink sweater, her hands cupping a mug of steaming coffee. She looked familiar. When she started to get up, Robards motioned her to stay. Beyond them the rain assaulted the wall of glass panes with a ferocity that looked deliberate.

"This is Lt. Cmdr. Cindy Silberblatt, U.S. Navy, retired—our dockmaster at the Gryphon Gate harbor. We always get the best," Rachel said, pulling out chairs around the oak table. "I believe you've all met before."

On several occasions the police had interviewed the dock staff who managed the array of costly yachts in the harbor. But they'd dropped it once they realized—even if the killer wasn't already in residence—it was as easy for an outsider to slip undetected into this "gated community" as it was to cross the United States border on foot.

"I can only stay a short time, Captain Robards," the dockmaster apologized. "I should be at the docks—we're having an awful time down there. The Coast Guard says this storm is shaping up worse than a nor'easter. We already have seventy mile winds, and building. Though we've finished hurricane season, the meteorologists are thinking of giving this one a name. I can already tell you what I'd like to call it!"

"Of course you must get back to work at once," Robards agreed, wondering how many hundreds of millions of dollars in designer vessels this poor woman was responsible for safeguarding on behalf of their spendthrift owners. She was beginning to sympathize with Leland Ford's security job. "But can you explain what it was that Mrs. Kaplan asked you to come here for?" Robards added.

"It's probably nothing," Cindy Silberblatt began.

This was Robards's favorite opening line, because it invariably meant that there *was* something. She gave the dockmaster an encouraging look to continue, as Rachel set cups of hot tea before them.

"I didn't think much of it at the time," Silberblatt explained. "Although my crew is responsible for oversight at the docks, owners who plan to be away for a long time will often ask other residents to keep an eye on things. I knew the Satterfields were staying in Europe for the month and that they'd given Doctor Vormeister the keys to their house and boat. He spent every afternoon on the waterfront working on his notes, so he'd have noticed anything out of the ordinary. And to reach the harbor he had to go right past the Satterfields' house at the sixth green."

The sixth hole sand trap was where Sigmond Vormeister's body had been found. Robards kicked herself for not searching that empty house the moment they suspected the body had been relocated from the murder scene to the sand trap.

"Why didn't you tell us about this earlier?" she asked the dockmaster.

"The detectives never questioned who might have had access to the boats—they were only interested in how an outsider might've entered the grounds from the port," said Cindy. "I didn't think anything of it until this storm started brewing yesterday. Then I realized that our key to the Satterfields' boat was missing."

Robards glanced at Leland.

"The dockmaster keeps a spare set of keys in a safe at the yacht club office," Leland explained, "so they can move the boats to leeward in the event of a storm."

As if to punctuate his remark, the wind ripped a branch from a tree across the terrace and flung it against the windows, smashing three panes.

All four people leapt to their feet and scurried away from the wall of glass, as gusts of rain swept into the kitchen. The storm seemed to be inside and out all at once.

"I *begged* Sigmond not to plant so many trees close to the house, with all these windows!" Rachel cried. She ran to the far wall, pushed the intercom button, and yelled, "Aaron! Come downstairs! Fast!—To the cellar!"

"I have to get to the docks!" Cindy Silberblatt hollered over the scream of the wind, as she yanked on her foul weather jacket and barreled into the hallway, followed by the others. Rachel shut the kitchen door behind them. They were all racing down the hall toward the front of the house when the lights flickered and went out, throwing the inner passage into momentary darkness. Just then all hell broke loose.

The front door opened and gusts of rain swept in—along with a very wet Tiffany in her colorful poncho, followed by Mrs. Kaplan in her long black cape. They collided with Aaron, who'd just flossed a backslide nollie off the railing from the second floor landing. The three sudden arrivals were tangled in a heap in the entrance hall, as Cindy Silberblatt tried to push her way past the shrieking Rachel and escape the premises to the relative sanity of her storm-tossed harbor.

"Halt!" commanded Diane Robards over the howl of the storm.

Leland pulled out his police whistle and blew a deafening blast. Everything stopped. Leland stepped over the pile of bodies and shoved the front door shut against the driving rain. With his back to the door he faced the motley crew.

"Captain Robards is trying to conduct a murder investigation here, and you all are behaving like a mob at a soccer game," he informed them with a firmness Robards had never seen before. She was impressed. "Now, up off the floor," he was saying. "I want everybody to take a seat on these hall steps—that's it."

Leland helped them extricate themselves in the gloomy light leaking through the entry glass. He got everybody seated in silence on the carpeted stairway.

Then he turned to Robards.

You're doing just fine, she thought. She smiled supportively, and nodded for him to continue.

"Mrs. Kaplan." Leland addressed the older woman, who sat dripping in her black cape on an upper step. "Captain Robards says you seem to think you've got this case solved. Our dockmaster, Lieutenant Commander Silberblatt here, has informed us that your son-in-law, Sigmond Vormeister, possessed keys to the Satterfields' vacant house and boat. She says the dock key for their yacht is missing, too. But we found no keys on his body. Can you explain that for us?"

Kaplan tossed back her black hood and glared at him with icy blue eyes. "Sigmond and I were conducting an important undercover investigation," she said. "We were using the vacant house as a meeting place. But when I got there last Friday, I found the door ajar. Sigmond was sprawled faceup on the floor, his head bashed in, deer chow sprinkled on his clothes—and his Palm Pilot was missing. I had to act quickly to try to apprehend his killer, so I removed the Satterfields' keys from his pocket. Then I put him in a golf cart and dumped him into the sixth hole sand trap."

Her testimony was instantly drowned out by a sea of gasps, protestations, a groan from Aaron, and Rachel's piercing scream, "Oh, Mother—how *could* you!?"

Leland glared until the noise died down, then Cundy added, "As for the dock key—I assume the murderer has it. I think you'll find the spare house key missing, too."

Diane Robards, at the railing, glanced quickly at Leland with raised brow.

"There's a safe in the clubhouse office with master house keys," he explained. "It's in case of fire or flood—they don't want their costly carved doors busted in. Only Mayor Drysdale has access to the combination."

Leland turned back to Cundy Kaplan. "Mrs. K., you've just admitted to meddling with evidence, moving the body, and disrupting a capital murder investigation—but you're claiming you didn't kill him? Exactly what was this secret project of yours, then, that got him killed?"

"It's an investigation of an enormous real estate scam involving Gryphon Gate," she told him. "Sigmond's Ph.D. in sociology was a perfect front for data-gathering from inside. We had evidence that some very highly placed people were knee-deep in the mud. Though we didn't yet have proof who the mastermind was, we were closing in. Then, unexpectedly, one of our top moles was killed."

Diane recalled Mrs. Kaplan's office visit—when she'd mentioned there were five murders, not four.

"You're saying someone was murdered *before* Sigmond Vormeister?" she asked.

"Yes," Kaplan replied. "Lincoln Sinclair. It was designed to look like an accident, but the stereo system that electrocuted him was tampered with by someone who had his confidence and access to his private office. We weren't sure yet, however, that his death was tied to our investigation. The obvious suspect would be his wife, Toni."

The wind was hammering at the front door, but everyone was quiet now, riveted to Cundy Kaplan's report.

"When I found Sigmond's body," she went on, "I was sure that both deaths were related. But luckily our killer knew nothing about *me*. So, at dusk that evening, when the greens were closing, I took poor Sigmond's corpse to the sand trap. Then I used the Satterfields' fax to notify the usual suspects—and I watched, with infrared binoculars, from the bay windows overlooking the sand trap, to see who would show up."

"The—usual suspects?" said Leland.

"Toni Sinclair, Vanessa Smart-Drysdale, the Upshaws, Senator Ned Carbury, Jerry Lynch, Lieutenant Colonel Lance McClintock—everyone who had something to lose and plenty to gain by silencing Lincoln Sinclair and Sigmond Vormeister. But my ruse didn't expose the killer. I saw Jerry Lynch lurking in the brush and watching as Toni Sinclair turned the body over, then covered her tracks. No one else showed up. But if either of them *had* killed Sigmond in another location and then found the body moved, he'd have been on instant alert of a trap."

"So you don't think Toni did it, either?" Robards interjected.

"Leaving deer chow as her calling card?" Cundy sneered disdainfully.

"But if Lance McClintock is dead," Leland observed, "and if Toni and Jerry are out of it, your scenario leaves us with only Vanessa Smart-Drysdale, Senator Carbury, or perhaps Lydia or Parker Upshaw as the—what did you say?—the mastermind?"

"Proverbs 11:13," agreed Cundy. "'A talebearer revealeth secrets, *but he that is of faithful spirit concealeth the matter.*' Our stumbling block was that one of those involved, an innocent, was concealing something, due to a misplaced sense of allegiance. So I hired Tiffany to hold a church service and I sent everyone invitations."

"You *hired* her?" Robards interrupted. "But how could you have known that the scheduled speaker would drop out? Professor . . ." A howl of wind interrupted her.

"Ahmed Djibouti, my grad school colleague at Johns Hopkins, and a good investigator himself," Cundy said. "At first we planned to have Achmed conduct the session, planting revelations from within the audience—but Tiffany was known in the community, which would seem less suspicious. It helped that she was already a seasoned free-lance operative with good credentials."

"But I didn't know that Mrs. Kaplan was my client," Tiffany chimed in. "I thought on the phone that it was Lincoln Sinclair's sister, Mrs. Clancy. I only found out the truth less than an hour ago when we met over at Lydia Upshaw's."

"Lydia was the one concealing something?" Leland Ford correctly guessed.

"She didn't come to the service," said Kaplan. "She stayed home, hunting for the information in her files that might prove her husband guilty or innocent—an answer she discovered only today. Though her findings would have helped the police investigation, we knew Parker Upshaw was innocent: He was working with us."

"Parker Upshaw? *Parker Upshaw?*" Diane jumped to her feet, grasping the banister in fury. She felt like screaming at the top of her lungs, which might be necessary soon if she wanted to be heard at all over the screeching storm.

Leland Ford put his hand over hers, trying to get her to focus. He could now see, only too clearly, where this all seemed to be heading.

"Mrs. Kaplan," Diane said in frustration, "is there anyone in this whole damned sinkhole of sin who *isn't* working for you?"

"My son Aaron isn't—or he wasn't until now," said Cundy, looking at the shamefaced skateboarder beside her. Aaron flushed beet red.

"For some reason, Aaron naïvely believed he could do business with the devil, and I learned of it only early this morning," said Cundy. The wind was howling so loudly now she had to yell to make herself heard. "If I had not intercepted him in the woods just then, my son might be dead right now. I have to blame myself—"

"*I* have to blame you, too!" Diane snapped, stepping forward to glare at Kaplan on the higher step. "You've withheld information and meddled with evidence from square one! Thanks to your manipula-tive secrecy, five people are *already* dead!"

"Five people are dead," said Cundy, "because Vanessa Smart-Drysdale murdered them!"

A gasp ran through the group, followed by an awed silence in which only the whine of wind could be heard. But Diane Robards hadn't quite finished with Cundy Kaplan.

"On character alone, Vanessa would certainly be my choice," Diane agreed. "But you said the killer had masterminded some big land scam involving Gryphon Gate. Vanessa's divorce cut her out of the pot financially. No motive. Furthermore—I'm sorry, Mrs. Kaplan—but I'm afraid I have trouble even *imagining* that a little twig like Vanessa could kill four big men and a tough, leggy brunette like Anka."

"I believe I mentioned before that you lacked compassion," said Cundy dryly. "Now it would appear that you lack imagination as well."

When Robards bristled, Cundy added: "Vanessa bribed her attorney, Ned Carbury—using her body and her husband Henry's money—to rig the land purchase of Gryphon Gate, which would make her rich. She wasn't expecting Henry Drysdale to dump her, but at least she got a chunk of the parcel: Forest Glen. That was four years ago. She's been in bed with Carbury ever since.

"When Lincoln Sinclair, through his computer research, found out about the scam, he should have phoned us first and blown the whistle on Carbury's crimes. Instead, Lincoln threatened Vanessa by revealing he was working with Sigmond Vormeister to expose the whole deal and those involved. Lincoln tried to blackmail her into cutting him in for a share of the pie to keep his information quiet. Vanessa crossed the wires in his stereo system—and kept him quiet instead.

"Her other murders," Cundy continued, "were managed by a stun gun and a blow to the head. But in fear that Lincoln might have revealed something to his wife, Toni, Vanessa planted deer chow on her next victims' bodies—and suspicion on Toni." Cundy folded her hands and added, "The rest of her crimes are quite simple."

"But why would Vanessa kill Charles Jefferson and Anka?" said Diane, trying to pitch her voice above the racket outside. "They had nothing whatever to do with Gryphon Gate real estate."

"I suspect Doctor Jefferson was in the wrong place at the wrong time," said Cundy. "Vanessa's faxes to Jefferson were intended to place more suspicion on Toni and to place the true father of her child at the site of a homicide. Instead, he arrived early and saw Anka's lifeless body being dumped in the koi pond. And perhaps Anka—just like my son Aaron here—believed she'd found a business partner in Vanessa, a patron who could provide keys to all the houses, stolen from Henry Drysdale's safe. Anka only had to get jewelry and information—information easy to snoop for, given her contacts with other servants—with no one ever realizing Vanessa was the final recipient. When Anka's activities were uncovered, so to speak, by the Lynches, Vanessa had to get rid of the foolish servant before she talked." Cundy paused and added, "But Colonel McClintock made the biggest mistake of all."

"You mean his fight with Carbury on the golf course?" asked Leland, who had plowed through his police notes more than once. "But that would make Carbury more a suspect than Vanessa. If the senator was getting payola from her to keep his mouth shut, it's unlikely he'd tell her that McClintock was about to blow the game."

"He didn't have to," said Cundy. "McClintock made that mistake himself, in front of others at the club—and thereby signed his own death warrant."

Diane's brain was pounding; the air in the foyer seemed to have vanished while the wind grew more ferocious, as if all the oxygen had been sucked outside. She thought she might black out.

What *was* it that Lance McClintock had said at the club? Camille had told her, but Camille thought it was Ned Carbury that her husband had been talking about. According to the police records, Carbury hadn't even been in the room at the time. But Vanessa was, Diane realized. And then it hit her:

"Give it back to the red Indians!" Diane yelled.

Everyone turned to stare at her.

"That's it!" she said. "This land doesn't belong to the Gryphon Gate Corporation! The papers Ned Carbury falsified were the land titles! But there *were* no land titles, at least, not private ownership: This was government land—*Indian* land!"

"A Native American sacred spring and ancient burial ground, as we believe," confirmed Cundy. "But the records had vanished and much of the surrounding land, due to its strategic location, was converted to military use."

"Lydia Upshaw must have noticed at once," Rachel said. "When the Department of Natural Resources showed up with zip—an endangered frog and a marsh mallow—that doesn't add up to a reason why land as valuable as this was never developed and was still available for practically a song. Environmentalists and ecologists embraced the whole idea because it was being preserved for natural uses. They never even guessed that there were no claims because the records had been destroyed."

"Vanessa Smart-Drysdale lived in this region all her life," agreed Robards, recalling her interviews. "She grew up in the Chesapeake area and knew the land inside out. Three guesses who stole the papers from the state archives at Annapolis, papers that would have proven its provenance? Who packaged Gryphon Gate, knowing that no one could ever contest the property rights without evidence?"

Rachel Vormeister had started laughing—a little hysterically, it seemed to Robards.

"Sorry," Rachel said, standing to face the others still on the steps. "I'm a Jungian, you see—and this is all so archetypal!" When no one spoke, she said: "Gryphon Gate: It's as mythological as its name. A gryphon—part lion, part eagle—exists only in imagination! Good God—don't you all see what it means?" she cried in tears above the storm. "My husband was *murdered for something that never existed!*"

Aaron slid down the stairs, between Tiffany and Lt. Cmdr. Cindy Silberblatt, and he went up to hug his big sister. "I'm sorry," he told Rachel, as if what she said had made any sense at all.

"I'm lost here," Tiffany shouted. "We know Vanessa is a horrible killer. The police are here to resolve the problem. What are we supposed to do now?"

"I know what *I'm* supposed to do," yelled Cindy Silberblatt. "I need to get down to the docks and secure those boats!"

Just then a gigantic crash came from the kitchen. The back hall door smashed open, and beyond it they could see the gaping hole where the wall of windows had been only moments before. Wind tore down the hall unimpeded. A heavy Bokhara runner was lifted from the hallway floor, and it was floating in the air like a serpent. The seven occupants of the entrance hall stood stupefied as china objects flew off the étagères and smashed into the walls around them. *People who live in glass houses shouldn't grow trees,* thought Robards.

"The basement!" Leland hollered.

But just then they heard the awful creaking sound of a giant tree falling, falling, the roots snapping with explosive cracks like gunfire.

There was another crash, right over their heads, that could only be the upper roof collapsing under the tree's weight. Bits of plaster from the ceiling broke away and started plopping onto their heads. All the light from the entry lunette was now obliterated by leaves and branches; the front had to be blocked by the fallen tree. Leland yanked the door open—a sea of water and branches crashed into the hall, knocking him backwards.

In the racket around her Robards thought she heard herself screaming—but it was Rachel, clinging to her shoulder. Cindy Silberblatt grabbed Rachel by the arm and slapped her once, hard in the face.

"Snap out of it," she told the pregnant woman. "Follow me—we have to get out of here before we're buried alive."

Right, thought Robards—*a navy commander. This chick could kick butt.*

Everyone followed Silberblatt back down the hall and into the garage.

Cindy disconnected the lock, but it took four of them to raise the garage door by hand, and when they did, they wished they hadn't. The two cars parked in the garage had been blocked by the police cruiser just outside—which in turn was crushed under the trunk of an enormous cypress.

It would take a crew with buzz saws a week to clear this, Robards thought.

"I can probably squeeze all seven of us into my Land Rover," the dockmaster yelled in Robards's ear. "If we can make it there. It's parked at the end of the drive."

"But *then* what?" Robards screamed back. "The whole neighborhood's a disaster zone!"

"My wheel base is high enough to clear most flooding, and the clubhouse is uphill," Cindy said. "I can drop you there en route to the harbor and then use our Coast Guard radio to get help. They should have issued an evacuation notice hours ago!"

Maybe they *had*, thought Robards grimly. But the power and phone lines had been out for hours and the cells were jammed—as always in emergencies, just when they were most needed. She prayed that the families with children had thought to take refuge at the clubhouse on high ground.

Silberblatt gathered the group into an arrowlike wedge to deflect the wind. They moved in cadence through Sigmond's dense forest of giant trees as branches crashed around them. At last they reached the main road and piled into the car. The dockmaster wasted no time, expertly weaving her way along the road, which had turned into a river of chocolate milk.

"I bet you never thought your navy experience would come in handy in a Land Rover?" Leland tried to joke. Nobody laughed.

The wind buffeted the car relentlessly as water sucked at the wheels. It seemed hours through the onslaught of rain before they could finally glimpse the clubhouse clinging precariously to the hill.

Silberblatt pulled the car up front and felt a *thunk* under the right tire. Leland hopped out of the front seat and the wind nearly tore the passenger door off. He looked at the ground in front of the car.

"Jesus! Don't go any farther!" he yelled to Silberblatt, staring at the mass of rubble just in front of them. "It's the portico! The columns have collapsed!"

The elegant former portico—beneath which the residents had pulled their Jaguars and Bentleys to keep themselves dry—was now nothing but a pile of stone and mud. The clubhouse didn't look much better: The windows that had afforded a magnificent view of the golf course and the valley were now nonexistent. Winds tore at the green velvet draperies that whipped from the gaping former windows of the Wild Goose Room. Not a creature was stirring—except the relentless storm.

By unspoken consensus it occurred to those seated in the Land Rover that the low ground might be a preferable solution. Leland crawled in again, and Cindy Silberblatt started to back out of the drive, when a blast from a car horn stopped her in her tracks. All seven passengers turned to stare as a tiny, bright red sports car came barreling by them through the water at a frightening clip. It headed downhill toward the port—directly into the jaws of the storm.

Though they could not see the driver, everyone knew the owner's name: The car belonged to Vanessa Smart-Drysdale.

Vanessa was ready to kill somebody. She had to laugh at the trite expression. Maybe she should say she was ready to kill *again!*

She was fed up with goddamned Henry Drysdale! After she had pushed her redial button for about the thirty-thousandth time and he hadn't answered, she threw her cell phone into the toilet, took the elevator down to the apartment garage, and hit the road for the beltway to the Wilson Bridge, and into Maryland. The ports had all been closed by the storm—and she had to get to that boat!

Who the hell did Henry think he was? She had made him rich. She had made him famous—*she!*—little Vanessa Smart who grew up poor and barefoot on the Chesapeake docks with nobody but her father—a poor fisherman. That bastard!

Her father that is—not Henry Drysdale.

Well, yes, Henry too.

And Lincoln Sinclair.

And all of them—*men!* The scumbags!

She'd *loved* imagining Lincoln Sinclair fry on his executive toilet! His death was the best of all. She played it over and over in slow motion in her mind—the sounds, the smell of singed hair and burning flesh. However, nothing she'd done to Lincoln, thought Vanessa, would compare with what they would do to him in hell. Especially after what her father had done to all those little girls.

No! No! Not her father! Her father only did it to *her*—*only* to her—because Mummy was dead. And Daddy was very lonely. . . .

Vanessa jerked the car back onto the road. Good heavens! This rain was deep!

Anyway, it all made no difference whatsoever. As long as Vanessa got those papers from the boat—the papers Henry wanted. The papers that *proved* how brilliant *she*, Vanessa Smart-Drysdale, really was! The papers that had made Henry rich. The papers that would destroy him completely—if he ever had the guts to cross her. The papers that would destroy that little girl Henry had dumped Vanessa for, the little girl he had spilled his big, fat diamonds on: his cute little trinket fiancée—little "Babs."

Vanessa drove the car into the belly of the storm.

She was ready to kill.

"Follow that car! It's Vanessa!" Cundy Kaplan cried, grabbing Cindy Silberblatt by the shoulder.

"Mother, my God!" said Rachel. "Gryphon Gate is being destroyed! There are families—*children*—trapped out there in the storm! What on earth are you thinking?"

"Hey," Tiffany interjected from the backseat, "let's just regroup for a moment. I mean, 'You take the high road and I'll . . .' etcetera. But unfortunately for us, Mrs. 'Rachel-the-Jungian-Expert' Vormeister— there *is* no high road. I mean, you've surely noted that our 'high road' here is about as imaginary as the 'gryphon' in Gryphon Gate?"

"Hey, Sis," Aaron told Rachel. "She's right, you know. That bitch Vanessa wiped Sigmond—she tried to wipe me too! She wiped a lot of dudes—you know?"

Rachel knew. She ruffled her fingers in her brother's wet hair.

"So let's go grab the bitch," said Aaron, "and crunk her entire case. You know?"

Everybody in the car agreed.

Vanessa seemed to be driving under water. She knew the port must be nearby because she'd passed the clubhouse minutes ago. A big car had pulled out like it was following her. She didn't give a damn. She had the key to the Satterfields' boat in her pocket. Nobody could stop her now.

Cindy Silberblatt screeched up to the dock. Actually, it was less a screech than a long, squishy slide. Everyone piled out of the car in the torrential rain. The scene before them was horrifying.

Boats were smashing against the piers—some had broken loose. As far as Leland could tell, all the residents who'd been trapped in Gryphon Gate were already gathered there. Lydia Upshaw, holding a tarp-covered basket, turned to him.

"Officer, can I put the twins in your car?" she asked, gesturing to the basket. "And the children—Miranda Sinclair and Samantha Lynch—they're here, too. Is there any chance that you can at least get the little ones out? Our houses are demolished."

Leland felt that sense of futility he had always felt as a cop—that he'd felt when his father died. He grabbed Diane Robards by the arm.

"I'll help the dock crew," he told her. "You get the kids out. And the mothers."

"What about Vanessa?" snapped Robards. "Have we completely forgotten why we're here?"

"Why don't you work on that issue with your friend, Cunegonde Kaplan?" Leland said. "I'm a cop. I'm here to save lives, not to take them."

He bent down unexpectedly and kissed Diane on the cheek.

Cindy Silberblatt tossed the car keys to Robards, touched her brow in an informal salute, and headed for the docks.

Just then—as everyone milled about in the storm in complete confusion—a boat started up. They watched as it pulled out into the harbor at top speed.

"No!" screamed Cindy Silberblatt. "Not the fuel dock!"

The Satterfields' little yacht had been lifted into the air, lifted higher and higher, tucked inside the curl of an enormous wave that was hurtling back toward the shore—right toward the fuel dock with its six high-octane gasoline pumps. They all watched in horror as they heard, over the sound of the storm, the boat's occupant futilely revving the boat's engine, trying to escape.

"Turn off that engine!" someone yelled meaninglessly into the wind as dockworkers scurried frantically away from the piers. But dockmaster Cindy Silberblatt, standing in the wind, knew it was too late.

When the boat smashed into the pilings, the dock collapsed into the water with a crash. The explosion of the Satterfields' costly boat was deafening. Oil sprayed everywhere, borne on the wild winds. One by one the docks and their valuable yachts were engulfed, swallowed into the violent sea of flame.

Leland Ford, with Robards and Silberblatt, was grabbing children and hauling parents back from the shore, but the sight of the wall of fire and the burning carcasses of boats, with the stench of gasoline and fire, was riveting.

It was half an hour before Silberblatt had made sure that all her dockworkers were accounted for and that no one was trapped in the burning boats. She rejoined the detectives, with the Vormeister-Kaplans and the others, where they'd taken refuge high on the hill.

Henry Drysdale stood with them in the rain, staring dazedly at the burning port, as if he had lost his mind or forgotten who he was.

Lydia Upshaw came up to the group, still carrying her basket of sleeping babies. Thank God the twins loved a storm! She put her other hand on Henry's arm, and he looked at her with bleary eyes, as if trying to recall who *she* was. He smelled as if he'd had a few drinks.

"That was Vanessa in the boat—wasn't it?" asked Henry, wiping the rain from his eyes. When Diane Robards nodded in affirmation, Henry added, in a strangely strangled voice, "I should have returned her calls."

"We know everything, Mr. Drysdale," Diane Robards told him. "Except for one thing: Why didn't you and Senator Ned Carbury come forward with evidence when people were being killed? You both must have understood—knowing what you did about Gryphon Gate, knowing that Vanessa had masterminded the theft of this land— that Vanessa herself would have had the best motive for the murders. Except for the two of you, that is."

Henry Drysdale had covered his eyes with his hands. Perhaps those were tears, not rain on his face, Robards thought. She'd have liked to feel sorry for him—after all, the man had lost everything. Sure, the wealthy residents of Gryphon Gate had seen their houses and manicured estates demolished, their costly yachts burned to a crisp—but those were only possessions and were insured. While Mayor Henry Drysdale, by contrast, had burned all his bridges and ruined other lives through his corruption and greed. She'd bet that Vanessa didn't have to browbeat him very hard to steal that land.

But Henry had taken his hand from his face, his eyes now riveted on Robards. His next words completely floored her. "These are just surmises," he announced. "The proof of your allegations—if there ever was any—has vanished in that yacht along with Vanessa!"

The man actually *smiled!* Robards felt her blood boiling. There had clearly been one murder too few in this slime bag of snakes!

"I'm afraid not, Henry," Lydia Upshaw, still holding her basket of babies, explained to the mayor. "The State of Maryland microfilms *all* historic documents, including ancient deeds. Early today, when I realized they were absent from the files of our last meeting, I entered the coordinates of Gryphon Gate into my database. I gave my printout to Mrs. Kaplan. Even if the original records are destroyed, it's *still* a matter of public record, Henry—all this land belongs to the Mattaponi Indians!"

"Mayor Henry Drysdale," announced Robards with great satisfaction, "you are under arrest as an accessory to the murders of Lincoln

Sinclair, Sigmond Vormeister, and Lance McClintock, and as accessory after the fact to the murders of Anka Kovacik and Dr. Charles Jefferson. . . ."

Robards was about to rattle off the lesser charges of conspiracy, grand larceny, and such, when Henry shrieked, "What about Carbury!? *He's* the one who falsified all the paperwork! He's the one who was blackmailing Vanessa and me for those goddamned documents!"

"So you're offering to work with the State in prosecuting Senator Carbury?" Robards said with a smile, as Leland Ford handcuffed the former mayor of the former Gryphon Gate. "Congratulations! That just might reduce your sentence to sixty years."

Leland Ford shoved the babbling Drysdale into the backseat of the Land Rover, then the security officer turned back to Robards, Silberblatt, and the group of homeless residents—all huddled there on the hill in the wind and rain. The raging oil fires on the docks below had almost vanished in a haze of acrid smoke that blanketed the river—all that remained of their magnificent possessions.

Leland put one arm around the shivering dockmaster and gave her a big hug.

"You saved our lives," he told Silberblatt. Then he took Diane Robards's slender hand in his. Diane looked up at him in surprise.

"I never knew how rich we really are, people like us," he told the two women. "No one can ever take away what we've accomplished tonight—saving lives and punishing evil, that's something real. Our lives are important because we give, we don't take. But you look at people like Drysdale and Carbury—everything they wanted was a mirage that vanished in less than an hour."

"A fantasy," agreed Robards, squeezing Ford's hand. Leland beamed down at her in the rain. "They must have felt, even from the beginning, that that's all it was," Diane added, smiling back at him. "I guess that's why they called it Gryphon Gate."